STARS FOR THE SHEIKH

A NOVEL BY

ANNABELLE WINTERS

Books by Annabelle Winters

The CURVES FOR SHEIKHS Series
Curves for the Sheikh
Flames for the Sheikh
Hostage for the Sheikh
Single for the Sheikh
Stockings for the Sheikh
Untouched for the Sheikh
Surrogate for the Sheikh
Stars for the Sheikh
Shelter for the Sheikh

STARS FOR THE SHEIKH

A NOVEL BY

ANNABELLE WINTERS

2017
RAINSHINE BOOKS
USA

Copyright Notice

Copyright © 2017 by Annabelle Winters
All Rights Reserved by Author
www.annabellewinters.com
ab@annabellewinters.com

If you'd like to copy, reproduce, sell, or distribute any part of this text, please obtain the explicit, written permission of the author first. Note that you should feel free to tell your spouse, lovers, friends, and coworkers how happy this book made you. Have a wonderful evening!

Cover Design by S. Lee

ISBN: 978-1975947941

0 1 2 3 4 5 6 7 8 9

Stars for the Sheikh

You don't travel through time.
Time travels through you . . .

1

"Fifteen thousand dollars is not nothing, my brother. Do not fall into the lazy billionaire's trap, where you start to lose track of the value of money."

Sheikh Rahaan stood from behind his worn and battered leather swivel chair, stretching his heavy, muscular body and grunting when he realized he'd been sitting for almost four hours straight. Not good. He needed to remember not to fall into the other billionaire's trap: where you overestimate the value of money, put it before everything else, lose sight of the fact that money in itself is fleeting and with no value other than what you gave up to get it.

Of course, Rahaan didn't need to work for his money, didn't need to give up those lazy afternoons sipping sweet tea on the grounds of the Royal Palace of Kolah, attendants and entertainments surrounding him and whichever rich and famous guests he chose to be with. He certainly didn't need to spend his days in a New York City office highrise, sitting behind a desk on the forty-sixth floor of the tower. He did it because it was fun, and it was even more fun when you owned the damned building. Rahaan had purchased the tower on Central Park South almost three years earlier, and although most of the floors were still on lease to old, white-shoe Manhattan law firms and investment banks, Rahaan had taken the entire forty-sixth floor for himself.

This was his Royal Palace in America, he always thought when he stood by his office window, which overlooked the length of New York City's magnificent Central Park, the expanse of perfectly designed green extending from 59th Street up to Harlem. One of the world's most beautiful vistas, Rahaan had always thought, though most of the time he had his back to the window, eyes focused on that forty-inch retina-display monitor with numbers scrolling across the bottom of the screen, intricately patterned black-and-white spreadsheets filling the main space like stars in their cosmic arrangements, sometimes reminding the Sheikh of those clear black desert skies and diamond-like stars above his kingdom of Kolah.

Three years after taking his MBA from the Harvard Business School, Rahaan had decided to take his talents to Wall Street instead of Camel Alley—which was the term of endearment Rahaan and his brother Alim used for the business district in the capital city of Kolah, their small, wealthy kingdom nestled in the grand dunes between Saudi Arabia and the smaller Sheikdoms of the Arabian peninsula. His talents and his gift. His gift . . .

Rahaan blinked hard and clenched his fists as he extended his thick, muscular arms out wide, his wingspan almost covering the large window, body casting a strange, bird-like shadow over the heavy teakwood desk. Perhaps a vulture—which would be fitting, Rahaan thought. After all, he was what they called a "vulture investor," always looking for dying companies to pick apart. Indeed, most of the companies he bought ended up being liquidated: all the employees fired and the assets sold off in parts. Profitable, yes. But that wasn't Rahaan's favorite part of the game.

No, Rahaan's real joy was when he was able to buy a company that only looked like it was dying but was instead just very sick, with a dim hope of recovery. Those companies could be bought cheap and nursed back to health before being sold again or taken public. Now those were the goldmines—provided Rahaan could do a good enough job convincing the owners that their baby was indeed on its deathbed, mortally wounded, where their only option was to sell it to a cold-hearted vulture like the Sheikh, who would squeeze out the last of its value and then put it out of its misery.

"We can consider it a gift, brother Rahaan," said

the younger Alim, blinking and smiling nervously as he glanced up at the much taller Sheikh, who was rubbing the heavy stubble on his thick jawline as he grimaced and then frowned at his younger brother. "Islam is a religion of charity, and so we can just consider this fifteen grand a gift. Yes? I am sure the woman needs it anyway. Come on, Rahaan. You are giving out gifts all the time!"

"There is no such thing as a gift," said Rahaan, his green eyes darkening as he glared at the soft-bodied, narrow-shouldered Alim. "Everything has a price, and nothing is given without expectation of something in return."

Alim snorted. "You donate to forty different charities every year. What do they give you in return?"

"I get the emotional satisfaction of using my wealth to help those less fortunate," said the Sheikh without missing a beat. Then he shrugged. "I also get a tax break. Everybody gets something. Everything is a transaction. There is no such thing as a gift. Remember that, Alim. You always pay a price, whether you know it or not. Whether you want to or not."

Rahaan held his gaze steady, those green eyes narrowed and focused, his jaw set. Alim was only a few years younger, but Rahaan was closer to a parent than a sibling when it came to the two of them.

Indeed, it had been just the two of them for most of Alim's life—he was too young to remember their parents. Their father and his three wives had been killed in an explosion on an oil rig in the Arabian Sea, leaving just the two sons, one of whom was merely an infant, the other a teenager who was forced to become a man very quickly.

Of course, the demands of being Sheikh were easily shouldered by the confident, intelligent teenager—and in fact the young Sheikh Rahaan welcomed the challenge, rejoiced in the work, loved to spend long hours in the Grand Library of the Royal Palace of Kolah, studying the laws and customs of his land and people, the history of his family, searching for answers to the hundreds of questions he had about being the supreme ruler of his ancestral kingdom.

But those were not the only answers the Sheikh had sought in those old family records. Because there was one question that had plagued Rahaan ever since that oil-rig accident made him an orphan. Ever since the night *before* the accident, more precisely, when the teenage Rahaan woke from a vivid dream, his lean brown body glistening with sweat, his green eyes wide in shock, his mind swirling like the thick black smoke he had seen in his dream, his smooth face burning from the white-hot heat of flames that had felt so real.

He had seen it, he knew. The explosion. The accident. He told himself it had just been a coincidence—after all, nothing like that dream had ever happened again. And certainly he had known beforehand that his father and the queens were to inaugurate a new oil rig with pomp and ceremony. Perhaps the young prince had been subconsciously anxious about that offshore journey his old father and the sheltered queens were taking. And that anxiety could have certainly been the root of that dream. The explosion? Ya Allah, it was a damned oil-rig! If anything was to go wrong, an explosion or fire would be the most likely result, yes? Yes. Of course.

So it was most certainly a coincidence, but still the young Rahaan had been overcome with a crushing guilt, a soaring paranoia, an overwhelming fear that perhaps a demon had taken up residence in him, filling his mind with visions of the future, tempting the young man with the gift of foresight in exchange for his soul! After all, that was the way of the *Shaitaan*, the great Satan, the dark one himself, was it not? To tempt and tease, offer and release, draw you willingly into his lair so his minions can slip into the seat of your soul and eventually turn you into a servant of darkness! We gave you a gift, and now you must give us something in return! The most ancient of traps!

Of course, Rahaan outgrew those religion-induced fears, and as he traveled the world and studied in England and the United States, that memory itself felt like a dream, like even his kingdom of Kolah was a distant land of myth and fantasy, part of a former life, part of a boy who was no more. Yes, Rahaan was still Sheikh, but he ruled in absentia, relying on his Ministry of Elders to administer the kingdom and only look to him for executive decisions of the highest importance or symbolism. It worked well enough. Kolah was small and its oil-reserves were vast. So long as the pumps kept going, there was not much to do besides allocate the monthly stipends and organize a few camel races for the younger generations who were hosting their European and American college friends. Ah, the black gold, the dark blood of the desert. Such a gift.

We gave you a gift, and now you must give us something in return, came the thought as Rahaan blinked away a feeling that had not emerged in years. It confused him, and he frowned and cocked his head as he looked at his brother and tried to refocus on their conversation. Alim had jokingly mentioned that he had been hustled out of fifteen thousand dollars in some online scam. No big deal. A learning opportunity if anything. So why was this conversation making those old, long-buried feelings bubble up in the Sheikh?

"Ya Allah, brother," Alim said with a groan. "Why did I ever bring this up? I thought you would see the humor in it, but I should have known I would simply get a lecture."

"The lecture has not even begun yet, I am sorry to inform you," said the Sheikh, holding back his smile as best he could. He stretched his arms wide again, turning and facing the window, planting his feet, finally lowering those arms and clasping them behind his back as he stood tall. "Now tell me, Alim. Who is this online scammer that has swindled the billionaire Royal Family of Kolah out of fifteen thousand dollars?"

Alim sighed and groaned again. "Ay, now it becomes about the family, does it? OK, brother. As embarrassing as it is, I will tell you everything, and I will take my lecture like an earnest student." He sighed for the third time. "And perhaps I deserve a lecture. After all, astrology is a scam as old as the universe itself."

The Sheikh turned, eyes wide, mouth twisted in amused surprise. "Astrology? Ya Allah, do you not remember your scriptures? Divination is the way of the Shaitaan, the work of the devil. If our old *maulvi* were alive, he would bring that camel-bone stick down hard on your knuckles!"

"Technically speaking it was not divination that I sought," said Alim, rubbing his eyes as his olive complexion turned dark with color. "It was illumination. More about the past than the future. An astrological chart based on my star sign, which is different from a sun sign and apparently requires quite a bit of mathematical expertise to get right."

"Oh, I am sure it takes some expertise," said the Sheikh, covering his mouth as he wondered if he should simply have the gullibility beaten out of his brother by the palace guards during their next visit to Kolah. "Well, let me see this fifteen-thousand dollar, expertly put together, highly mathematical chart of my brother's star sign. I hope there is a rainbow drawn on it as well. Some color to please the eyes, yes?"

Alim's face was the color (and perhaps even the texture) of a sun-ripened tomato as he crinkled his brow and twisted his mouth, rubbing his eyes again before exhaling and looking up at the Sheikh. "Actually the chart only cost eight thousand dollars. But I never got the chart, and when I asked about it, she told me that she did in fact send it and perhaps it had been lost in the mail."

The Sheikh just stared at his brother, not sure if he felt anger or pity at where he suspected this was going. "Lost in the mail," he said quietly, nodding slowly as he rubbed his chin. "No UPS or FedEx tracking, of course. Please, Alim. Do go on."

Alim's voice went soft, like a child's. "So I asked her to send out another copy," he said weakly. "But she said each chart was hand-drawn and she didn't keep copies because it was against her code."

"Her code," the Sheikh said, his voice deep and drawn out as his eyebrows slowly moved up. "By God, Alim, you are one in a million. But please. I cannot wait to hear the rest, even though I have already guessed it."

"If you have already guessed it, then why force me

to embarrass myself?" Alim shouted, finally losing his cool. "You can finish the story, can you not? Please, brother! I feel foolish enough as it is!"

The Sheikh sighed, rubbing the back of his head, fingers pushing through his thick black hair that could use a trim. He tilted his head back, looking down at his visibly uncomfortable brother. The boy had learned enough from this, he thought. Now there was someone else who needed to be taught about the consequences of their actions, that every action has a consequence, that just like no gift is given without an expectation of something in return, no offence is tolerated without swift and unequivocal retribution. It was the way of justice. It was the way of Wall Street. It was the way of physics, science, and the natural world. But most importantly, it was the way of the Sheikh. It was his goddamn code.

"Eight thousand dollars for a chart you never got," Rahaan said quickly, glancing at an alert that popped up on his computer screen. "And then she asked for another seven thousand to re-do the hand-drawn chart. A special one-thousand dollar discount. Of course, you never got that either. And now she is fifteen-thousand dollars richer. She is also gone like the morning mist. It is a classic con-artist strategy. Two strikes and then disappear. Poof!"

Alim was huddled in the leather armchair near the side wall, almost laughing as he shook his head. "Actually, brother, she offered to draw me the chart for a third time. Only five thousand dollars for this one."

The Sheikh looked up from the screen, cocking his head as he wondered if he had heard right. Then he roared with delight, clapping his hands three times, the sound ricocheting through the large office like a whipcrack before he slammed his heavy fists down on the table and laughed again. "Ya Allah, that is priceless! The balls on that woman! The standard con is to do it twice and then disappear. But this one tried for the triple! The goddamn hat-trick! By God, that takes guts." He settled himself down and shrugged. "Or recklessness."

"Is that not the same? Guts and recklessness?"

The Sheikh shook his head and pointed his thick index finger at Alim, looking back at the computer screen for a moment before turning again to his brother. "Recklessness is when you take a risk without having a clear idea of what you are risking. Guts is taking the very same risk but with your eyes open, with an understanding that the odds are against you but there is still a chance of victory." He punched out a quick note on the computer, now straightening up and putting his hands on his hips, thumbs stroking his thick black leather belt which was as well-worn as that swivel chair. "OK, Alim. I was going to end the lesson here and turn back to more pressing matters. But now I am intrigued. I almost want to know if this astrologer has guts or whether she is simply reckless, like so many desperate con-artists. Indeed, I am curious about this code she speaks of. A con-artist with a code is an interesting twist."

"Takes one to know one," muttered Alim, almost to himself.

"I heard that," growled the Sheikh. "And I take it as a compliment. Now tell me where this astrologer keeps her offices."

"Her offices? Ya Allah, brother. You need to get out more! Spend some time with people who are not CEOs and CFOs and CGOs!"

The Sheikh raised an eyebrow. "What is a CGO?"

"I have no bloody idea," said Alim. "But anyway, I told you I have never met this woman. She may not even be a woman, in fact. And who knows if the address on her website is even real. Probably not, if she is a crook."

"A con-artist is not quite the same as a crook," the Sheikh said glancing back at his computer screen and frowning as this latest email stole his attention. He'd been targeting a struggling company in the southwestern United States, feeling out the CEO and owner, trying to see if he could convince the man that his company was beyond saving. This way Rahaan could buy it cheap, turn it around, and make a killing. Rahaan had almost given up on the deal—it had been months since he last put in a bid. But now the CEO was asking for a meeting, and the Sheikh knew what that meant: He was ready to sell.

Rahaan began to type—a short, professional message that would not betray his excitement to do the deal: *I am busy this week. Perhaps I can visit on Thursday if one of my other deals goes through quicker than anticipated. Where did you say you are located again? I am still a tourist in America when it comes to any place outside of New York and Boston.*

Of course, Rahaan knew quite well that the company was based in Albuquerque, New Mexico, a place Rahaan had never been near but one that often came to mind for some reason. Perhaps it was the unusual spelling of the name: Albuquerque started with "Al" and could almost be an Arabic name—like Al-Buquerque. Maybe it was because he knew that the Southwestern United States was a sprawling landscape of beautiful desert, something Rahaan did miss now and then, much as he hated to admit.

"New Mexico," said Alim.

"Yes. What of it?" said Rahaan, still distracted as he sent off the email and watched his screen for a response.

"That is where this astrologer keeps her offices, dear brother," said Alim. He looked at his phone and frowned. "Al-byu-kwerk-kyu. What a name for a city, by Allah." He frowned again. "Actually it could almost be an Arabic name, yah? Al-byu—"

Rahaan sat back in his chair and stared up at his brother and then back at the screen as that old feeling came rushing back with a suddenness that knocked the wind out of him. It felt like he had been pulled back into that boyhood dream, like he was in a dream right now, living within a vision or an illusion. He forced himself to take a deep breath as he heard his computer beep again, alerting him to a new message.

It was the CEO: *We're in the fine city of Albuquerque, New Mexico, Sheikh Rahaan! Desert Country, USA! Thursday would be great. I'll have my secretary book a suite for you downtown right away—there's some kind of New Age conference happening (that stuff goes on all the time here—New Mexico is weird that way), and hotel rooms are scarce this week. Looking forward to it, Sheikh Rahaan.*

Rahaan blinked as he read the email and looked back up at Alim, who was scrolling through his phone, his face still flush with embarrassment.

"Well," said Alim, looking up and holding the phone facing out. "It appears she did not lie about her name or address. She does indeed live in Albuquerque. Her name is Hilda."

"Full name, please," grunted the Sheikh as he turned on his swivel and faced the sprawling expanse of Central Park once again.

"Hogarth," said Alim. "Hogarth is her last name."

"Hilda Hogarth," said the Sheikh as he rubbed his stubble again. "Hilda Hogarth, the Astrologer from Albuquerque."

2

Hilda Hogarth polished her crystal ball and tried to catch her own reflection in its hazy surface. Was her face really that round? Was this crystal ball really this filthy? Was she seriously in her thirties, unmarried and childless, polishing gypsy trinkets in this sad excuse for a... what was this place, anyway? And what was she? The sign outside said "Hilda's Astrological Readings," but it could have said, "If you're gullible enough to come in here, I'm going to take you for everything you've got, with the stars as my witness."

Hilda giggled as she put that silly prop back on the small round table that sat against a wood paneled side wall, beneath an oval mirror with a beautiful old silver frame. She walked to the mirror, deliberately avoiding looking into it, instead just running her red-painted fingernails along the smooth bumps of the ribbed silver frame. This had been her only inheritance, the only gift from her parents before they moved away and then moved on—first leaving New Mexico for a Florida retirement community (really?) and then leaving Earth to take their place amongst the stars.

And the mirror wasn't even a gift really. Hilda had to pretty much steal it from her parents' cluttered apartment when she was helping them pack for Florida. So that meant the only gift Hilda had ever gotten from her parents, her family, her bloodline was . . .

Stop it, she told herself, turning from the mirror and walking across the empty store to the far counter. She lit some sandalwood incense and sighed, turning and standing tall, all five-feet-not-much of her. Hands balled into tight fists now, firmly placed on her wide hips, eyes closed as she reached inside herself for what she had once been told ran in the Hogarth family, traced back at least three generations, when her great grandfather had told fortunes on the street corners of Brooklyn, New York, in the days after the War, earning enough to raise a family. He had looked the part, Hilda thought with a smile, thinking back to those black-and-white photographs that had faded to sepia: a young Bertrand Hogarth wearing what appeared to be a black cloak of some kind— something an evil viscount might have worn in an old romance novel. He had a big gap between his front two teeth, which highlighted his canines in those old pictures. Hilda had always thought the man looked like a grinning vampire with his cloak and fangs! Of course, Bertrand Hogarth had been a showman, and although the family legends were that he did indeed have a gift, they were just that: legends. The man was a salesman, a marketer, even a con-man if that's what he needed to be to put food on the table. There was honor in that: a man providing for his family, doing what it took to protect his woman and child.

"Well, I may not have the much-bandied Hogarth gift of visions and foresight or hexing and vexing or whatever the hell Bertrand supposedly had, but I can certainly look the part," Hilda said out loud, smiling as she looked down at the green-and-gold paisley harem-style pants she had on with a fitted black top stretched tight over her boobs that were still firm but admittedly a bit less buoyant and perky than when she was in her twenties. She sighed, looking down at the healthy curve of her not-so-flat belly, that black top bunched up a little around her waist, tucked sorta haphazardly into the elastic waistband. She took a breath and got into character—or perhaps a caricature of a character—turning to the door and flashing an inviting smile at no one. "Ah, a visita-aurr! Come eeen! Come eeeen!" she whispered in an accent she was sure would offend at least three different ethnic groups. "Madaaaam Heeeldaaa vill tell you your fyoochaur, read your faurchooon, interpret your dreeeems . . ."

Dreams, Hilda thought as she blinked and shook her head, wondering if she should just close up for the day and get back to that bottle of red wine that would certainly turn to vinegar if it wasn't finished off within the next couple of hours. After all, it had been sitting open since ten this morning, when she had downed a quick glass (was it two?) with her eggs and sausage. The French drank wine at breakfast, didn't they? Sounded right.

"Nobody actually goes to stores these days anyway," Hilda muttered as she walked back to her ornate, dark-wood desk in the back, where her old gray laptop was silently waiting. "All the money is online now. At least I was able to read the tea leaves on that one," she said as she clicked open her browser and checked on her website traffic. A few hundred new visitors this morning, but no new inquiries about personal horoscopes or stardust-and-rainbows hocus-pocus chartamajiggies. People just peeking in to read the free bullshit horoscopes she'd made up while finishing a bottle of that lively Pinot Noir last Saturday night, with Sabbath sitting quietly on the purple armchair, staring her down with those green eyes of his.

"Where are you anyway, Sabbath?" she called out as she opened her email and started to delete the junk messages. "Come hither, Sabbath! Come, or I swear I'll trade you in for a goddamn dog. Maybe one of those tiny lap dogs that are sooo cute, and soo—"

Now she heard movement at the foot of her desk, and hey, presto, the cat was on the tabletop in a flash, green eyes shining brighter than that crystal ball ever did, black coat shimmering in the dim yellow lamplight of the cluttered space.

"Jealousy and paranoia," said Hilda as she smiled and tickled Sabbath under his bristly chin. "Works every time. Perhaps next time you'll come to me not out of fear but out of love, Sabbath. Love! You know what that is?"

Hilda sighed again as she pushed her old red-cushioned swivel away from the desk and pulled out her phone. God, she thought. I cannot bear to swipe through these losers on Tinder or Bumble or whatever other ridiculous dating site I've signed up for. Who are these weirdos who keep showing up as "OMG it's a 99% match!"? Half these dudes look like they'd be Dungeons & Dragons grandmasters if they weren't so strung out on whatever the hell pills they've been stealing from Grandma's Medicare prescription box. Goddamn it. I'm never gonna have a kid, am I?!

A chill ran through Hilda as she tossed her phone onto the table and stood up again. Why did I even think that, she wondered, touching her belly. Am I in my "Dirty Thirties" now? Is my body shouting out to me that it's getting close to that time, that I'm still prime but spoiling fast, still peaking but close to the precipice, that if I don't take care of business, my business is going to go bad, my business is going to—

"How is business, Ms. Hilda Hogarth," came the voice now, clear and resonant, deep and booming, smashing through her self-imposed cloud of self-pity and melancholy with a vigor that startled the hell out of her—certainly startled the hell out of Sabbath, who leapt off the desk and disappeared into the shadows of the store.

"Sorry, what?" Hilda stammered, wondering if she should straighten her top or fix her hair first. She chose hair, which was wild and untamed and needed one of her many paisley scarves more than ever. Where was a scarf when she needed one! Her thing was the Cute Gypsy Woman look, not the Crazy Wild Witch of the West! "I mean hi! Hello! Come on! I mean come in! Not come on! Come inside!"

"I am already inside, Ms. Hogarth," said the man, and she could see his silhouette as he stepped into the store and stood in front of the doorway, the light of the New Mexico afternoon sun streaming in behind him, lighting his frame in an almost surreal, certainly spectacular way.

God, he was tall, Hilda thought as she squinted to get a look at his face, which was clouded in shadow. And shit, he was broad. Were those really his shoulders?! And the way his muscular outline tapered down in that masculine V shape. Tight waist, strong legs, great posture. Oh. My. God. Tell me this guy matched me on Tinder and I just don't remember because I blacked out from the wine last night! Come on, universe, where's my gift? Show me some love for the faith I've put in you, doing your work of mystery and wonder!

"Would you like a reading?" she asked weakly, swallowing hard as she wondered why she felt so goddamn nervous. Usually she felt confident and in charge when she was on her own turf. Of course, her usual customers didn't look like this . . .

"On the contrary," said the man, and now he stepped out of the shadow and into the light. "I am here to speak of your future."

"Ohmygod you're here to kill me, aren't you," she said as she stumbled away from the cramped space behind her desk and straightened up to full height and full curvy, doing her best to pull in her stomach and stick out her bum, cursing herself for not wearing the one bra that made her boobs stand up right instead of flopping about like a couple of badly-stuffed sacks.

The man was handsome, his skin a deep, smooth olive, his strong jaw lined with well-manicured stubble, his black hair short and even, like he had just had a haircut. Who gets a haircut before going to kill someone?

He cocked his head to the left, taking a half-step and stopping. He wore brown linen trousers and a white shirt that Hilda could tell was fine Egyptian cotton. The clothes were tailored, fitted perfectly, the trousers hugging his tight hips, the shirt hanging lightly on his broad shoulders, three buttons open, heavy pectorals clearly visible.

Hilda found herself frozen as she stared at the man, her gaze slowly drifting down along his body, past his flat stomach, stopping briefly at the old leather belt that seemed vaguely out of place with the pristine clothes. She allowed her gaze to rest on his full crotch for a moment before realizing what she was doing and quickly blinking and looking up, suddenly finding herself staring directly into his eyes. Green eyes, dark and piercing, full and open, clear and . . . familiar?

He held her gaze, his head still cocked to the left, a slow smile breaking behind those dark red lips. Beautiful white teeth showing now, and before she knew it she was smiling too, somehow, for some reason . . . for every reason.

"I do believe that was not a serious question," he said slowly, his voice betraying an accent that was clearly Middle Eastern but with hints of the West in it. "But given the world we live in, allow me to be clear: I am not here to kill you, Ms. Hilda Hogarth."

The man's confident smile and the easy, smooth delivery of his words were hitting home, and Hilda could feel her composure returning fast. "Well," she said, somehow managing to hold his gaze as well as her own smile, "then please stop calling me by my first and last name. That's a total serial-killer thing."

The man frowned. "I thought having three names was the hallmark of an American serial killer."

"Those aren't mutually exclusive," Hilda said, folding her arms under her boobs and trying to push them up as discreetly as possible. She felt her knees go weak when the man clearly let his gaze fall to her bosom before he looked back into her eyes without flinching, like he couldn't give a damn that she had just seen him check out her tits. Oh, God, she could feel a tingle beneath those harem pants of hers now. Oh, shit, get a hold of yourself, Hilda!

"Mutually exclusive? You are a student of logic?" the man said, glancing around the dimly lit store, his gaze quickly sweeping past the crystal ball props and the tie-dye tapestries. He stared at that old mirror for a long moment before looking back towards Hilda. "I suppose that makes sense. In America they teach logic in the philosophy departments, and philosophy seems a reasonable course of study for a fortune teller."

"Astrologer," said Hilda firmly, looking down at the maroon fake-Persian carpet and taking a breath before narrowing her brown eyes and looking back up at him. "And actually I studied physics in college."

"Really," he said, not sounding particularly impressed—which actually impressed Hilda in a way: she couldn't count the number of first dates she'd been on where the guy said some patronizingly sexist shit about being a woman who studied physics. "Where did you attend college? I do not see a degree on your walls."

Hilda blinked and frowned. Had he really scanned

the walls in that much detail with that one sweeping glance of his? There was a lot of crap on the walls, and even some framed certificates from those bullshit seminars she'd taken. But no—there was no degree on the wall. "University of New Mexico. And yeah, I didn't graduate. I—"

"UNM at Santa Fe? They have a surprisingly good physics department, if I remember correctly."

"Why is it surprising?" Hilda said, feeling the strangest annoyance rising up in her, like she was angry suddenly, angry that her hair wasn't at its best, that her eyes felt tired, that her boobs felt uneven and saggy. It had been so long since she'd even been near an attractive man, and it felt painfully obvious to her that this man's type was almost certainly not a short thirty-something hippie with paisley harem-pants and a big butt. "And how do you know my name anyway?"

"It is on the sign outside," said the man, his smile leaving his lips, eyes narrowing just enough to let on that he wasn't going to back down just because Hilda was getting angry.

"That's just my first name. I don't publish my last name, and so—"

"Well, I am sorry to inform you that Google publishes your last name, whether you like it or not," he said crisply.

Hilda felt a chill run down the curve of her back,

and she involuntarily tightened her buttocks as she stared up at the man. So a handsome, muscular Middle-Eastern man had googled her, and now he was in her store. Ohgod, no! That guy Alim she had just milked for fifteen grand?! Was this him?! The name Alim sounded Middle-Eastern enough, didn't it? Shit, this was him! Oh, God, she was screwed!

Stop, she told herself as she swallowed hard and tried to get her lower lip to stop trembling like it used to when she was a little girl. She wasn't a moron. She had always planned for something like this happening. Yes, she only pulled bigger cons like this with customers too far away to actually drive down to New Mexico. But she wasn't a moron. She knew that someday some pissed-off customer was going to walk in here or at least try to sue her, and she knew she needed to be ready.

"You're Alim," she said quickly, forcing a smile that she hoped would hide her panic. "Is that right?"

The man's eyes widened for a flash, like he was surprised at how quickly Hilda had gotten there. And then that wide, warm smile of his was back, melting through her anger, pushing past the paranoia, making her want to push her boobs up right again. God, she really was in her dirty thirties, wasn't she? Was every man she met now a prospect? Was every man now a candidate for knocking her up? Was she that pathetic? That desperate?

"I am here on behalf of my brother," said the man, still smiling as he folded his arms over his broad chest and looked her up and down, his eyes shamelessly taking in the contours of her body once again, making it clear that this was a man who didn't apologize to people, a man who looked where he wanted, perhaps did what he wanted. "He is gullible and easy to deceive, and—"

"Oh, perfect!" Hilda said loudly, raising her arms and smiling, now turning and hurrying back to her desk, to the long, somewhat unstable shelf against the dark red wall. She pulled an incredibly large, thick paper envelope from the middle shelf. "That'll save me the trouble of mailing this out to Mr. Alim! I don't use FedEx or UPS as a matter of principle, and for some reason we've had so much trouble with the mails. Here you go."

She confidently handed the envelope to the man, smiling and holding eye contact as she watched his expression change. Surprise in his eyes. Now he was thinking. Finally a glimmer of something, like he had figured out exactly what Hilda had done, what she was doing, how she was playing this con-game like a goddamn pro.

Because I am a goddamn pro, she reminded herself as she thought back to how she always had an unnecessarily complex, hand-drawn star-chart ready to go for every customer she scammed, just in case something like this happened. It had never happened before, because usually she only charged ninety-nine dollars and she was careful to pick folks who would just say screw it and let the hundred bucks go or even just forget about it when she pulled the oh-it-was-lost-in-the-mail bit. Of course, she'd never caught a fifteen-thousand-dollar fish like Alim before, and never pushed it to three rounds either, and so she'd been extra careful to make his bullshit-ass chart look good enough to earn a place in the Swindler's Museum of Fine Scams.

The man's green eyes twinkled as he took the envelope from Hilda, and he held the gaze as he tore it open and pulled out the chart. Slowly he glanced down at the hand-drawn nonsense, with star-maps and correspondence-numbers intricately put together in what Hilda knew was an indecipherable masterpiece. The man took a long look at the chart before shaking his head in wonder and looking back into her eyes.

"Ya Allah," he muttered, and she saw him flinch, like she had actually gotten to him in a way that surprised both of them. "By God, you are good, yes? Damn good."

"The best," she whispered, narrowing her eyes and holding his gaze, feeling a strange sense of familiarity, perhaps an unspoken recognition between one con-artist and another. "That'll be five thousand dollars, please. I take American Express."

3

The Sheikh couldn't stop smiling as he placed his heavy leather wallet on the dresser of his bedroom in the Presidential Suite of the Albuquerque Hilton. He flipped it open and stared at the American Express card, his grin widening as he pushed the wallet away and clapped his hands once, shaking his head as he thought of that curious, curvy, devilishly smart woman who he was certain could give any fast-talking gypsy a run for their money.

Ya Allah, she got me, did she not, Rahaan thought as he undressed and headed for the shower, his smile still wide as the hot steam rose up around him, enveloping him in white mist, adding to the surreal, mystical sense that had enveloped his goddamn brain all day.

The meeting with the CEO seemed faraway and meaningless to the Sheikh as the warm water ran down his hard, naked body. Usually a deal like the one he had just made would have gotten him wired and focused, giving him that feeling of power, of being a titan in his chosen field, a goddamn winner! But all of it barely registered, and all he could think of was that curvaceous, bodacious, vivacious fake-gypsy woman in her harem-pants and that tight black top that highlighted the swell of her bosom in a way that made him weak.

Was I staring, he wondered as he felt himself get hard almost immediately at the vividness of the memory. Usually Rahaan didn't stare—indeed, he'd always considered it a sign of weakness to stare at a woman's assets like a depraved, sex-starved animal. But by Allah, he did feel like a depraved animal right now!

For a moment he wondered if he should go back there, to the woman's store. He could charm that curvy little con-artist back to his hotel room, couldn't he? She may have had dollar signs in her eyes when she saw him, but there was most certainly attraction in those baby-browns of hers as well.

So why did you not charm her when you had her right in front of you, great Sheikh, he wondered as he reached for a thick white towel and walked to his bed, water rolling in heavy beads down his broad back, his cock bouncing gently as he took a breath and glanced down at his thick, filled-out shaft, reminding himself that it was also a sign of weakness for a man to pleasure himself like a pubescent little boy. A man takes his pleasure from a woman, not his own hand, and there were plenty of women on the menu back in New York City. Women who knew the rules. Women who knew his rules.

Still, it would be fun to have that curvy little cutie

between his sheets, would it not? Certainly she would not be at the store at this time of the evening, but he could easily get her home address.

And then what, you fool, he asked himself as he glanced once more at his erection and then shook his head and got into bed. You will show up at this woman's house with a smile and a hard-on? It is too late, dear Rahaan. You should have pulled out the charm when you had the chance. But she turned the tables on you, surprised you with the level of her game, and now you are five-thousand dollars lighter, and stuck in New Mexico with heavy balls and no goddamn release.

I could stroll down to the hotel bar and be back here in twenty minutes with some businesswoman with a toned ass and perky boobs, the Sheikh thought as both he and his cock stared up at the ceiling. Or maybe one of those young New-Age types who had overrun the hotel, with their blue beads and blonde dreadlocks and no bras. It would not even take twenty minutes, he thought as he imagined one of those modern flower-children bouncing on his mighty cock.

But for some reason the thought made the Sheikh feel sick inside, the feeling confusing him as he furrowed his brow and tried to interpret its source. Now again that overwhelming, dreamlike sensation came back to him, that cloudy feeling that had him moving trancelike all day, the only clear memory being that of Hilda Hogarth in her harem-pants, her pretty round face so clear in his mind . . . those light red lips all full and clean, big brown eyes exuding both innocence and intelligence, sharpness and softness, fierceness and . . . familiarity?

His frown deepened as he turned off the light and lay there in the darkness, that dreamlike cloud descending on him as the leftover steam lazily drifted around the room. It occurred to him now that the feeling inside was something resembling . . . resembling *guilt* of all things! Like the thought of walking down and bringing up some unknown woman to share his bed would be somehow wrong! Ya Allah, perhaps it had been too long since he had breathed some clean desert air! The smog of the city had clogged his brain as well as his lungs! Since when was Sheikh Rahaan concerned about the moral implications of consensual sex with a stranger?!

He pushed away the image of Hilda that seemed to be getting even clearer as his confusion deepened, and he tried his best to ignore that rising sense of familiarity, that he had seen her before, looked into her baby browns before . . . before this day, before this time, before this . . . life?

4

Hilda grunted as she pulled out the cork and tried to read the label on the bottle. She could make out the logo, but the text looked blurry. Shit, she thought as she looked over at the two empty bottles on the counter near the sink. Was she already at the "Shut one eye to see straight" phase?

Screw it, she thought as she poured herself a glass and sat back in the wooden chair. She grinned like a madwoman when she realized she was sitting at her kitchen table, hair all mussed, drunk off her ass on red wine, a chubby, annoyingly smug cat staring at her.

"Yup," she said to Sabbath, taking a sip and shrugging. "I'm now that woman. Who woulda thunk? At least I don't smoke cigarettes!"

She had smoked cigarettes through most of her twenties, of course. Then when thirty came around, she got this crazy idea that maybe she was going to be a mom in the not-so-distant future, and she needed to quit so she'd be ready.

"Talk about putting the cart before the horse," she muttered out loud as she drained her glass and hastily poured another. "Putting the baby before the bathwater. Or somethin' like that."

God, that guy was hot, wasn't he, she thought as the image of him rolled through her mind. I'd totally have been up for it if he'd made a move. Maybe. I dunno. Yeah. No. Whatever. Doesn't matter whether I would've or not, because he's gone.

Gone without making a move, even though he'd absolutely checked out her boobs. Should she have been a bit more open? More inviting? Would that have sent things down a different path? Maybe she'd be in a ballroom gown right now, footmen and butlers quietly standing against the walls of her dream-date as she danced the night away with this mysterious man.

"He'd swing me, dip me, *twirl* me!" she cried, rising and stepping away from the table, loping left and then right, wine sloshing in her glass as she smiled at the fantasy. "Then he'd whisk me away to his carriage and we'd ride through the night, the horses trotting in perfect rhythm as he kisses me in the privacy of the backseat, grabs my boobs like he can't stop himself!"

"Of course," Hilda said, her expression going stern as she pointed right at Sabbath, who seemed only mildly impressed. "I'd stop him right there! No more, Mister Man! I'm not that sort of woman! And who do you think you are, anyway?"

She hiccuped and cocked her head as it occurred to her that she didn't even know the guy's name, and here she was fantasizing about . . . wait, what was she fantasizing about? What the hell was this lame-ass, old-fashioned fantasy that made her feel like she was in a different place, a different time, a different . . . life?

The fantasy kept building, and as she drained the last of the wine and collapsed into bed, Hilda Hogarth felt herself slip closer to that different place, that different time, that different life.

Only it didn't seem like a different life, came the thought as the man kissed her again in her dream, smiling down at her as he spoke through the mists of her fantasy.

"Did you know that I am a king?" said he, leaning close as those horses cantered through the night. "I am a king and you are my queen, Lady Hogarth."

"I thought you were not yet king. And so how am I your queen?" Hilda replied, and she was in that half-asleep half-awake stupor, not sure if she was talking aloud or if it was all dream.

Dream or not, he kissed her again, and she swore she felt the kiss, warm and wonderful, raw and real.

"I have always been a king," he said as the dream sucked her in whole, pulling her down to that place where reality and fantasy are one, where everything is real in the same way nothing is real. "And you have always been my queen."

5
<u>HIS DREAM</u>

"You have always been my queen," said the Sheikh in his dream, and he smiled down at her as he kissed her again.

Her lips tasted like strawberries. Her tongue felt sweet and warm. Her skin was smooth like cream, like untouched snowfall. In her big brown eyes he saw himself, the reflection clear and unwavering, just like the love he felt for her in that dream.

"Kiss me, my king," she said to him. "If I am your queen, then kiss me like a queen. Kiss me like a king kisses his queen."

Rahaan felt himself smile in his dream, and Hilda smiled with him, her face lighting up like the sun as he leaned in and kissed her gently, carefully, every sense focused on her, on how it felt to hold her, kiss her, touch her, love her.

"I love you," he said to her, feeling his heat rise as he undid her bodice and caught a glimpse of her cleavage. "Oh, God, I love you."

"Is that what you say to every lady you bring in your carriage?" she said, her breath catching as he undid her all her way and touched her naked breast, pinching her plump red nipple until it stiffened between his strong fingers. He grasped her other nipple as he descended on her, taking her right breast into his mouth, sucking hard on the pert nub as Hilda squealed in surprise.

"I have never said it to anyone," the Sheikh growled as he looked up briefly into her eyes. "This is the first time. You are the first time. The first woman. The first love. The only love."

She gasped as he ripped through the last threads of her bodice, and he was on her now, kissing her breasts, sucking her nipples, his hands working their way around her smooth stomach, her lower back, into her skirts, grabbing fistfuls of her buttocks, pushing her onto her back as the carriage rollicked down the country roads of that dream.

"The only love," she moaned as he pulled her knickers down past her knees, grunting as he pulled off her boots so he could get her underwear all the way off. "That sounds nice. Though I swear you've said that before to someone."

"I have indeed said it before," said the Sheikh as he pushed the lady's skirts up over her wide hips and looked into her eyes. "I have said it before to you. Many times. Again and again."

6
__HER DREAM__

"Again," Hilda said to the young man in her dream. "Oh, do that again."

He kissed her again and she giggled, moving her little round bottom against the hard old mattress they had found in the attic. It smelled old and musty up here, but it felt clean. All of it felt clean. Even though she knew what she was doing was dirty. So dirty.

"If Pa hears you he'll be up here with his shotgun so fast we ain't gonna have time to—" she began to say as she felt him touch her small breasts through her thick nightclothes, the oversized shirt which was a hand-me-down through four sisters. His hands caressed her sides, her hips, her thighs, strong fingers that she could feel through the long-johns that were thankfully new but felt awfully wet right there, like she'd peed herself or something—though she knew she hadn't. She was too old for that.

"Then we'd better get on with it, yea?" said he, grinning wide as he found the buttons to the front of her nightshirt and began to feverishly undo them.

"Oh, you are horrible," she giggled. "You promise you'll marry me, yes?" she said as she felt the cool air swirl around her bare chest as her young lover took her shirt off and gasped at the sight of her breasts, little pink nipples all stiff and ready . . . ready like she was, ready to do something she knew was wrong but somehow didn't feel wrong. Not with him. Him.

He looked down at her, his green eyes shining in the dim moonlight coming in through the tiny attic window. "We're already married. I told ya. We don't need no minister or judge to say it's true. Didn't I ask you to marry me three months ago, when we was picking strawberries and we saw that rainbow even though there weren't no rain?"

"Yes," she whispered as she looked up at him. He was only three years older, but he looked like a man in the dim light of the secret night. His black hair was thick and wild, those green eyes shining something fierce. There was no lie in those eyes. There was no betrayal in that voice. There was no doubt in the moment. "Yes," she said again.

"And if your Pa don't like it, then we'll run away together. I told ya. I ain't gonna live without you. You're my wife now. Nobody can say you aren't!"

She felt a warmth rise up in her as he kissed her breasts, gently sucking her nipples in a way that made her want to squeal in pleasure. But she held her tongue because she knew the walls were thin.

She held her tongue and bit down on her lip as she felt him pull her long johns down past her bottom, all the way off, and she could smell herself now as he touched her down there, carefully, gently, like he truly did love her, like he truly was married to her. This was what married people did, yea? And so there was no reason to feel guilty. She could enjoy it, couldn't she?

"Tell me again how you're going to be a king and I'm gonna be your queen," she whispered as she felt him touch her there with his fingers like he had done before, sending her into that half-dream state where she truly was a queen and not a farmer's daughter, where he was a king and not a tailor's son.

"I already am a king," he said to her in the darkness, his voice sounding deeper, older, different. "And you already are my queen. The rest of the world just don't know it yet."

7
<u>HIS DREAM</u>

"The rest of the world does not need to know," she said to the Sheikh through the mist of the dream. "We can wait until—"

"We will keep it secret until the child is born, but then the world will know it. I will make damned sure the world knows it!"

"A child out of wedlock," she said, her big brown eyes looking up at him, like they were searching him for something. "On top of what we are already doing. There will be no righting this! Your father would—"

"It is not my father's life. And it is not my father's child. It is my child! Our child." He smiled down at her, marveling at how beautiful she looked even though they'd been riding for days, through rain and sun, dust and wind. It was the two of them, the prince and his commoner-bride, with a small group of loyal servants, setting out on a self-imposed exile, a choice that seemed mad on the face of it but had been so easy to make. Indeed, it felt like he had made the choice before, would perhaps make it again: The choice to put his woman and child before anything else, before *everything* else.

A week ago he had met his arranged bride for the first time, the golden-haired Princess Diamante, the only royal child of a small but powerful kingdom in the foothills of the Pyrenees mountains. The girl was sharp and ambitious, beautiful and gracious, and would certainly make any prince proud. Any prince but him.

And that was what he had told Diamante, right after making it clear he would not be going through with the marriage, that he was promised to another. It was a promise that could not be broken, he had said. A promise written in the stars, he swore.

He had expected that Diamante would appreciate his candor, respect his private, discreet confession. After all, he had a younger brother who could take his place, should the royal families still wish to pursue the alliance-by-marriage. He had thought telling her face-to-face would be better than simply declining the arrangement from afar, which might give rise to misunderstandings at a political level, implying that the alliance itself was being rejected. But it was a mistake: Diamante took it as a personal rejection, a rejection of not the alliance but of her—her beauty, her grace, her womb even.

"And who is the woman more suitable than I to

bear your children?" Diamante had asked, her forwardness surprising the prince, something about her tone warning him that he should perhaps not add to his error by speaking the name of the one he loved.

Somehow the prince had navigated his way through that conversation, racing back to his kingdom and telling his father the king of what he had done, what he was going to do.

"It is the only way now," the prince said to his father. "I will leave, and you must announce that I have been exiled for my insult to Princess Diamante. I know the alliance is crucial for our kingdom, and my selfishness has brought us to—"

"What is done is done," the king said, his dark eyes steady and unwavering. "A king does not apologize for his actions. You have made your decision, and you are backing up your act of selfishness with an act of sacrifice. That is the way of a king. The king you will be one day."

"How, Father?" said the Sheikh in his dream. "How can that be when I am to leave in exile? When it is time for a new ruler, it will be my younger brother and Diamante who will ascend, yes? How will I be king?"

8
<u>HER DREAM</u>

"**I** don't know how I know," said Hilda in the musty attic of that dream. "I just know. OK? Oh, God, are you angry? I swear I didn't mean for it to happen!"

"It's not your fault," he said to her, smiling even though she could see the worry on his young face, the concern in those green eyes of his. "I'm the man, and I'm responsible. I'm responsible for you, my wife."

"Am I really your wife?" she whispered up at him. "Do you really mean that?"

"How many times are you going to ask me that?" he said as his expression softened, though the concern still showed in his eyes. "I already told you. We don't need anyone else to tell us we're man and wife. Especially now. Now that . . . oh, God, are you sure?"

"I . . . I think so. I haven't bled for more'n two months, and I been getting sick sometimes, just like my sisters did when it happened. They stopped bleeding too when it happened, they said."

"You told your sisters?" The worry rushed back into his voice.

"No, silly! Of course not! They used to talk about it, that's all. I just remember."

"You're smart that way," he said, his smooth brown forehead crinkling up as he looked down at her, petting her dark hair gently, undoing a beast of a knot in her tresses as she smiled and blushed at the compliment. "We're gonna need your smarts when we set out on our own."

"What do you mean?" she asked, even as the terrible truth dawned on her. It was one thing to be married in secret, without anyone knowing. But if she was with child now, then there'd be no hiding it soon. And then what? What would Pa say? What would Pa do?!

"I mean, once your Pa finds out, he ain't gonna let . . . he ain't gonna let . . ." He sighed and smiled, rolling off her and lying next to her on that hard mattress in the attic. Now he turned and held her hand, raising her arm and pushing up her sleeve. He paused for a moment, and then he kissed her smooth white forearm and pulled back his own sleeve.

"What do you see?" he asked, placing his bare arm next to hers. "Tell me what you see."

"I dunno," she said, frowning as she looked at the smooth brown skin of his arm pressed up against the creamy white of hers. In a moment she understood, and she glanced into his eyes, her hand reaching for his face, her fingers caressing his dark cheek as he smiled at her in the night.

"You see, don't you? You see what your Pa will see. You see what the town will see. What they already see when they look at me."

She blinked away the tears welling up in her brown eyes. "But that don't mean nothing! I know what they say around town, but it's not true. Your ma and pa are white as anyone else in town! Whiter'n my parents even, I bet!"

He took a deep breath, slowly exhaling as he brought her hand to his lips and kissed her fingers, one by one. "They ain't my real parents. They didn't tell nobody 'cause they know how it is in these parts. They just tell everyone my grandpa had black hair and dark skin. And all us boys are browned from the sun anyway. My folks said let people talk. So long as nobody knows for sure, we're all right. People talked, but nobody cared enough to start any trouble. But now . . . ? Not now. Not with this."

She swallowed hard as she tried not to cry. The tears rolled down her smooth round cheeks, but her voice was firm as she spoke. "It don't matter. Once I tell Pa we're married, it'll be OK. He ain't gonna shoot you!" She said it with a forced smile.

He snorted and shook his head, his expression hardening, his young face once again looking older, like he was a man and not a boy—not anymore at least. "I ain't worried about that so much as I'm worried about you!"

She snorted. "Me? What's gonna happen to me?"

He took a breath as his gaze moved slowly down along her body, and he gently reached out and placed his right hand on the small round of her belly. "They ain't gonna let this happen. They just ain't. There's folks in town who got ways. I heard about it."

"Oh, God!" she squealed, immediately clamping her hand over her mouth and closing her eyes tight. "Oh, God," she whispered. "They wouldn't. Pa wouldn't let them. Ma wouldn't let them!"

He exhaled and shook his head. "They ain't gonna have no choice. Like you said, your pa ain't gonna shoot me." He grunted. "He'd for sure wanna shoot me, but he ain't gonna do it. And he sure as hell ain't gonna let me marry you for reals. Which means there ain't no choice for him. They'll do it quiet, so no one knows. Take the baby outta you before the rest of the town finds out. You in more danger than I am, you see? And you're my wife. I gotta protect you. I gotta protect our child. That's what a man does, you hear? A man protects his family. I can't protect you here, and so we gotta run. You, me, and our baby."

She closed her eyes and took a breath, holding it in as long as she could. When she opened her eyes and exhaled she could feel something different about her, like something had changed, like she had made a decision that was monumental but somehow so easy. It was almost as if she'd made the decision before, many times before, in different ways, again and again . . .

9
HIS DREAM

"Again . . . tell me again how you're going to be a king," she whispered as the carriage bounced its way through that mystical country road in the Sheikh's dream.

He could barely see straight, his arousal was so strong. She was magnificent, he thought as he caressed her naked hips, reveling in how her thighs shuddered each time the carriage went over a bump. She was perfect, just perfect, he thought as he leaned close to her bare sex, his entire body stiffening as he took in her feminine scent. He kissed her soft inner thighs as she moaned and placed her palms on his head. By God, this woman drove him wild! To the world she was quiet and shy, sophisticated and well-mannered. But with him she was a goddess, a wallflower opening up into full bloom just for him— only for him. Like she had done once before, three years ago. Did she remember? Did she know it was him?

"Is that the only reason you allow me so close, grant

me such access, spread for me thus, my lady," he whispered as he kissed her secret curls, breathing deep of her musk again as he gently parted her brown triangle with his tongue. "Because I am to be king?"

"Oh, dear," she muttered as the tip of his tongue touched the mouth of her slit. "Oh, dear!"

"There we go," he whispered against her, kissing her full on those dark nether lips of hers before sliding his tongue into her glistening slit as she moaned.

Slowly he moved his tongue back and forth, in and out, faster and faster, his warm lips working her labia as his tongue drove deep into her cunt. He could feel her body shudder with each stroke, shiver with each stab, shake with each roll, and he could not hold himself much longer, he knew.

Feverishly he undid his breeches, groaning into her crotch as he released his cock. He was harder than he could possibly believe, his shaft feeling thick like a lamppost as he massaged himself while he brought her close with the fury of his tongue.

"No," she muttered when she saw what he was doing. "What if I get pregnant?"

"That is the point, my lady," he grunted as he released his engorged manhood and pushed her down flat against the cushion. "That is the whole damn point!"

"Oh, Lord!" she whispered when she saw his masthead burst into view, dark red and swollen full, glistening, gleaming, terrifyingly thick, supremely erect. "Oh, my dear God!"

10
<u>HER DREAM</u>

"**O**h, God!" Hilda screamed through her dream as the Sheikh pushed his manhood deep into her sex, his thick cock forcing open the slender mouth of her slit, widening the walls of her vagina as he drove hard, thrust long, pumped strong.

She gasped for air as she felt him kiss her hard on the mouth, ravishing her face with his warm lips as he took her, those powerful hips driving his cock into her with a force that shook her. She moaned into his mouth as he pulled back halfway and then drove back in, again and again as the horses pulled that carriage through her dream, again and again as she moaned and wailed, again and again as she got closer, closer, until she was there, coming suddenly, coming hard, like a lady and a whore, a saint and a sinner, a lover and a wife, a peasant and a queen.

And as she came she could see the lampshades above her, gypsy lanterns swinging wildly from the motion . . . the motion of the carriage, the motion of their lust, the motion of his thrust, the motion of . . . time.

Suddenly Hilda was in her store in Albuquerque as the Sheikh took her, and she was also in that horse-driven carriage with a man who said he was to be king, somehow still that girl on a hard mattress in a musty attic with a boy who swore he would be king, now riding through the night with a prince who might never be king because of her . . .

Three dreams in one, three lives in one, three women in one . . .

"Oh, God, what's happening!" Hilda screamed as she sat bolt upright in her bed, back arching as her climax whipped through her, making her scream, making her howl, making her shout and sob, writhe and bob, thrash and flail. That green-eyed cat ran for all nine of his lives as the world shattered and rebuilt itself in that little room, as the earth shook, the universe shuddered, space and time bent over and twirled around, all of history and herstory dancing a cosmic dance with Hilda Hogarth as the dancefloor.

"Oh, God, what the fuck is happening," she sobbed as that orgasm still roared through her stricken body like he was in the room with her, his green eyes looking deep into hers as he took her, again and again, the Sheikh, the king, the boy, the girl, the dream.

"Oh, God, what's happening," she muttered as she finally surrendered and let the climax take her back to that dream, the dream that was in full color, vivid and alive, burning and true, more real than life, perhaps because it was more than life, perhaps because it was all of life.

Oh, God, what's happening . . .

11

"Ya Allah, what is happening!" he roared, the sound of his own voice waking him, and he was in his hotel room but still in that carriage with her, alone in his room but also in that musty attic with her, naked and in bed but somehow riding free with her. With her!

He almost passed out from the force of his orgasm, the release coming so hard and with such violence that his heavy torso raised up off the bed as the Sheikh exploded into the sheets, his seed pouring into white linen even as he swore he felt his body pressed tight against hers, his release flowing directly to her depths, his heat somehow flooding her valleys, pouring deep into her canals like it always had, like it always would.

He came like it was coming from somewhere else, like it was going to somewhere else, and as the dreams swirled through his crazed mind, his body racked with a fever so raw, the Sheikh clearly saw her face, clearly tasted her lips, clearly knew her name, all her names, the girl, the woman, the queen, three names, three women, three dreams.

Three dreams in one. Three lives in one. Three women in one.

Hilda. Hilda. Hilda.

12
<u>**TWO MONTHS LATER**</u>

"**H**ilda," she said to the doctor after following him into his private office adjoining the examination room—which was where she'd been a couple of weeks earlier, when she came in for a checkup, wondering if all that cheap-ass wine had finally done some real damage. "Just Hilda is fine. Certainly not *Mrs*. Hogarth. I think I'd remember if I had gotten married."

The doctor turned bright red and blinked hard, rubbing his chin and staying strangely quiet until she took a seat. He went around the desk and sat down as well, nodding again and blinking hard. "My mistake. The nurse must have written it down wrong. So sorry."

It's always the nurse's fault, she thought as she tried to stop herself from giving him an over-the-top eye-roll. Nice to have a ready made scapegoat, yes, Doctor? Well, let's see if you can give me something or someone to blame for why my body seems to be going nuts over the past couple of months, ever since . . .

No, she thought as she tried to block out the insane thoughts that had been invading her mind ever since she'd missed her period twice and then taken a home pregnancy test that was obviously and positively fake or broken. Or perhaps she was broken, she eventually decided when all the dumb-ass pregnancy tests seemed to say the same thing—the impossible thing, of course. So now she was here, wondering if her thirty-something hormones were getting out of whack from the wine and the junk food and the wine and her weight and the wine and the cat-hair. Cat hair! That must be it! Some messed up cat allergy from the little green-eyed devil!

Of course, "cat allergy" hadn't showed up as one of the many reasons an otherwise healthy woman would suddenly stop getting her period. Hilda had gone down the list twice: Severe stress? No more than usual. Hard drugs like heroin or crack? Just red wine and caffeine, with a chaser of sugar. Low body-fat? Um, nope.

She didn't even consider testing for being preggers until the second missed period and the random morning-sickness type stuff that was most certainly something new. Of course, the pregnancy tests were more for entertainment, she had told herself when she bought them from the Walgreen's across town. (She had been careful not to be seen in the drugstore down the block buying something that pretty much confirmed you were a whore . . . hey, even a gypsy woman cares about the fake-ass morals of society!)

But now she was here, exhausted and at the end of her rope. Two months without her period. Two weeks of consistently lighting up those infuriating pregnancy tests with positive readings that seemed to say, "Yes! You are a whore! A drunken whore at that! If you weren't, then at least you'd remember sleeping with whichever guy knocked you up!"

Yeah, she blacked out sometimes if she didn't eat before going through a bottle of Pinot. But usually that resulted in her waking up with a hangover and a messy kitchen from some awesome-sounding internet recipe that she didn't remember attempting. Hilda knew that blacking out wasn't great, but she always felt the appropriate amount of self-hatred after those nights. And she never got that drunk when she was out at a bar or a party. Certainly not on a date! She was a lady! Besides, the last date she'd been on was over seven months ago. And Videogame Grandmaster Wizardski Potbelly (who didn't look anything like his Tinder pic, btw . . .) didn't get his dragon even close to her ladylike dungeons.

But clearly I missed something . . . or someone, she thought as she watched the doctor's thin lips move in slow motion, the words forming one by one in the ether as she felt a sickness rise up in her.

"Well, there's nothing wrong with you, Mrs.—I

mean Miss—Hogarth," he said. He swallowed hard and blinked again and his face turned that Pepto-Bismol pink once more. "Or perhaps I should say congratulations? Is the pregnancy a surprise?"

And now it came, the sickness that had been building to a head, the awful feeling of being pulled into a nightmare, a world where nothing made sense, where *she* didn't make sense!

"Oh, God, this is impossible," she muttered as she gasped and blinked four-hundred times in rapid succession and then wiped her mouth while the doctor weakly called for his nurse. "Fucking impossible!"

13

"It is impossible, Sheikh Rahaan. It simply cannot be done."

"Impossible . . . cannot . . . these are words that do not make me happy," said the Sheikh, putting his sunglasses away and squinting down at the much-shorter, and certainly rounder, foreman overseeing the construction of a new, state-of-the-art oil rig in the Arabian Sea, just beyond the mouth of the Gulf of Oman. Rahaan and Alim's father had wisely held on to the drilling rights off the small coastline that their ancestors, the founders of the Kingdom of Kolah, had fought to acquire almost a hundred years ago, when land was still being taken by force. The powerful Islamic nation of Saudi Arabia had offered to buy the drilling rights decades ago, and in fact the offer still stood and was valued at tens of billions of dollars now. But Rahaan's father had refused to sell, and Rahaan somehow felt compelled to uphold his father's decision.

Though now it seemed like selling might have been the wiser choice, the Sheikh thought as he took a breath and walked to the deck-railing of the thirty-foot boat that was bobbing about a hundred meters away from the still-under-construction rig. They were almost a year behind schedule already, and now he was being told it would take another ten months before they could start pumping!

"It looks almost ready to me," said Alim, shrugging as he tugged at his goatee and glanced over at the Sheikh.

"I agree," said Rahaan, holding a straight face as he saw the foreman almost melt into a puddle of muted anger. "You have two months. I am already setting a date for the opening ceremony."

"By Allah, great Sheikh! Two months is madness! There was a reason your father could not build a rig in this part of the ocean! The sea bed beneath these waters is shifting sand, and we have to dig deep and wide to secure the foundation for an oil rig this size! I implore you, do not make us speed up the process. Remember what happened the last time one of our oil rigs was rushed to completion."

Rahaan's jaw went tight as he turned and looked down at the foreman. Did the man really just say what he said?! By Allah, what gall!

The Sheikh saw Alim raise his eyebrows, and Rahaan placed a hand on his brother's shoulder, staying him.

"Your name is Yusuf Iqbal," Rahaan said to the foreman, looking at him closely, realizing that although the man was short and round, he was powerfully built, with a strange confidence—even defiance—in his sand-colored eyes.

"Yes, my Sheikh," said the man, holding eye contact for several seconds before looking down towards the Sheikh's feet. "My apologies for my thoughtless, insolent statement. Please, I am—"

"You are barely older than myself," said Rahaan, frowning and touching his chin as he tried to read the man, size him up. The Sheikh could usually make a solid, accurate character assessment in a moment—something that came in handy when he had to make quick decisions about firing deadweight executives from the struggling companies he purchased. But he couldn't get a clear picture of this man for some reason. Almost like the man was in a state of flux, blocking the Sheikh's powers of perception.

"I am two years older than the Sheikh," said Iqbal, bowing his head once more and then looking up and holding Rahaan's gaze in a way that was respectful but far from submissive.

"I was fourteen then, and so you were sixteen during the time of the great tragedy," Rahaan said slowly, his voice deepening, his green eyes steely and unwavering as he stared down the man. "You were a teenager as well. What can you possibly know about an oil rig's state of readiness back then? Speak, Yusuf Iqbal."

Yusuf Iqbal finally blinked and looked past the Sheikh. "Of course I was a boy. Like you, my Sheikh. But I paid close attention, because like you, I too lost my father in that explosion."

The Sheikh's eyes narrowed as he tried to think back. Yusuf Iqbal. Iqbal. The name did ring a bell. It had been years since Rahaan had been to the Hall of Archives in Kolah's Royal Palace, but he had studied the reports of the tragedy so many times as a youth that he could almost recite them word for word. Finally it hit him, and his body stiffened for a moment before he spoke. "Yezid Mohammed Iqbal," he said softly. "Your father. He was the head of Kolah's Royal Corps of Engineers. Educated at Jamiah Milliah University and then at the California Institute of Technology. He worked in the oil industry in Texas, USA, for some time before my father offered him the position in Kolah."

"Not offered. Ordered," muttered Yusuf Iqbal, making sharp eye contact with the Sheikh before looking down at the deck and nodding quickly.

"Speak freely, Yusuf Iqbal," snapped Rahaan, a sudden anger rising in him as he watched this man's body language. The Sheikh was feeling a vague discomfort from all this, from this man himself, and he did not like it. "I would rather my people speak their dissatisfactions or concerns directly and honestly than mutter under their breath and give me sharp looks that I am supposed to interpret like I am a goddamn psychic. Speak freely. I assure you, I will not have you thrown to the sharks if you offend me. It is just the three of us within earshot, and you may speak your mind. Clearly there is something you want to say. Spit it out, Yusuf Iqbal. Speak to my face like a man instead of mumbling like a schoolboy!"

Alim glanced over at the Sheikh, his eyes wide, and Rahaan realized that he'd been speaking at the top of his voice, almost shouting at Yusuf Iqbal. It was not like him, the Sheikh thought as he blinked and tried his best to soften his expression.

But Yusuf Iqbal did not seem fazed, and he held his head high and began to speak, his voice sounding deeper, different, like something had changed in the man over the last few moments, as if they had all stepped into a different reality—different in a subtle, almost eerie way.

"My apologies again, great Sheikh," said Yusuf Iqbal. "I mean you no disrespect. You have been a gracious and generous Sheikh as long as you have reigned, and I would not stand to hear a man say otherwise. My sharp tone was misguided, and my behavior is inexcusable."

Rahaan smiled, exhaling and looking past Yusuf Iqbal and towards the distant shores of Kolah, just a golden strip on the horizon, past the deep blue swell of the Arabian Sea—the sea that was a graveyard to many, he remembered. Strong emotions ripple through the years like the waves, rising and falling, changing form, he thought. But emotions that deep never truly go away.

"And perhaps my tone was harsher than it should have been, Yusuf Iqbal," he said quietly. "As a boy I carried anger and grief for a long time. Allah knows it is still in me somewhere. I only imagine it was the same for you. Come, sit with me. I will call for tea. We will talk. Of course, first let us take a moment and remember our fathers and the other innocent souls whose final resting place is beneath these very waves."

"I remember my father every day when I wake up and go to work across these waves," Yusuf Iqbal said quietly, placing his thick arms by his side and looking up at the Sheikh. The man's long white tunic billowed in a sudden gust of breeze, the extra cloth around his shoulders and sleeves rising up like wings for a moment. "And since we speak of work, I must get back to my engineers now. We have to do one year's work in two months, and so I must beg the Sheikh's leave and respectfully decline his offer to leisurely drink tea above the graves of our fathers."

The Sheikh held the man's gaze for a long, strange moment before nodding once and giving him permission to leave, choosing to remain unmoved by the last comment. He watched Yusuf Iqbal walk to the aft of the boat and quickly descend the metal ladder to the dingy that would take him back to the oil rig.

Once the dingy was far enough, Rahaan nodded at a white-clad crewman who stood silently on the forward deck, and the man spoke quickly into a walkie-talkie. In a moment the powerful engines of the boat roared to life, and the Sheikh placed both hands on the side rail and watched the dingy and the oil rig fade into the distance as that odd dreamlike feeling came closer, closer, too close perhaps.

The Sheikh exhaled hard as he turned away from the sea, trying to turn away from his thoughts as well . . . thoughts that had made him question his own sanity over the past two months. Thoughts of that night in New Mexico. Thoughts of that dream. Three dreams in one. Three women in one. One woman in three dreams perhaps.

"At least there are no more wet dreams," he muttered, trying to make himself smile even as he fought that intense need to go back there, to be close to her, a closeness that he still felt to her, a closeness that made no damn sense just like a dream should make no damn sense when you're awake.

But the dream is the only way it makes sense, he thought as he turned towards the shoreline and put his sunglasses back on. It is the only way to explain this feeling of closeness.

14

"Not too close now," said Hilda, placing her hands flat on the round table in the center of her store, palms facing down, head slightly bowed, big brown eyes dramatically narrowed as she stared into the candle-flame and tried to make it seem like she could see visions of this suburban stoner-chick's future.

The candle flame danced before her, and perhaps it was because she was sober as a judge's chauffeur, but the words came to her easily now, making her almost believe in the crap she was spouting to this dazzled nineteen-year-old with a platinum debit card.

"He is tall, but not too tall," Hilda said in a low, deep monotone, doing her best not to go full gypsy on the girl—not yet, at least. Wait for a sign that you've got a hit first, then you can lay it on and pull her in for the "special" session reserved for stoners with platinum debit cards.

"Perfect," the girl mumbled, her glazed eyes mesmerized by the candle-flame. "Tall is sexy, but too tall freaks me out. Is he rich?"

Hilda gently closed her eyes and opened them,

allowing a low hum to come from her throat as she nodded. "It is coming to me . . . give it a minute . . . ah, I see . . . I see a car, two cars, a garage full of cars, a house, big, very big, with grounds, lawns, beautiful and exotic. You are with him, the two of you holding hands."

"Ohmygod, what about a ring?! Do you see a ring?" the girl shrieked, her tongue hanging out, making her look like a teenage tennis player trying to concentrate on serving right.

Hilda did the vibrating-hum again, blocking out the annoying thoughts that she was pregnant without a ring. She hummed again, wondering if this girl would use her own version of the humming technique to get the future she envisioned. Ohgod that was so mean. Not every woman's a whore like you, Hilda, she reminded herself. Not every woman gets knocked up without a fucking clue who the baby-daddy is!

You do have a clue, came that annoyingly persistent thought from the back of her even more annoyingly sober brain. The only problem is it's impossible! You're further gone than Stoner-Girl if you believe a man can knock you up in a goddamn dream!

"A ring," Hilda muttered quickly, forcing herself to get back to business even though her mind was wandering again. After all, she was gonna be a mom in six months. Mom to what, she didn't know yet. Perhaps an alien lizard king. That was about as plausible as a good-looking Arabian stud doing the deed in a dream.

Except the man is real, came the voice in her head that she wished was actually a voice—that way she'd know for sure that she was crazy! Yes, the man is real, the orgasm was real, and the dream was . . .

"A ring," Hilda said again, raising her voice to a squeak and almost breaking the spell for Stoner-Girl. "Yes, I see a gorgeous, shining ring. Gold band, with—"

"Oh, yeah, that's what I'm talkin' about," gushed Stoner-Girl as she got sucked in again.

"Thick gold band," said Hilda. "Diamonds studding the sides. I see it clearly on his right hand. Maybe an Ivy League college ring. No, it's a sports ring! From a sports title, maybe even the Superbowl—"

"Wait, the ring's on *his* hand? What a bummer!" cried Stoner-Girl, and now Hilda knew she'd lost the game. Hilda had read Stoner-Girl as someone who was already rich and so perhaps would be more impressed with someone famous, but no: Stoner-Chick just wanted a no-name rich dude with a ring for her. Shit. Shit. Shit! That's what you get for being too creative.

Hilda tried to turn it around, but the buzz had officially been killed, and Stoner-Girl paid the advertised discount fee and strutted out, staring at her phone on the way.

"Goddammit!" Hilda said, slamming her palms back down on the wood, making the table jump and almost knocking the thick red candle over. "Almost had her for the full-price menu! Gotta remember that even a modern hippie-chick wants her diamond ring. Ring me! Ring me! Ring me!"

She screamed out the last bit of her private rant, slamming her palms down on the table again, biting her lip as she tried not to cry. God, how was she gonna do this? She wasn't bad with money and she could probably figure that part out, especially now that the wine budget had been freed up. But more than that, how was she going to handle this mentally! Being a single mom was one thing. But like this? Hell, she couldn't even tell her two or three friends about it, because what would she say when they asked the obvious question?!

"Who's your daddy," she muttered, giggling as she ran her fingers through her hair, clawing open the braid she'd artfully done along one side. "Who's your daddy!"

"Sorry, am I interrupting?" came a man's voice from the door, and Hilda started in her chair and blinked through the candle-flame as she tried to shake that eerie sense of being someplace else but still here, of being someone else but still herself . . . just like she was pregnant but still celibate. Was she carrying the new messiah? The devil's spawn?

Alien abduction and secret government experiments is more like it, she thought, squinting at the man and wondering if she'd stepped into the X-Files and this was a secret government agent who was going to explain what was going on and then erase her memory with a radioactive tampon.

"No," she said, still squinting as she tried to make out the shadowy figure standing in the doorway. For a moment she thought it might be him . . . the man of her dream, the man she'd taken for a cool five grand, the man whose name she didn't even know.

Ohgod wait, she thought as it hit her that the handsome Arabian guy had paid with his American Express card, which meant she actually did have his name on the receipt somewhere! Had she seriously not looked it up for two months? Talk about denial. Wait, what was she denying? It can't be denial if it's ridiculous to begin with, yes? Oh shit, where was that—

"Hilda? Hilda Hogarth?" said the man as he stepped forward, the yellow light illuminating him finally. It was not him, Hilda thought with a sinking feeling that almost pissed her off as much as it confused her. Was she sitting here pining for some guy she barely knew?!

"Yes? Sorry, I don't know—oh, shit, Professor Norm! Oh, wow, I didn't even . . . what are you doing here?" she said, standing and stepping away from the round table, her face going red as she tried to casually hide that crystal ball with her left hand. She shook her head and stared into the soft eyes of her physics professor from UNM-Santa Fe. He'd aged a little—after all, it'd been almost ten years since she'd dropped out of college—but it was certainly Professor Norman: that uneven, orange-brown beard, soft, light-brown eyes that were earnest and intelligent, sandy hair that was most certainly on its way out, thinning terribly at the top. "How are you, Professor! It's been what . . . nine, ten years? What are you doing here?"

"Oh, God, please call me Norm," he said warmly, stepping forward like he was going to hug her but then hesitating and extending his right hand for an awkward handshake. He blinked as she shook his hand, now smiling as he glanced around the chaotic little store, eyes resting on that crystal ball before he looked back at her. "Well, the wife and I are in town for a seminar, so I thought I'd say hello."

"Well, I'm . . . I'm . . . I mean it's great to see you, Prof—I mean Norm," said Hilda, pulling at her hair and squinting a little. "I didn't think you'd even remember me, let alone know where I worked, what I did." She took a quick breath and glanced at the crystal ball, going a bit red again as she frowned and looked back at the middle-aged physics professor who seemed to be trying very hard not to laugh. "Go ahead," she said finally, smirking and placing her hands on her hips. She'd always liked the professor's gentle demeanor and earnest way, and so screw it, she thought. Let him laugh. "You can laugh now. It can't be healthy to hold it in like that."

Now they both burst into laughter, the professor doubling over and shaking his head, squeezing Hilda's arm warmly as he rubbed that crystal ball and giggled himself back to calmness. "Well," he said finally, taking a deep breath. "This is actually the reason I remember you so well, Hilda. My best students usually want to work for Intel or NASA, so you've always sort of stuck out in my mind."

"Your best students usually graduate too, I bet," Hilda said, brushing off the compliment as she remembered that she'd actually done pretty darn well in Professor Norm's classes. Not so good in the rest of her classes though. Yeah, Einstein supposedly flunked math and history too, but he probably didn't have a scholarship riding on his grade point average. "And they don't fail math, history, English, and psychology. Not to mention most of the other physics classes I took."

Norm pursed his lips and shrugged, nodding and shrugging again before smiling that gentle, easy smile. "I remember. Made it kinda hard for me to convince the scholarship board to make an exception for you."

"You tried. I know that. It was good of you, and I always appreciated it." Hilda waved her hand at him. "College just wasn't for me. Couldn't drag myself to those boring classrooms, which is kinda important if you want to not fail. But whatever. What about you, Professor? You said you're here with your wife? When did you get married?"

Norm cocked his head and looked up at the ceiling. "Three . . . no, four years now." He frowned, reaching into his pocket and pulling out a very large, clunky phone. "Which reminds me, I should . . ." He trailed off as he poked at the screen, looking up when he finished. "Di will actually be really interested in hearing about what you do. It's right up her alley. Oops—getting ahead of myself here. Sorry. I didn't even ask. You up for lunch with me and Di? Our treat. Come on."

Hilda took a breath as she glanced towards where Sabbath was sitting, over on the shelf near the back of the store, coolly surveying the scene in his who-gives-a-shit way, those green eyes of his wide and unwavering.

"You gonna be all right, my little monster?" she said, walking over and reaching for Sabbath, lifting him gently off the shelf and holding him at eye level. "Oh, shit!" she cried out when she looked into the cat's eyes, shock ripping through her when she saw that Sabbath's green eyes were somehow, someway, for some reason . . . not green anymore!

A chill crept through her as she looked at her cat, and she cocked her head as she wondered if it was just the weird light in the room that was making Sabbath's eyes look red and not green. What. The. Hell. It was most certainly Sabbath and not some imposter cat—she knew that for sure. But those eyes . . . how? How?!

Hilda carefully placed Sabbath on the paisley patterned rug, watching him slowly walk towards his litter box in the back. Yes, it was most certainly her cat. She was just seeing things. Maybe it was the hormones. Maybe it was being sober. Or maybe it was because this was a dream too now.

She turned as the front door opened again, and as the warm outside air rushed in, Hilda felt that weird sensation again, like it wasn't just the air swirling around, like it was time itself, space itself, reality itself twisting and turning, spinning and swaying.

The woman who'd walked in was tall, with dark red hair open and long, sharp features and narrow eyes, a pronounced jawline that matched her lean, almost muscular body. She looked athletic and strong, with boyish hips in tight black jeans, a loose gray shirt with a black tank top underneath. Was this Professor Norm's wife? Whoa!

"Hey!" said Norm, blinking as he looked over at the woman. "That was quick. Di, this is Hilda. Hilda, my wife Di—"

"Nice to meet you," Di said without a smile or a handshake. Her voice was friendly though, and Hilda smiled. "I love your cat. I'd have ten of them, but Norman's allergic so we only have three."

Hilda glanced at Norman, seeing a flash of annoyance show itself on his soft face before he relaxed and shrugged. Was she kidding or . . .

"Let's go. I'm hungry," said Di, flexing her long, tight arms like she'd just worked out or something. "And thirsty. God, it's hot today! Come on. Chop chop, people."

"Hold on," Norm said slowly, looking over at Hilda, eyes almost apologetic. "Hilda hasn't said she's available right now. She might have appointments, and so—"

"Do you?" said Di sharply, eyebrows raised as she glanced over at Hilda, who was uncharacteristically quiet as she tried to shake that trancelike feeling of being in a dream where her green-eyed cat suddenly had red eyes and not green eyes.

She opened her mouth to answer, but was forced to look towards the door. It was opening again, someone else walking in as that surreal feeling got stronger. Hilda frowned and stared, wondering if that door was a portal through time as she looked into his green eyes.

Wait, what? Whose green eyes? What the hell was happening?

"How is business, Ms. Hilda Hogarth," he said in that booming, resonant, accented voice as he walked into the store through that magical doorway.

Hilda's mouth stayed open as she stared at the tall, handsome, Middle-Eastern man who stood there in the doorway, surrounded by light, like perhaps he'd been beamed down from that spaceship just to make sure she knew that she was one hundred percent crazy. Loco. Mas loco.

Please see him too, she thought desperately as she glanced at Norm and Di. Oh, please tell me you see him too!

"Sorry, we're closed for lunch," Di said turning to

the man and then pausing when she saw him full, her eyes going wide for a moment, her body stiffening as she quickly touched her hair and stuck out her tight butt and smiled so wide Hilda would have puked if she hadn't been so damned relieved that she wasn't bat-shit crazy.

The man looked into Di's eyes, a confident half-smile breaking on his face. "It is funny," he said to her. "I was about to tell you the same thing, because I have a lunch appointment with Ms. Hogarth." He looked over at Hilda, that half-smile turning to full when he looked into her brown eyes, everything about him so real and so surreal, so familiar and so foreign, so clear and yet so damned impossible.

"What?" she muttered as she blinked and took a step back, still not sure she was seeing right, not sure if she was hearing right, not sure if she *was* right.

"Why don't we all go to lunch?" Hilda heard Di say in a voice that was way too sweet to stomach. "Then you can have your appointment with Ms. Hogarth in the afternoon. Come on. I just got tenure and I'm celebrating. It's not too early for champagne, is it? Oh, look at that! High noon! Come on, people. Chop chop!"

"I do not drink alcohol," said the man firmly, keeping his eyes on Hilda. "And I have a very full schedule the rest of the day. I do not have time to—Ya Allah, are you all right, Ms. Hogarth?!"

"Stay back. I got this," said Di from behind her as

Hilda felt her world spinning around and around, the walls closing in so fast she couldn't even think about getting to the bathroom before the morning sickness rose up as if to remind her that yes, she was still crazy. Still crazy, and still pregnant.

"I'm OK!" she muttered, shaking her head and straightening up again as she held on and forced an embarrassed smile. "I'm OK. Thank you." She raised her arms and placed her hands on her head, pulling her brown hair back straight until she could feel it pull at the roots, a wonderfully clarifying pain radiating across her scalp. She gulped down several deep breaths as she surveyed the room, the professor and his wife, the Middle-Eastern stranger, even Sabbath the little monster. The room felt remarkably still, like everything had stopped and was waiting for her to make a decision.

"You know what," she said, pulling her hair back tight and then letting go so her thick brown tresses opened up full and wild. "Screw it. Let's eat."

15

"I do not want to eat. Thank you," the Sheikh had said on the flight back to the United States the previous night, not even looking at the tray of freshly prepared hummus, organic almonds, cold-pressed virgin olive oil, and soft, fluffy pita bread that his personal attendant had placed before him. "More tea, and then you are relieved from duty until arrival."

The white-clad attendant had bowed and taken the tray away, returning minutes later with a silver teapot from which he poured the hot sweet tea that the Sheikh had relished since he was first allowed to taste the strong brew as a child.

Rahaan sipped his tea and watched the clouds slowly move by as the silver jet cut through the sky. They had been flying for almost eight hours. Alim was asleep, as were most of the attendants. But the Sheikh could not sleep. And the Sheikh could not eat. That meeting with Yusuf Iqbal had awoken something in him—something that took Rahaan back to the tragedy of his father and the queens, to the accidental explosion that ended the lives of almost thirty people, irrevocably changing the lives of so many others along with it. Everyone had looked for someone to blame at the time. Indeed, Yusuf Iqbal's father's name had come up several times—after all, Yezid Mohammed Iqbal had been the Lead Engineer on the project.

But even as a grief-stricken teenager wielding supreme power, Rahaan had decided not to place blame on anyone. Certainly there had been a lengthy investigation by the Royal Engineers of Kolah, and an independent Saudi engineering firm had been hired as consultants as well. But although foul play was more-or-less ruled out, the specific cause of the explosion could not be ascertained. And so the young Rahaan, still racked with the guilt of that dream the night before the explosion, had simply blamed himself.

"To say nothing and do nothing is also a decision," Rahaan said aloud, looking towards the window through the rising steam of his tea. He stared into the empty space of the open skies, his thoughts drifting like the clouds. "And just because something cannot be explained does not mean it does not exist," he said. "After all, for centuries people could not explain how birds can fly. But no one could deny that birds do fly! Eventually we discovered the science of aeronautics, and now a ninth-grade science student can clearly explain the physics of flying, from how a sparrow flies to its nest to a how a Boeing 747 traverses the globe." He drank his tea and poured another cup, nodding and clenching his fist as he felt himself come to a decision. "And so perhaps someday science will explain why as a boy I saw an event that had not occurred yet—and that too in a dream. Certainly history is full of anecdotes of people seeing snippets of the future, either in dreams or in waking trances. Shamans under the influence of hallucinogens see visions. Monks in the silence of mediation see the birth of the universe. Priests in the rapture of their faith witness the glory of God. None of it can be explained, but it is hard to argue that it does not exist. With so many stories through the ages . . . Ya Allah, not all those stories can be lies! Not all those people can be insane or delusional!"

I ignored one dream long ago, and people died. So I cannot ignore the dream from two months ago, he had told himself as the plane flew through a cloud, the white swallowing up the deep blue of sky. I cannot ignore that the dream felt vivid and real, like no other dream except the one of the explosion, when I did nothing, I said nothing, I believed nothing: when thirty people died. This dream did not seem to foretell any tragedy, and it is not clear if it foretells anything except a passing lust. Either way, what is the harm in following up? What is the worst that can happen?

No, Rahaan, he told himself as he smiled at the thought of that curvy con-artist, that feisty fortune-teller, that gorgeous gypsy of the south. That is not the question to ask. That is not your way. You do not ask, "What is the worst that can happen." You ask "What is the best that can happen!"

And just as his smile broke, the plane shot through the other side of the cloud, and the Sheikh almost shouted in delight as the blue of sky and the gold of sun burst through the window as if something out there was agreeing with him, as if everything out there was agreeing with him.

But how to walk back into this woman's life after two months, thought the Sheikh as he heard the cabin door behind him open, which meant his brother Alim had awoken. I cannot simply show up at this woman's store again, two months after that brief meeting that she may not even remember! Do I walk in and ask her out to lunch? She will think I am mad! Yes, there was an attraction I felt in the air when we met, but bloody hell, that was two months ago! We are a bit past the stage where "strike while the iron is hot" applies, yes?

Then make the iron hot again, the Sheikh told himself. Engineer a situation where this woman and you are forced to spend some time together so we can see if there is indeed something here or whether that vision was just a schoolboy's wet dream that should be laughed at and forgotten. Some kind of a trial period with this woman to see if the attraction returns. That would be perfect, yes?

He thought of the company he'd just taken over in Albuquerque. He'd already put new management in place and the company seemed to be on the road to recovery. Rahaan was a dealmaker, not a day-to-day manager, but certainly he could find a way to involve himself in the company, creating a reason for him to be in Albuquerque. He was the goddamn owner, yes?

But that is business and this is something else, he thought as he watched Alim stretch and clap his hands to summon his attendants, one of whom would massage his feet while the other would scroll through the list of movies on the big screen until Alim picked one.

Slightly annoyed at being distracted from his thoughts, Rahaan frowned as he watched his younger brother sigh and grunt and stare blankly at the big screen. Alim was no longer a child, Rahaan thought as he wondered when his brother would step up and find some worthwhile pursuit to occupy his mind.

"The mind atrophies just like the body if it is not exercised every day," Rahaan said out loud, pushing away those thoughts of Hilda Hogarth and prophetic dreams and instead focusing on his brother. "You spend all your time staring at screens like a zombie, eating unhealthy food. When was the last time you read a book that did not have pictures in it? When was the last time you visited a gymnasium? You are blessed with a sharp mind and a naturally healthy body, but soon enough your youth will no longer mask the evidence of your degeneracy."

Alim glanced up at his brother, eyebrows raised. "Ya Allah, brother! I have only just awoken and you greet me by called me a degenerate? Now what have I done? What is the topic for today's anti-degeneracy lecture?"

Rahaan took a breath and forced a smile, recognizing that he was directing some of his inner turmoil outwards. Yes, Alim was a bit lazy and directionless. He did not read much and he preferred chips and pizza to hummus and pita. But he had never fallen into drugs or alcohol, and was virtually a saint when it came to women. He was a good young man, Rahaan thought. He just needed a bit of a kick to get going, something to spark a sense of urgency, force him to focus on something big, something important.

In a way the shock of that tragedy forced me to become the man I am, the Sheikh reminded himself. I had my fun in college, but I was always forced to be cognizant that I was Sheikh and supreme leader, not just a spoiled heir of some Arab billionaire. I never took alcohol, never experimented with drugs. My only vice was sex, which I obtained easily and often and still do, though with a bit more discretion nowadays. And although I now spend half my time in Manhattan and have a reputation as a ruthless dealmaker, I do not cross certain lines when it comes to how I negotiate a deal. Yes, I play psychological games of misdirection and deception, but I do not lie to anyone who has not lied to me, and I do not cheat anyone who has not tried to cheat me. I have a code.

That last thought reminded the Sheikh of something Alim had said two months ago: "It would be against her code," he had said about Hilda Hogarth, and as Rahaan stared at his brother, he felt an idea slowly swirl into form.

Being unexpectedly forced to take over as Sheikh had made Rahaan the man he was. Could he put the innocent, directionless Alim in a similar situation and force the kid to wake up and get serious? It would not actually come to pass, of course. Just find a way to make Alim think he was going to have to be Sheikh in say . . . six months. Six months would be enough time.

The idea was taking solid form now, and Rahaan's keen dealmaking mind began to put the pieces together—all the pieces. By God, he realized as he turned to the window and stared into the clouds of white mist, there is a way to accomplish all of it with one move. A move that will need another participant, but she is a dealmaker too, is she not? I will be able to convince her. She will agree if the price is right.

The Sheikh took a breath and decided abruptly that yes, he was going to do it. What the hell! Why not! So he snapped his fingers and dismissed Alim's attendants, smiling and narrowing his eyes as he glanced at his surprised brother.

"I will be informing the Ministry of Elders of this in the next few weeks, dear Alim," the Sheikh said with quiet seriousness, "but I wanted you to know first so you can start preparing yourself mentally."

"Preparing for what?" said Alim, frowning as he picked up the seriousness in the Sheikh's tone.

"For taking over as supreme Sheikh of the land of

our ancestors, the kingdom of Kolah," the Sheikh said, delivering the line perfectly, no inflection in his voice, no break in eye contact.

Alim stared at his brother as if the words had not registered. Slowly he broke a grin that looked suspiciously like panic. "You are joking, Rahaan. And it is not even a good joke. What—"

"I am engaged to an American woman, and by tomorrow I will be married to her," the Sheikh said, a shiver going through him as he said it even as he made a mental note to call ahead and have a diamond ring waiting for him in Manhattan. "And by the laws of Kolah, a Sheikh's first wife must be from an Arabian royal family. If a sitting Sheikh takes a first bride who is not of Arab blood and royal lineage, the Sheikh must abdicate the throne one day before the *nikaah* ceremony. That is what I will be doing in six months, the day before we have the official Islamic wedding. In six months you will be Sheikh, little Alim. In six months you will need to get off your lazy arse and be prepared to administer your kingdom. In six months the throne of Kolah will be yours."

16

"So is there really a throne in your palace?" Di asked as the Sheikh unwrapped his triple-decker roast beef sandwich and pulled away the top slice of the thick, nine-grain bread so he could inspect the meat.

"This is beef and not pork, yes?" he asked Hilda, who was seated right across from him at the four-person table in the center of the clean, well-lit café around the block.

"Um, hello, I asked you a question," said Di, snapping her fingers in front of the Sheikh's face until he slowly pulled his eyes away from Hilda's and looked at the suddenly sparkly redhead, whose body was almost entirely turned away from her husband and towards Rahaan.

Indeed, Di had been asking all the questions thus far, most of them directed towards the Sheikh. Her ridiculously obvious (and inappropriate—even if her husband weren't there, Hilda thought . . .) body language aside, Di's questions did cover a lot of ground. Now Hilda knew his name, what he did, where he was from, and the interesting tidbit that the man was supreme Sheikh of a Middle-Eastern kingdom called Kolah. Yup. The dude was a king. Hilda had scammed five grand from a king. Not to mention another fifteen from his kid brother, who was a prince. "Off with her head," anyone? Oops.

"There is in fact a throne, but it is exceedingly uncomfortable and I only use it for the most formal of ceremonies," said the Sheikh graciously, his eyes darting back towards Hilda as he answered Di.

"Fascinating," gushed Di, fluttering her eyelids in a way that seemed strangely at odds with the lean, no-nonsense, sharp beauty she'd projected when Hilda had first seen her. In fact she seemed like a different person suddenly, and a quick look at Norm seemed to confirm it. The man appeared more surprised than jealous or angry, which made Hilda think Di didn't usually turn into a sparkly girlie-girl whenever an attractive man showed up on the scene.

Well, he's more than attractive, he's . . . he's . . . OK stop, she told herself as she took in his strong jawline outlined by that dark, trimmed stubble, those cheekbones like ridges of smooth granite, thick black hair that fell in lazy waves that made her heart speed up, those dark red lips she could swear she'd tasted before, would taste again . . . oh, God you need to stop! Open your mouth and talk!

"So are you a professor too, Di? You mentioned getting tenure," Hilda said, taking a bite of her veggie-wrap and smiling with a full mouth, cursing herself for starting to talk right when she needed to chew. Could she be any less ladylike and attractive right now? Should she just burp and scratch her armpits while she was at it?

"You've got something under your chin, dear," said Di, barely looking at Hilda, only turning to face her when Rahaan turned away to take a gigantic bite out of his roast-beef sandwich. He smiled at Hilda as he chewed, giving her a quick wink that felt so familiar it almost made her choke. It was a look two playful lovers might pass to one another across a crowded room, a knowing look, a familiar wink, like they had an inside joke going, something between just the two of them.

Which is impossible, Hilda told herself as she blinked and looked away from the Sheikh, directing her focus back to Di, if only for poor Professor Norm's sake. "That's actually another chin," she said cheerfully, feeling light-headed and relaxed after that warm look from the Sheikh. "Another chin under my chin. Double chin. Get it?"

Rahaan snorted through his sandwich, his green eyes dancing with delight as he stared at her. It took all of Hilda's will to keep from turning back to him, and she could feel his eyes on her, his gaze taking in every feature of her smooth round face, her open hair, her full lips, the curve of her neck. And although her mouth was full and there were crumbs on her black top, the way the Sheikh was looking at her made Hilda feel attractive. She sat up a bit straighter, feeling her breasts rise in a way she could tell affected the Sheikh. It affected Di too, it seemed, whose jaw went tight and eyebrows seemed to cross for a fleeting moment as she turned to Hilda and forced a smile.

"Sorry, you were asking me something. Yes, I am a professor. Actually I'm the only full professor right now—Norm's still an associate. There's a bit of a backlog in the physics department, and Norm's tenure has been pushed back. He won't be called up for a couple more years," Di said nonchalantly.

"Next year, Di. You know that," Norm said quietly, smiling at Hilda and nodding. "Yes, Di is a professor of history at UNM."

"Oh, really?" said Hilda. "What kind of history? European? U.S.? Asian? Af—"

"Science, actually," said Di, poking at her salad and putting her fork down without taking a bite. "The history of science. My research covers how science evolves through the ages, like how science now explains simple things that our ancestors would say were caused by ghosts or God or magic." Di's eyes lit up as she spoke, and Hilda could immediately see the woman was whip-smart and genuine when it came to her field. "From which it follows that phenomena we now consider to be unexplainable or perhaps even impossible, will eventually be explained by scientists of the future."

"Or scientists of the present," said Norm, beaming as he looked at his wife and then at Hilda. "We're writing a book together, Di and I. We're taking the latest discoveries from quantum mechanics and applying it to ideas commonly thought of as impossible or even . . . well . . . magical."

"Magical? Like what?" said Hilda, still conscious of the way the Sheikh seemed to have eyes only for her. What was he up to? Why was he even here?

"Well, like what *you* do," Di said matter-of-factly, finally taking a bite of her salad. "Reading fortunes. Telling the future. Or pretending to."

"Di!" Norm said, frowning at his wife and then looking apologetically at Hilda.

"No, it's fine," Hilda said quickly, noticing that the Sheikh was interested now too. "I get the point. It's either fake or coincidence, right? Even if I really do predict a future event, we currently have no way to explain it except by one of those options. If I see the future and it's not fake and it's not coincidence, then science can't explain it right now. It might as well be magic. Perfectly logical."

Norman narrowed his eyes like he was thinking, rubbing his mangy orange beard as he stared at Hilda. He turned to his wife now. "You know," he said. "We should ask Hilda to read the manuscript. She'd be perfect, actually. She understands physics, but she hasn't studied it at an advanced level. She'd be able to give us a sense of whether the book can reach both a scientific audience as well as the public." He shrugged as he looked at Hilda. "The smart, intellectually curious public, of course. The ideas are still a little beyond, say, your average romance novel aficionado."

"You'd be surprised how sophisticated your average romance reader is, Professor," said Hilda with a playful edge in her voice. "And as a scientist you shouldn't be making assumptions that can be easily disproved. If you looked at the demographics and education-levels of romance readers, I assure you that—"

"OK, OK, I take it back," Norm said hurriedly, throwing his hands up in the air as he turned red. He exhaled when he saw Hilda relax and smile. "So will you do it? Read the manuscript and see if it makes sense to you?"

Di shifted in her seat, glaring at Norm for a moment before finally nodding and shrugging and looking over at Hilda questioningly.

"Sure," said Hilda. "I'd be happy to. What's the name of the book?"

"Sideways Through Time," said Norm, beaming again as he leaned back. "We're focusing on a topic that's always been fascinating to people. You see it in movies and books all the times. Science fiction. Romance novels even."

"Sideways through time," Hilda repeated as she

glanced quizzically at her veggie wrap and then slowly looked at the two professors staring her down while the Sheikh looked on. "You mean like time travel? You guys are writing a book that explains time travel?"

Norm took a breath and blinked as he stared at his hands for a moment. "Technically, we've already written the book," he said, his sharp little eyes gleaming as he glanced at his wife and then at Hilda.

"What is the main idea?" said the Sheikh suddenly, breaking his silence, his face peaked with a strange excitement, an excitement that Hilda could feel rising in her as well. She couldn't explain it, but she could sure as hell feel it. And that was Norm and Di's point from earlier, wasn't it? Just because you can't explain something doesn't mean it isn't real. Oh. My. God.

Di turned to Rahaan. "Well, ask any physicist about the science of time, and they'll tell you that time is an illusion, that every single moment in the history of the universe actually exists right now—has always existed, in a way."

"And not just every moment we've experienced in the past or will experience in the future, but every *possible* moment as well," said Norm, touching his nose even though it appeared he'd traded in his glasses for contacts.

"Parallel universes," the Sheikh said. "That is what you mean by every possible moment being in existence?"

"Correct," said Norm, glancing at the Sheikh in surprise, perhaps even envy, as if a man that rich and good-looking shouldn't know anything about physics. "So at this very moment, there are a whole bunch of parallel universes out there which are similar to ours. And we actually exist in those parallel universes. In real flesh and bone, living real lives! Some of those worlds are almost identical. Others have tiny differences—like maybe you have green eyes in this world and blue eyes in another world. And—"

"Wait, what?" Hilda said as she thought of Sabbath her green-eyed cat who'd looked very much like a red-eyed cat earlier that day.

"So anyway," said Di, ignoring Hilda and nodding furiously as she leaned forward, looking at the Sheikh. "These parallel worlds are real, and in fact the past and future are just parallel worlds too. It's all parallel worlds, in a way. Which means that once we understand how to move forward and backward through time, we'll also know how to move sideways through time!"

Hilda blinked hard and took a breath. This was going over her head, and she couldn't get that image of Sabbath and his new eyes out of her mind. "Sideways. You mean move from one of these parallel universes to another? Where you have green eyes your whole life and suddenly you wake up and your eyes are blue, but everything else is the same?"

"Yes," said Di, turning and looking into the Sheikh's

eyes. "Here, Rahaan. Let me see," she whispered to him. "Still green. Damn. I'd hoped we had moved into a parallel world where—"

Hilda stared wide-eyed as Di just about managed to stop herself from saying what was clearly on her mind, and the Sheikh frowned and looked away from Di, focusing on Hilda again. He seemed lost in thought, like he was somewhere else. Truth was, Hilda felt like she was somewhere else too, and she heard herself asking Di another question.

"So how would that work," Hilda said slowly. "This sort of sideways time-travel? Once the science gets sorted out, they'll invent some machine in the future that allows us to—"

"No machines," said Norm firmly. "That's the entire point of the book. That's the biggest flaw in popular conceptions of time travel: that to travel through time we need to transport our bodies through time. It's not going to work that way."

"No bodies. Then what? Are you saying it is just the mind that moves between times, moves between parallel universes?" said Rahaan.

Di nodded. "The consciousness, more precisely. The secret is that there will never be a machine that transports our bodies through time. Think about it this way: If a scientist a hundred years from now invents a time-travel machine, then by now we would have clear, verifiable cases of people from the future coming back and explaining exactly how all of this works. The fact that we have no legitimate cases of humans from the future popping out of a phone booth or whatever means that we're missing something in how we understand time travel."

Norm jumped in now. "And what we're missing is that time travel is already happening! We're already doing it, both when we're awake and when we're asleep."

"Asleep?" Hilda said, her voice almost a whisper. She couldn't even look at the Sheikh right now. He'd see it all over her face—even though she couldn't be sure what he'd see. "You mean in a dream?"

"Yes," said Di. "We haven't worked all of it out yet, but we believe that in a dream state, the consciousness is disconnected from the body in a way that frees it. So the consciousness opens up and gives us glimpses of the other worlds and universes in which we're living lives that are as real as this life—just one dimension backward, forward, or sideways from our current reality."

Norm nodded. "Most of the time we don't actually remember these dreams—which could be a survival mechanism that has evolved in humans. After all, if we're waking up every morning with clear, vivid memories of the other lives we're living, it would be confusing as hell. So our brains just sensibly block those out from the waking mind so we don't go insane."

"But you said our consciousness is doing this time travel when we are awake as well," said the Sheikh, stroking his stubble as he leaned back, straightening his back and stretching his long, muscular arms out wide. The sleeves of his white linen shirt rode up over his bulging brown biceps, revealing a tattoo on the inside of his right arm. It looked like Arabic letters, but when Hilda squinted and tried to focus on them, she thought maybe they were some kind of symbols etched into his skin. Weird. Kinda sexy. OK stop.

Norm nodded and exhaled. "Yes, it happens during the day when we are awake too. We travel between parallel universes every day, but most of these parallel universes are so close to our current reality, that there's really no practical difference. The differences appear consistent and logical, and so we don't notice."

"You mean like the green eyes to blue eyes thing?" said Hilda. "Um, I think I'd notice that."

Norm laughed. "Actually the green eyes to blue eyes would never happen, because a parallel universe where you have different color eyes would probably also have a few other things that would be different. So a universe where you have different color eyes would actually be several dimensions away from your current world. Almost zero chance your consciousness will pull you into that parallel reality. Too big of a jump."

"Almost zero chance, but not a zero chance?" said the Sheikh, asking the question on Hilda's mind. "So it could happen?"

Norm went quiet, and Di shifted in her chair and then pulled out her phone, frowning and putting the phone on the table before looking up and tossing her hair back. But she stayed quiet too, exhaling slowly and then picking at her salad.

"Well? Could it happen?" said Hilda. "Or is this the cliffhanger part of the book? Trust me, the romance readers are gonna skewer you for this! They hate cliffhangers."

Norm grinned and nodded. "Scientifically speaking, it is possible. But practically speaking, it would never happen. The probability is just too low. Never gonna happen."

Di shifted again, her face tightening as she glanced at Norm and then folded her arms over her toned chest and looked up at the ceiling, smiling and shaking her head.

Norm rolled his eyes. "In case you guys can't tell, Di and I disagree on this one."

"Do tell, Ms. Diana," said the Sheikh, and he turned and smiled at the redhead in a way that made Hilda's neck-hairs bristle up. She narrowed her eyes at the Sheikh, relaxing a little when it hit her that God, he was totally faking that smile for her so she'd talk.

Di softened and blinked at him, touching her hair and shrugging. "Well, Norm is right that the probability of passing between parallel worlds that far apart is pretty unlikely. But not as unlikely as he thinks. That's where his scientific training is a disadvantage. But the philosopher in me can easily imagine it."

"Imagine what?" said Hilda.

"OK," said Di, leaning forward and shifting in her

chair again. "I'll try to explain. Remember how we said that time is actually an illusion, that all of time actually exists right now? That's actually kinda hard to imagine for some people, right?"

"Yes," said Hilda. "Sure."

"So think of it this way. Think of time more like you think of space, like you think of geography or a world map. Just like New York and London both exist but are at different places on the map, all moments in time also co-exist but are simply in different places on a map. A cosmic map, if you will."

"Oooh," said Hilda. "OK, wow, that's . . . I mean please go on."

"So in other words, the different lives we're living in different times are actually all being lived right now, just like London and New York both exist right now but at different spots. Our consciousness connects all these lives together, and Norm is right: As humans we block out any waking memory of these other lives or else we wouldn't be able to function in our world. But at a subconscious level we are in fact aware of these lives. We do get glimpses of these other lives in dreams," said Di.

"Just so we're clear, I agree with Di on all of this. That's not where we disagree," Norm interjected.

Di smiled. "What we disagree on is the role of emotion in all of this. Science doesn't have a way to deal with the power of emotion, and so Norm just ignores it. Whereas I think emotion can change the probabilities in dramatic, almost magical ways. I think strong emotions that are mirrored through several different dimensions can create strong ripples through time, perhaps even pull your waking consciousness into other realities that are quite different."

"Green eyes to blue eyes?" said Hilda, trying hard to smile nonchalantly even though she wanted to faint and wake up in a parallel life where she wasn't pregnant and her cat didn't look like Satan's minion.

"Yes," said Di matter-of-factly nodding. "Perhaps even more, if there are deep emotions being experienced in several lives at once. You could see very strange, even impossible events occur in your life because the emotional ripples from other lives have pulled you into a different parallel world. I believe it absolutely can happen, and I believe it does happen. I just think that when it happens, most people can't explain it so they pretend like it didn't happen. For others, they may actually go insane or experience psychological problems including schizophrenia. No one would believe them, and eventually they stop believing themselves or get turned into medicated zombies and forced into social isolation. Extreme cases could lead to suicide, crime, maybe even murder. Who's going to believe a psychotic killer with some crazy story that they swear is true?"

Hilda's mouth hung half open as she listened to all of it. She didn't even want to start thinking about . . . ohgod, where would she start? The dreams? The pregnancy? Where?

Start with him, came the answer from somewhere

in her subconscious, and it sounded so clear that Hilda almost gasped in shock. Was she finally going to go insane? Were the voices finally coming?

But there were no voices. Just feelings. Just emotions.

Start with him, she thought as she glanced at the stranger across the table from her. Why was he here? What did he want?

She nodded in a daze that made her feel like she was behind a veil, watching reality unfold, watching her life unfold, watching all her lives unfold. That dream from two months ago was hazy in her memory, but she saw that bumpy carriage on that mystical country road. She felt the excitement and fear of those teenagers on the run. She sensed the danger and tumult in the dream of the prince who gave up his kingdom after rejecting Princess Diamante for his true love.

Through the veil Hilda saw Norm write down her email address so he could send her the book. Then she saw Di flutter those eyelids in that strangely out-of-character way as she asked for Rahaan's email so she could send him a copy as well.

And as they all stood and said goodbye, Di looked over at Rahaan and said in a voice that drifted clearly into this very real world:

"Oh, by the way, Rahaan: Di isn't short for Diana. My real name is Diamond, believe it or not. Or, as the say south of the border: Diamante."

17

Hilda stared at the diamond. Then she closed her eyes and opened them again. Shit. He was still here. And so was that diamond.

"It is a diamond," said the Sheikh, holding the ring up to the sunlight streaming through the front window of the café. "See?"

"Yes, I see it's a diamond," said Hilda, glancing at the twinkling stone, then briefly into Rahaan's eyes before blinking and looking away. Had she now bounced into a new parallel world? Was she totally and completely unhinged in space and time? An alien abduction might actually be a relief right now. "That wasn't what I meant when I asked what the hell that is. I meant why the hell are you showing me a diamond ring in the middle of a café? I meant why the hell are you even here? Who are you anyway? What's your game? If this is about the five grand or the fifteen I got from your brother—"

"Ah, so you admit it was a con," said the Sheikh, placing the ring on the table far too casually. Somehow a diamond ring the size of Jupiter shouldn't be sitting near a plastic salt shaker, Hilda thought.

"The only con here is whatever you're trying to pull," Hilda snapped, not sure where the venom was coming from. "Am I missing something, or did you show up at my store a couple of hours ago pretending to have an appointment. Then you bullied your way into my lunch meeting, and—"

"Actually, it was you who said 'Let us eat!'," said Rahaan, leaning back in his chair and placing his hands behind his head. There was that tattoo on the inside of his right bicep again. Definitely not Arabic letters. Some kind of symbols for sure.

"What is that on your arm?" she asked without thinking, gesturing with her head. "The tattoo."

He shrugged and looked away for a moment, a half-smile showing on his face. "From my college days in England. Let us say that I was not the most humble nineteen-year-old king at Cambridge."

Hilda frowned. "Were there other nineteen-year-old kings at Cambridge? Or are you just being humble?"

The Sheikh grinned. "Can we get back to the topic at hand? I did not come here from Manhattan to relive the pomposity of my youth."

"You're coming across as pretty damn pompous right now," Hilda said as she watched the Sheikh lazily drape that tattooed arm over the back of an empty chair as he pushed his own chair away from the table and commandeered a third chair to use as a footrest. "Are you just going to take up the whole damn café? The way you're sitting is called manspreading these days. I take it you don't ride the New York City subways much."

The Sheikh raised an eyebrow. "Why would I ride the subway?"

"Um, to get to work? You know what, never mind. This conversation is ridiculous. This whole day has been ridiculous. I gotta get back to feed my cat anyway, so—"

"Your cat had a full bowl two hours ago. And it did not appear to be in imminent danger of starvation."

"Wait, did you just call my cat fat? How dare you?"

"You are correct. This conversation is ridiculous indeed. Now may we get back on topic?"

"What topic?!" Hilda snapped, almost shouting in frustration at what the hell was going on. Why was she sitting here with this guy she didn't know at all, who had randomly showed up after two months, had just casually joined her for lunch, and five minutes ago, after Norm and Di left, had pulled out a diamond ring and said, "Ms. Hogarth, I have a proposal for you."

"The topic of my proposal," he said, green eyes twinkling, dark lips twitching mischievously like he was trying his best not to laugh. Obviously he was messing with her. Strange way to mess with someone you don't know, but hey, the guy was a king from the Middle East. He might just be some eccentric lunatic. Probably inbred too.

Screw it, she told herself finally, taking a sip of her now-cold tea. Just stop thinking, Hilda. That's the solution. Stop thinking, or else you'll turn into one of these lunatics yourself.

"OK, I'll bite," Hilda said, exhaling and putting the cup down. "So I took five grand from you two months ago, and fifteen from your brother. Clearly you're rich enough that you don't give a shit about that, and—"

"Do not insult me by implying I do not take the value of money seriously," the Sheikh said firmly. "My brother may be guilty of that, but I am not. How money is obtained and how it is spent is meaningful. There are moral implications of every transaction, whether it is fifteen thousand or fifteen billion." He took a breath and shrugged. "Though you are correct that I am not here to attempt to recover the five thousand or the fifteen thousand. That money is yours, and you are morally entitled to it."

"Morally entitled," said Hilda, rolling her eyes even as she felt an involuntary smile break. "Well, that's a relief. OK then. So what's with the ring? You've decided that you're morally entitled to ask me to marry you now? That was quick, Your Highness. I know I'm beautiful and charming, but this is a little early in our courtship, don't you think?"

Hilda almost choked on her tongue when she heard herself spout words like marriage and courtship. OK, so maybe "Stop thinking" wasn't the best advice to give yourself. You need to maybe think a little teeny bit before you toss out gems like that. Though speaking of gems being tossed out, that rock could solve a lot of problems. This alien baby ain't gonna pay for its own fucking college.

Stop it, she told herself as she felt her mind squirreling its way down a path that seemed morally dubious at best, downright criminal at worst. Conning a billionaire out of fifteen or twenty grand was one thing. But coming up with a way to relieve this guy of a ring this big? That would be . . .

"I can already see the wheels turning back there," said the Sheikh, a lazy half-grin hanging on his gorgeous face. "So I will tell you point blank, with no jokes, no bullshit, in all honesty, with Allah as my witness, that in six months this ring can be yours. I will give you papers detailing the history of the diamond and its valuation. I will formally assign ownership of the ring to you, and I will legally designate it as a gift, which means that I, not you, would pay tax on the transfer. It will be clean and legal. Six months, Ms. Hilda Hogarth. Six months."

"Great," she said, pretty much ready to just give up trying to understand anything about what in holy hell was going on in her goddamn life right now. "I assume there's a catch?"

"Of course there is a catch, Ms. Hogarth. No gift comes for free. Everything is a transaction."

"All right, what's the deal?" Hilda said. "My life couldn't get any stranger right now, so give me your best shot. What do I have to do?"

"Wear it," he said.

"Wear what?" she said.

"The ring. You wear that ring for six months, by my side, and that is all." He shrugged. "You convince people that you can tell the future and that your indecipherable star-charts actually mean something, yes? So for six months you must convince people that you are my wife, and that our relationship actually means something. Six months, and then we go our separate ways. Back to our parallel universes."

18

Ya Allah, it is more like a perpendicular, upside down, bloody mad universe, the Sheikh thought as he heard himself follow through on the ridiculous scheme that he had come up with while flying back to the United States. It did occur to him that there might have been an air-pressure leak on his private jet and he was suffering from altitude sickness, which is known to induce madness if not treated.

But what was more insane was that this woman seemed remarkably calm. Or perhaps calm was not the right word. Unsurprised was more like it—not in a way that made it seem like she could have guessed any of this was coming, but still like it was not as shocking as it should be. Now the Sheikh recalled her saying her life couldn't get any stranger, and he wondered what she meant. Yes, his life had taken a turn for the strange too, had it not? And this woman was in the middle of it. The woman, the dream, the ring . . .

And as the Sheikh sat back, he felt as if a veil had come down in front of him, and suddenly he was watching the world as if he were a step removed from it. Not outside his body but within it, somehow deeper within himself in a way he couldn't understand.

He watched and listened as Hilda went back over what he'd just explained to her. She was smart, he thought. Clear-headed and analytical in a way that seemed so much at odds with her choice of career, even her choice of clothes. Those harem-style pants with their paisley brightness had given him a goddamn headache when they were walking to the café from the store. Of course, he didn't need to look at the pants, but by God he couldn't help glancing at the way her buttocks moved beneath that thin cotton. He had caught sight of her panty-line as she walked, and he had forced himself to look away before he got hard right there on the goddamn street!

Slowly the Sheikh forced himself out from behind that veil before he lost track of both his body and his mind, and he exhaled when he found himself back in the moment, back in the world.

"So all of this is to teach your brother a lesson," she was saying. "This elaborate scheme is to teach your brother some responsibility? Why not just get him a puppy?"

"If you are not going to take this seriously, then I will offer the job to someone else," said the Sheikh, trying to speak as firmly as possible. "I think I will be able to find another American woman who will accept a three-million-dollar payment for six months of fairly pleasurable work."

"Um, pleasurable? Listen, buddy. Maybe it's the harem pants that gave you that idea, but pleasure isn't part of any goddamn deal," she said, leaning forward on the table.

"Ah, so we have a deal then?" said the Sheikh, purposely not answering her question, keeping his eyes focused on her face even though the way she was leaning forward on the table in that v-neck black top was making it very difficult. Was she doing that on purpose? Was she already playing this game? Winding his cock up so she could grab him by the balls? Ya Allah, this woman was a dealmaker too, was she not? What a game this would be!

"I didn't say that," said Hilda. "I need to understand this a bit better. You do realize it sounds sketchy as hell, yeah? I mean, this is a classic setup where I end up dead in some pit across the border. Or worse, it's a setup for the cheesiest romance novel ever written. The lame-ass, Fake Marriage plotline!"

"Earlier you were defending romance novels," said the Sheikh, glancing down her neckline and quickly looking back up, the blood surging through his hard body as he blinked away the overwhelming image of her smooth, heavy cleavage. "And now it is a fate worse than death?"

Hilda groaned and rubbed both her eyes at once,

and the Sheikh took the opportunity to glance at her breasts again. Ya Allah, what was wrong with him?! He was acting like a guilty schoolboy around this woman! Ogling at panty-lines and hints of cleavage!

"Oh, God," she muttered. "What the fuck is happening?"

"Are you all right, Ms. Hogarth? Please. My comment about the romance novels was a joke. I am not expecting anything beyond a professional arrangement. No part of this deal involves private intimacy." He paused and took a breath. "Though of course, it does not preclude it."

"Wait, what? Does not *preclude* it? I can't believe you just said that."

"Fine," said the Sheikh, and his eyes narrowed and his mouth went tight as he realized they were wrestling for the upper hand. "If the possibility of intimacy is so offensive to you, then we *will* preclude it. No matter what, it will *not* happen."

She stared at him like he had turned into a giant bear before her eyes, and for a moment the Sheikh was certain she was going to pass out right there. He wondered if her fainting would actually be an excellent chance for him to get out of this ridiculous situation he was engineering himself into, but he knew he was not going anywhere. Dreams, parallel lives, and distracting cleavage aside, he was actually starting to have fun. By God, this was fun, was it not?! And that was the point of it all, was it not? To experience emotion. To feel joy. To play. To have fun! The point of life, yes? Parallel, perpendicular, past and future lives—all of them!

It was the reason he did the work he did, the deals he did—it gave him a kick, a rush, a sense of adventure. And did this scheme not have all those things built in? And the risk was not even that much: Three million for the ring was pocket change. But the reward? Ya Allah, there was some upside here, was there not?

He felt his cock move as he watched her run her hands through her hair, touch her neck, lean back in her chair and fold her arms beneath her breasts. Yes, there is some upside, he thought as he caught her glancing at that ring once again. This woman is my equal in so many ways—nothing like the women who enter my private chambers in Manhattan. Those women may be educated and intelligent too, but they lack something that this curious woman in those harem pants seems to have. It is a depth of some kind—not just intellectual, and not as simple as her personality. It is a depth that feels holistic, even though I suspect this woman can be as shrewd as my fiercest boardroom adversary. It is a depth that feels honest even though this astrologer has manipulated Alim and me into paying her twenty thousand dollars. It is a depth that connects to something similarly deep in me, like she is the answer to a question I have been asking for twenty years.

Ya Allah, that is it, yes? Deep down I believe that what happens with Hilda Hogarth in the next six months will answer the question of whether the teenage Rahaan truly saw a vision of the future or not. Is that what I am chasing here? The hope that she contains the answer, whether she knows it or not, whether she believes it or not, whether I believe it or not.

"I can't," she muttered, staring past the Sheikh and slowly shaking her head. "It's too messed up. All of it. I just need to step back and figure this shit out. It's just too much right now. I can't."

The Sheikh watched her as she whispered to herself, and something inside him said he needed to act. Fate, destiny, past and future be damned, Rahaan knew enough about physics to understand that the only thing real is the now, the present, the moment. And in a moment this woman was going to say no unless he acted.

Time moved in slow motion as the Sheikh calmly looked around the café. It had filled up a bit, and to their left were three teenage girls with their phones out as they chattered and giggled and selfied and shared. To their right was a young couple, the man staring out the window, the woman reading a book. Both their phones were lying on the table near their coffee cups. Behind Hilda was a middle-aged woman sitting alone, smiling as she scrolled through her phone. The perfect, camera-ready audience, thought the Sheikh. Do it, Rahaan. Do not think and just do it. The most vivid part of the dream was the physical part, was it not? Consciousness and possible worlds be damned, the one thing that is guaranteed to be real is the body, is it not? It can be felt and it can be touched. It is real, simple as that. So stop thinking and just do it. You start from this world, start from this moment, start from the physical.

You start with her, and you do it now.

And just as Hilda blinked and focused on the Sheikh, her lips slowly parting as she started to mouth the word no, Rahaan pushed his chair back so hard it slid across the café, making every head turn. Then he rose to full height, dramatically kicked an empty chair out of his damned way, grabbed that ring from near the plastic salt shaker, and went down on one knee as oohs and aahs and eeks and omgs rose up from the audience as they grabbed their phones and swiped to their cameras.

"Hilda Hogarth," the Sheikh said as he looked up at her and took her hand in his. "Will you marry me?"

And as she sputtered and gurgled like she was going to faint either in rage or shock, Rahaan pulled her close, slipped the ring onto her finger, and kissed her full on the mouth.

By God, he kissed her.

19

The kiss rippled through space and time as Hilda gasped for breath, the world slipping away as she felt herself kissing him back, kissing him like it was their first kiss and their last kiss, like it was their only kiss, the only kiss that ever existed, the eternal kiss that exists outside of space and time, that is created anew every time lovers meet, that is fresh and pure even though it is ancient and old, old as time, old as the universe, old as man and woman, old as life and death, sunshine and rain.

"Oh, God," she gasped as she broke from the kiss and blinked. The sound of applause and cheers rose up around them, and she tried to focus, tried hard to focus even though everything was twisting and turning, swirling and swaying. She could feel her body tingle with electricity, burn with a fever, dance with a joy that made no sense. She could feel herself floating and sinking at the same time, soaring and crashing at once, being born and dying all in the same moment.

Now focus slowly came, and she looked into his eyes, green eyes warm and familiar, eyes looking out from the face of a stranger whom she swore she knew, had always known, would always know, again and again.

Start with him, came that whisper from inside her, from a place that seemed more real than reality, more vivid than a rainbow in the sun, a place where a part of her lived forever, where perhaps all of her lived.

"Say yes!" came the voices from her left.

"What're you waiting for?" came the squeals from the right.

"Ohmygod, this is so beautiful!" came the whimpers from behind.

Now she was back in that dream, floating through that fantasy, dancing through that vision, careening in that carriage, running through the night, riding through the mountains. Somehow she could still see his eyes, and now she realized she could only see his eyes, and she saw all of it in his eyes, saw herself in his eyes.

Start with him, came the whisper again. Start with him.

And she closed her eyes as she saw him lean in for another kiss or perhaps the same kiss. She closed her eyes and said yes.

"Yes," came the word, and it carried with it a gravity that rippled its way through the cosmos along with that kiss, and it sounded like a chorus as she said it, the chorus of every woman who'd ever said yes to her lover, women old and young, dark and fair, past and present, future and forgotten.

Yes.

20

"**N**o!" she shouted as she tried to close the door fast enough that the cat couldn't get out and the Sheikh couldn't get in.

"A deal is a deal," called the Sheikh from behind her, sticking his heavy foot in the door and stopping Sabbath the cat dead in his tracks before he could make a run for it. "I do business the old-fashioned way, where a handshake means everything."

"We didn't shake hands," she said firmly, turning and trying to stare him down even though she had to look up to do it.

But Rahaan's eyes were steady and his gaze was cool steel as he smiled and pointed to her left hand. "That ring says otherwise." He pushed his way into the store and stepped close as Hilda backed up to that dark wood shelf by her desk. "And so does this," he whispered as he leaned in to kiss her again.

She clenched her teeth and *slapped* him as he came close, shocking herself at how fast she'd done it, her body whipping almost all the way round as the Sheikh took a step back in surprise.

"Bloody hell!" he roared as her grabbed her right wrist and whipped her around so she faced away from him. He pulled her tight against his hard body as he trapped both her arms and pinned them across the front of her body, down against her thighs. "Are you mad, woman?! Are you bloody mad?!"

"Fuck you," she snarled as she tried to fight herself free, her head spinning from the adrenaline coursing through her system, her entire body feeling alert and alive, effervescent and electric.

She felt him breathe against her neck from behind, his rock-hard chest moving against her back, his hips pressed against her soft bottom. She could sense him trying to control himself, breathing hard, and she felt herself breathing hard too as she became acutely aware of how tight their bodies were pressed together. Slowly his breathing steadied, and her own breaths fell into rhythm with his, slowly, up and down, in and out, back and forth until they were breathing together, sighing together, moving together.

She tried to pull her arms free, but his grip was too tight, and she felt her body stiffen as she realized that God, she felt so secure being held like this, so safe even though she was pinned down by this muscular, hard-bodied stranger who'd just put a ring on her finger and kissed her without asking.

"Damn you," she muttered as a sense of being overwhelmed rushed in, making her weak at the knees, forcing her to lean even more of her weight against his body. "Damn you for coming here. Damn you for coming here at all. This isn't real. It isn't real. You aren't here and this isn't real."

"I am here and this is real," he whispered fiercely against her neck, and she could feel his unmistakable hardness against her ass as she rotated her hips in a rhythm that she wasn't sure was intentional or inevitable. "And I am about to make it more real. Real the only way I know how. Real with my touch. Real with my kiss. Real with me and you, Hilda. Right now. Right here. Just like in my dream. I ignored my need to come to you for two months, Hilda. It sounds mad but it is true. I cannot ignore a dream that vivid, that real, a vision that captured both body and mind, emotion and action. I ignored a dream like that once, and it was a mistake I will not repeat. No, I will not wait to see if our dream comes true. I will make it come true. That is the goddamn answer. You are the answer, Hilda."

"What?" she muttered as she felt her heat rise beneath those harem pants, and only now did she realize how wet she was, how hot she was, how ready she was. "What did you just say about a dream?"

She moaned as she felt him push his cock hard against her soft buttocks as he slowly let go of her wrists. He circled one arm tight around her waist, just beneath her breasts, and he slid his other arm down along the front of her body, hand sliding down the elastic waistband of those hideously fluorescent harem-pants, fingers pressing against the front of her black cotton panties, pushing the soaked cloth into her slit as he massaged her mound roughly, grinding his cock against her ass as he began to kiss her neck from behind.

"What are you doing," she whispered as she felt his other hand rise to her breasts. "What are we doing?"

"Making our dreams come true," he muttered, and as he said it she felt him pinch her nipple hard through her top just as his other hand slid down the front of her panties, two strong fingers pushing through her matted brown curls, spreading her dark nether lips, driving smoothly and carefully up the canal of her cunt like he knew the way.

21

She almost fainted against him as she came, the orgasm arriving without warning, silent like a cat in the night. Hilda was so shocked she couldn't even cry out, couldn't make a goddamn sound, and it was in that wave of shocked silence that the first climax rose up and took her.

Somehow a peace descended upon her through the silent chaos of that subterranean orgasm, and she felt herself go limp in his arms as he massaged her clit with his thumb, curled his fingers in her pussy, gently stroking the front wall of her vagina with his fingertips as she shuddered and shivered, shook and stammered, sighed and finally, completely, absolutely . . . surrendered.

Surrendered to the madness. Surrendered to herself. Surrendered to him.

Now sound came roaring back in along with a fresh wave of arousal even though she swore she was still coming. The Sheikh slid his hands out from her panties and pushed her forward towards her broad wooden desk. She flung papers and pencils, pen-holders and peacock feathers out of the way as he turned her and sat her up on the desk, leaning in and kissing her hard, kissing her full, kissing her like he meant it, like he wanted it, like it was all he wanted, all he'd ever wanted.

"Oh, God, what are we doing," she muttered as she felt herself kiss him again, her tongue rolling against his, her lips warm and secure from the pressure.

He grasped her breasts full, grunting like a beast as he plucked at her nipples through her black top, drawing them up into hard points between his thumbs and fingers, pinching and twisting as she felt those dark red nubs of hers go rock-hard and stiff from his ferocious touch.

"I had this dream," he muttered as he feverishly pulled her top up over her breasts, groaning again as he glanced at her full breasts nestled in her beige bra. She could see his cock pushing like a goddamn tentpole against the front of his fitted brown trousers, the outline of its head looking massive as it pushed against the heavy cloth. "It sounds mad, I know. There was a dream, Hilda. Two months ago. I cannot forget it. I cannot ignore it. But I cannot explain it either." He stopped for a moment, straightening up and looking down at her, his handsome face dark with the blood of his arousal, eyes focused completely on her, his gaze taking in everything about her, her eyes, her face, her lips, her smile. Her neck, her shoulders, her breasts.

She could smell his arousal coming to her with his masculine scent, a deep mix of musk-oil and betel, fresh tobacco leaf and dark sage.

"Don't try to explain it then," she whispered up to him, realizing she was more shocked that she wasn't shocked at what he'd just said. Right now she was so gone, so over the edge, so hot, so ready, that everything made sense and nothing made sense and all of it was right and all of it was wrong and it was fine, it was good, this was right, who gives a shit, who gives a damn . . .

She almost fainted as she tried to push away the thoughts clamoring for attention behind her glazed-over eyes: an unexplained pregnancy, an unexpected visit, an unbelievable proposal . . .

"Don't," she said again as she watched him reach for her breasts and lift her bra cups over her boobs, releasing her globes. He pressed her naked breasts with such force she arched her back and moaned, smiling as those thoughts were dismissed by the commanding presence of her arousal, an arousal that was in control of her now, in control of everything perhaps, body and mind, space and time. "Don't explain anything, goddammit. Just . . . just . . . kiss me again, Rahaan. Please. I need it. I need this. Oh, God, I need this right now. I just—"

The kiss came before she could finish the sentence, and he pushed against her so hard she was knocked backwards. But he grabbed her by the back of her head and stayed with the kiss, pushing her down on her back on that wide table, spreading her legs with his strong hips, pressing his peaked crotch against her mound as he put his weight on her.

"I cannot stop," he muttered as he ravaged her lips, kissed her cheeks, licked her neck, sucked her boobs. "I am not stopping."

"Good," she muttered as she felt him caress the curve of her belly as he searched for the waistband of her pants, getting there quickly and pulling the elastic down past her wide hips.

The Sheikh pulled away from her as he yanked those harem-pants down past her thighs, down to her knees, stopping at her ankles. He didn't pull them all the way off though, and Hilda gasped in shock as he raised her legs up and bent her knees back over her chest, exposing her underside as her panties rode up into her slit and crack. The harem-pants were still around her ankles, holding her legs together, and she felt the Sheikh slide his fingers between her rolled up panties and her slit and pull them aside.

"Oh, God," she whispered as she felt his breath against her wet cunt. The position he had her in made her feel so exposed, so filthy, so . . . so sexy that she didn't know what to do, where to turn, what to even feel. She was too aroused to be embarrassed, too turned on to be ashamed, too hot to possibly stop this stranger who'd just put a ring on her finger from doing anything he wanted.

She could smell herself now as he kissed her between her legs, at that dark place between her slit and her crack, licking her with long, firm strokes as he pulled her soaked, rolled up panties to the side. Her thighs were pressed together still, but she could feel the Sheikh's stiff tongue push its way through her secret folds, somehow sliding into her slick depths.

He licked her as she stared up at the ceiling, tremors rolling through her body, her buttocks shuddering, her thighs twitching. She could hear him tasting her, and it felt so damn filthy she thought she was going to come again, all over his face, and the thought got her even hotter, even wetter, until she was moaning loudly, groaning with abandon, licking her lips and smiling.

She was still smiling when she felt him lower her legs and pull those pants from her ankles, tossing them away as he yanked her panties all the way down and off. She gasped as he leaned in for a quick kiss, making her taste herself on his lips, swallow her own sweetness from his tongue. She felt so free and wild, like she was an animal running naked through the forest, moonlight and starlight lighting her way, her body shining silver in the glow of the night, her hair open and flowing, bare feet falling on soft grass, bare skin greeting the cool breeze.

God, she thought as she felt herself spread wide for him, without shame, without self-consciousness, without guilt, without guile. Nobody's first time together is like this, this open, this free, this familiar. It's like we already know each other's bodies, trust each other's touch, know each other's need. How can I be so open and free with him if he really is a stranger? How can he get me so hot, so wet, so . . .

"Oh, God," she muttered as she watched him back away from her and rip his white linen shirt off, tossing it against the wall and stretching his arms out wide. Hilda was bare bottomed and naked from the waist down, her beige bra pushed up over her boobs, which were hanging down as she propped herself up on her elbows and watched this man unbuckle his heavy belt as the muscles on his brown torso glistened under the yellow overhead light.

She watched in muted awe as the Sheikh dropped his brown trousers and stepped out of them, pushing his black underwear down over the tremendous peak of his hardness. Hilda almost choked in shock when she saw his cock spring into view. It was monstrous, a beast of a cock, thick and heavy in the middle, round and massive at the top, hard brown shaft glistening in the yellow light, the head dark red and oozing his fresh, clean oil.

She felt her pussy tighten as he drew near, and she slowly lowered herself down onto her back as the Sheikh grasped her thighs, kneading and squeezing with force, spreading her full and bending his face down, kissing her once again between the legs, breathing deep of her musk, his stubble rubbing gently against the tender skin. Her wetness was flowing like a slow, steady stream, and Hilda could feel the lips of her slit thickening and opening up like a flower opens for the rain. She could smell them both, man and woman, Rahaan and Hilda, and the scent of their combined sex took her back to that dream again.

"Maybe this is the dream," she muttered to herself as she watched the Sheikh raise his head from between her legs and look her in the eye, asking her if she was ready for him, asking without words, like he already knew her body just like she knew his need.

She nodded to him, to her lover, to her stranger, to her madness, to her arousal. She said yes to all of it. Yes to the man. Yes to the woman. Yes to the dream.

Then he climbed on top of her, looked into her eyes, and slowly but with power, carefully but without hesitation, as if he'd done it before, like he knew what she'd feel like, like he knew she could take him, the Sheikh pushed into her, deep into her, all the way into her, every damned inch.

22

This does not feel like the first time with this woman, the Sheikh thought as he slowly pushed into her. The first time could never feel this intimate, this close, this connected. It is like I know her, every inch of her. It is like I own her, every inch of her. The kind of ownership that can only come with the deepest trust, the most careful intimacy, following the most magical courtship. It can never be like this at the beginning with two people.

He looked into her eyes as he felt his cock slide all the way into her warm valley, his entire body tightening as he felt himself somehow get harder from her heat, wilder from her wetness, delirious from her need. He could smell her scent, and it was from his dream, he thought as he flexed inside her and heard her moan.

Or perhaps this is the dream, he wondered as she opened her eyes and looked up at him, big brown eyes looking into him, her pretty round face framed by the brown tresses that were wild like a country schoolgirl's, flowing like the ocean waves. She smiled as he leaned in to kiss her again, and the Sheikh felt his cock drive deeper as he pushed his tongue into her mouth.

She groaned and clenched, her smile fading to a grimace of ecstasy, her eyes rolling up in her head as Rahaan began to thrust, slowly at first as he tried to control his need. But the need was strong, and soon he was pumping harder, kissing her face as she gasped and shuddered, her soft, womanly body writhing beneath his weight, skin sliding smoothly as he rose and fell against her, driving harder now, deeper now, his jaw clenching as he felt her pussy tighten around his cock.

"Ya Allah," he muttered as he felt her legs wrap around him and pull him deeper into her. "By God, this is cannot be the first time. It cannot even be real. How can it be? How can it be?!"

But he knew the answer, he realized, listening to her moans get louder as he pumped his hips with force, pushed into her with power, drove into her with all the desire in him. *I know the answer and she is the answer*, he thought as he grasped her hair and held her tight as he started to come. *She is the answer. Yes, even if we do not understand it yet, she is the answer. She, us, and this. This. This moment, this meeting, this miracle. This.*

And then he came, his heavy balls tightening as they thumped against her flesh and clenched, his shaft flexing to the extreme as his thick semen barreled its way to that explosive release, his own eyes glazing over as he felt the climax smash its way through him, a climax stronger than he thought possible, louder than thunder, more powerful than lightning, unstoppable like an avalanche, glorious like a volcano at midnight.

He came. By Allah, he came. Like fountains and rivers, geysers and waterfalls, furious and fast, his heat so vivid he could not be sure if he was shouting, could not be certain if she was screaming, did not know if any of this was real, did not care two damns about whether it was real or not.

He felt his fingers pull at her hair as he erupted into her depths, his cock flexing back and forth in her cunt as he poured his semen down her canals, flooding her valleys, bursting through her dams, breaking all barricades, destroying all her defenses.

The Sheikh looked into her eyes as he came, and in them he saw peace through the ecstasy, joy through the madness, stillness through the chaos. She was his, he thought as he felt his balls tighten again, somehow pushing more of his seed into her. She was his before he ever touched her, perhaps before he ever saw her.

"Are you all right?" he managed to say as he pumped out the final draw of his load, barely descending from his peak, still hard inside her, still throbbing within her. "You are so still and quiet. Did I hurt you? I was so mad with desire I lost all sense of—"

She just stared up at him with wide eyes, her full lips trembling, her round face streaked with red from her arousal and his savage kisses. Still she did not speak, and now the Sheikh realized that Hilda, this woman from his dream, this fake gypsy in her hideous pants, this curvy firecracker who'd taken his money and slapped him across the face, this vivacious vixen who was somehow the answer to the only question he cared to ask . . . she was about to come.

"I have you," he whispered as he stayed inside her, stayed on top of her, stayed with her. "I have you, Hilda. So come to me. Come to me. Come."

23

She came with the stillness of the forest in the morning, with the silence of an owl in flight, his voice just a whisper above her but loud as thunder, a thunder that shook her as she felt his seed pour into her wells, flow through her valleys, flood her canals.

"Oh, God," she groaned as she felt her lips tremble while he kissed her like he owned her, kissed her like he knew her, kissed her like he loved her. "Oh, God, this can't be real."

Of course it isn't real, she told herself as the full upward force of her orgasm hit, pulling her far from any glimpse of the real world, ripping away any semblance of order, wiping away the pathways of reason, blowing down the walls dividing sanity from madness, dream from hallucination, life from death.

She came again as he flexed inside her, delivering the last of his load, filling her so completely she thought she'd never be able to move again, spreading her so wide she was certain she'd never close up again, reaching inside her so deep she wondered how it was even possible.

It's just a dream and so anything is possible, she told herself through her delirium as she tightened her legs around him and held him there, barely even realizing she was doing it as the head of her climax hit finally, closing her eyes for her with its warm fingers, sliding into her like tentacles of ecstasy, reaching places inside her that couldn't possibly be reached except from within.

"I had the dream," she heard herself say, her voice sounding muffled, like she was listening to herself from behind a curtain, a veil, the wall of a cocoon. "I had it too. This dream. I had this dream."

And the last thing she saw before the crescendo of her climax claimed her was the Sheikh's green eyes going wide in confusion, wide in disbelief, wide in . . . joy?

And then they collapsed together in silence, exhausted and exhilarated, the ceiling fan gently circling above her, that red-eyed cat nonchalantly prowling the perimeter like it had seen it all before.

24

"So I think we've already broken the major clause of our fake-marriage contract," Hilda said to the Sheikh. She watched him reluctantly pull his trousers back on after finally realizing the front door was still unlocked and some stoned teenagers could walk in to the sight of a muscular brown beast having his way with the gypsy of the valley. "Usually that doesn't happen until the last scene in a romance."

Rahaan turned and looked at her, smiling as he buttoned his pants beneath his flat, rock-hard abs. He shrugged as he reached for his belt, his gaze taking in a last glimpse of her stiff red nipples before she pulled that now out-of-shape beige bra back down over her boobs.

"Then perhaps this is the last scene," he said with another shrug. "The courtship is done, and we are man and wife. The end."

She giggled and brushed away an obstinate strand of hair from her forehead. "Um, we're not married yet! That was just the engagement! You can't cheat the audience out of the wedding! What kind of a man are you?"

"Ruthless," he said, deepening his voice and straightening his back. He stepped forward and reached for her breasts just as she pulled her black top down and slid her naked ass off the desk. "And efficient. The engagement was done an hour ago, and now our fake marriage is complete. We are pretend-husband and imaginary-wife as of this moment. But the ceremony will be in six months, so the audience will have to wait for the wedding, I am sorry to say. Yes, ruthless and efficient." He grinned. "Also insatiable. Come here, my gypsy fake-wife. Let me—"

"Oh, God!" came a cry from the doorway, and Hilda pushed the Sheikh away in a panic before realizing that she had no pants and no goddamn panties. Quickly she stepped behind Rahaan's broad body now, clutching his arms as she hid her shame and slowly peeked out from one side.

It was Di, red and ripe, lean and indignant, like somehow she was the one whose sense of decency and privacy had been violated.

"Turn around and step back outside," said Rahaan smoothly, his voice calm but commanding. "You may come back later or wait outside if you wish, but—"

"This'll only take a minute," said Di, taking a step to her left and glancing at Hilda with a strange look that was part envy and part contempt. "Hello there, Hilda!"

"Leave!" said the Sheikh, and Hilda could feel him tense up as he moved his body to shield her from Di.

"This is inappropriate and indecent, and you will damned well turn away and get the hell out before I—"

"What is it, Di?" Hilda finally said, feeling secure enough behind the Sheikh's massive body that she thought to hell with it, just deal with this strange woman and get it over with. Di. Diamond. Whatever. What is it?

"New ring?" said Di, just as it occurred to Hilda that shit, her hands were still clutching the Sheikh from behind, so of course Di would see the diamond. "Didn't know you two were that close yet. Congratulations. I'm sure Norm will be thrilled. But listen, Rahaan, I tried to email you the manuscript, but the address bounced and so maybe I got it wrong. Just give me your number and I'll text you a link where you can download the book. Here, you can just type it into my phone. I hate taking dictation."

"And I hate to repeat myself," said Rahaan, his voice rising but still steady and even, like he was used to giving orders, used to being obeyed. "You will do what I say or—"

"Or what, Sheikh Rahaan," Di said, her voice getting closer as Hilda wondered if this woman was seriously unhinged. What was that stuff she had said about people going schizo or straight-up insane? Takes one to know one, maybe . . .

"Or what, great king?" Di said again, her voice

sounding different as Hilda listened from behind the Sheikh. "You can't really move much, can you? And I am not a particularly movable person anyway. So it appears you are stuck between me and her, between a rock and a . . . a soft place."

Hilda squeezed Rahaan's tight, thick arms as she felt his temper rise. Enough, she thought. Whatever the hell was causing this weird tension was not going to get sorted out with a shirtless Arab manhandling an "immovable" white woman in broad daylight while a fortune teller displayed her goddamn pussy to the entire world.

"Just do it, Rahaan," Hilda said. "Give her the damn number so we can all move. This is ridiculous. Ridiculous!"

"I am not known to be movable myself," the Sheikh said slowly. "And I do not give out my private number. To hell with your book, and to hell with you. Now get out!"

"Fine," said Di. "Then neither of you is getting the book. The file needs to be released by both me and Norm, with separate passwords that we don't share with each other. So neither of you gets the book."

"Who gives a damn about your—"

"I want the book," Hilda shouted, clutching the Sheikh as she felt him move forward, dragging her along with him. "Rahaan, stop! Please! Listen, I want the book. I do. I told Norm I'd read it and offer my opinion, and it's important to me that I follow through. Please, Rahaan. Do what she says."

Hilda almost added "do it for me," at the end, but she managed to stop herself. God, she thought, I can't believe all three of us are still basically strangers to each other, and here we are fighting tooth-and-nail about some nonsensical crap, with emotions running through the goddamn roof! What is going on?! What the hell is going on?!

Emotions, came the thought as she listened to the Sheikh angrily punch in his phone number and toss Di's phone down on the round table to their left.

"Nice crystal ball," Di whispered as Hilda heard her grab the phone and walk out the door.

Emotions, Hilda thought again as Di's own words came swirling back into view. Strong emotions can force jumps between parallel worlds, cause someone's consciousness to get pulled into a new world that's still in the present but a few degrees removed . . . like moving sideways through time.

Sideways through time, Hilda thought again as she heard the Sheikh's phone vibrate in his trousers.

"She is right," the Sheikh said as he went and locked the door behind Di. He turned and pointed at the round table, diverting his eyes as Hilda stumbled into her crumpled harem-pants, underwear be damned. "It is a nice crystal ball. Perhaps it will tell us what in bloody hell happens next."

25

Di didn't stop shivering until she got back to the hotel room, ran herself a hot bath, and slipped into it with a loud sigh. Norm was at the seminar's afternoon sessions—thank God for small mercies. She couldn't even think right now, let alone talk about how she'd behaved today. What. The. Hell.

"It's just the fucking hormones," she said out loud. "You're almost forty and you've had three miscarriages in the last five years. This is probably your last shot at getting pregnant, and you're freaking out. Don't underestimate how hard this is. Just because you've been strong all your life doesn't mean you can handle everything your biology and chemistry throws at you without missing a beat. You know that one of the effects of these fertility drugs is that it jacks up your sex drive. And you're a scientist, so you know that a fertile woman is more attracted to musculature in a man. Just like a man can't help being turned on by a specific waist-to-hip ratio in a healthy woman."

Di took a breath as she smiled at the memory of Hilda trying desperately to hide her waist-to-hip ratio behind Rahaan's musculature. God, what the hell was I thinking! That wasn't me! Yes, I'm an aggressive woman—hell, Norm would've never had the balls to make a move if I hadn't pretty much dragged him to our first date.

And where did that get you, she found herself thinking again as she took a breath and tried to the shake the image of her smart but soft-bellied, sweet but passive, cute but not handsome husband. Not like that man Rahaan. Oh, God, what a man! Should she have held out for a man like that instead of cashing in her chips on Norm?

You can still do it, came a whisper from some awful part of her mind, perhaps her body, perhaps both. You're still attractive—hell, you've heard your students talk about how tight your ass looks in your black jeans. Both male and female students—which is a pretty good sign you've still got some pull, that you can still trade up from Norm.

But of course you can't do that, she told herself as she reached for the plastic glass of white wine by the tub. No, you can't even let yourself think that way. It would be wrong. So wrong.

Would it be wrong? Wasn't it wrong for Norm to convince her he was on his way to becoming head of the Physics Department when they'd first started dating? Then they were married and suddenly it was, "Oops! I didn't realize that academics was mostly politics, and now even my tenure is in doubt, along any ambitions of being department head!" Wasn't it wrong for Norm to put on forty pounds, most of it around his belly, while she ate goddamn arugula and spent her Saturdays doing planks and squats, keeping that ass tight. And for what? Sex had become a chore now, especially with the fertility stuff going on. And Norm didn't even particularly want a kid, whereas it was all she could think about now. That seemed to be the missing piece. She had her career. She had her health. She was financially secure. Sorry, why was she still married to that underachiever?

Di poured herself another glass of wine and took a sip, smacking her lips as a gentle buzz crept into her head. She shouldn't be drinking while trying to get pregnant, but what the hell. She'd just gotten tenure. And she'd turned in an epic performance of bizarro-land behavior with that magnificent Sheikh and the fortune teller with the fat ass. Yeah, maybe she'd been wound too tight.

"She does have nice tits though," Di said out loud, draining the glass and pointing at the bathroom ceiling. She poured another and kept talking out loud, liking how her voice echoed off the walls in the tiny bathroom. "Yup. Nice rack. I'll give her that. So I'll forgive you that one slip-up, my king in waiting. I don't know what the story with that ring is, but it doesn't seem right. I've known men like you in the past, Rahaan. I looked you up. A billionaire king who's never been married? And you're probably in your late thirties, even though you look timeless with that smooth brown skin and that warrior's body. That musculature, scientifically speaking."

Musculature, she thought, giggling like a madwoman as she finished her third cup of wine and dunked her head beneath the warm water, coming up gasping and sputtering, still laughing.

"Oh, God, you've lost it," she sobbed, not really crying but somehow still sobbing, gulping mouthfuls of air. She felt so strange, like it was more than just hormones or fertility pills or wine or stress or a marriage that felt boring and dead. It was deeper. Weirder. Older, she thought as she rolled up a towel and rested her head on the ledge of the tub, sighing and slowing down her breathing.

Timeless. Like musculature and birthing hips. Marriage and babies. Kings and queens. Princes and princesses.

And as her breathing slowed and her head buzzed, Di slipped into a dream, and she saw mountains and rivers, palaces and fountains, kings and queens, a prince and a princess, a princess marrying a prince . . . but not the prince she wanted. The wrong prince.

26

"Prince Alim sounds much better than Sheikh Alim," pleaded the prince, who looked more like a boy than ever as Rahaan glanced up from the computer screen in his Manhattan office. "Sheikh Alim sounds so serious."

"It is serious," said the Sheikh, narrowing his eyes and pushing his chair back. "And it is time for you to get serious, my little brother."

But am *I* being serious, the Sheikh wondered as he turned away from his squirming brother and towards the view of Central Park, the strip of green stretching north-south before him like the cultivated grounds of the Royal Palace of Kolah. Everything is in doubt now, even though it should be the other way around after what happened with Hilda in New Mexico.

In a way he could not blame the woman for backing off again, Rahaan thought as he watched his brother raise another objection, plead again, rub his beard that seemed to be growing a bit uneven around the cheeks. Yes, the sex was sublime, surreal, real. And perhaps that was why she pushed him away again after that woman Di broke the spell with her bizarre behavior.

The Sheikh tried to think back to that dream from two months ago, but the memories were hazy at best. Certainly he remembered Hilda quite clearly, her beautiful brown eyes looking at him through the faces of those ephemeral women: Hilda with him on some bumpy carriage ride; Hilda with him in a musty attic; Hilda with him as they rode through the forest, mountains in the distance. Certainly he could still feel the emotional imprint from those dreams, still see her brown eyes looking into his, still feel her body pressed against him, still feel her love as if it were real. But the details had faded away now . . . names, places, none of that remained. Just the feeling. Just the emotion.

Emotion is the connector, the Sheikh recalled as he thought back to the manuscript he'd read since returning from New Mexico alone two days ago, his own emotions in turmoil, his own mind in flux, his own world suddenly feeling strangely out of control. Out of his control, at least.

"It's just too . . . too out of control," Hilda had said right after she told him she couldn't wear the ring, couldn't make that deal, couldn't commit to something like that after what happened between the two of them. "The idea of faking an engagement is laughable enough. But now that we've . . . now that we've . . ."

Stars for the Sheikh

"Made love," the Sheikh had said, his eyes hardening as he looked at her sweet face go all serious, her brown eyes flashing a firmness that told him she was every bit as stubborn and immovable as he. "You can say it, Hilda. We made love. Had sex. We damn well fu—"

"Stop!" she had said, covering her ears like she was a nun from the 1600s. "I don't know what we just did, Rahaan. But it wasn't . . . it wasn't . . . it wasn't real!"

Rahaan had jerked his body back as she said it, his hands going to his hips as he snorted in disbelief. "It was not real? What does that even mean, pray tell? Are you implying that it simply did not happen?"

"No, of course I'm not saying that, Rahaan," she whispered. "I just . . . I just don't know what's real anymore, OK? There's just some craziness going on in my life that I need to figure out, and that's not going to happen if I add more craziness to the mix. Do you understand?"

"I do not," the Sheikh had said firmly. "Explain it. Putting aside the fact that you dismiss what we just shared as craziness, tell me what other craziness is going on. I will solve it for you. I will bring sanity to the rest of your life so you can step into this new craziness with me and make good on our deal—which you have already agreed to, by the way."

Hilda had looked at the ring which was still on her finger, and she'd blinked hard and pulled at it. But it didn't budge, didn't move an inch, the diamond staying right there, stubborn and tight, obstinate and immovable like the two of them.

"Oh, for heaven's sake," she shouted, pulling so hard the Sheikh had to grab her hand and stop her before she dislocated her finger. "OK, hold on. I've got some soap in the bathroom. I'll get it off in a—"

But the Sheikh held her in place, smiling as he drew close to her. "I think it is a sign, Ms. Hilda Hogarth. That this deal is meant to be. A transaction written in the stars. A contract made in heaven."

"Hell is more like it," she had muttered grimly, but he could feel her melting as he wrapped his arm around her waist and pulled her close, held her tight, kissed her hair that smelled like flowers, tasted her lips that he swore were fresh strawberries, savored her scent which already felt like a drug to him.

They had made love again, without speaking a word, the two of them moving together against the dark red walls of that dimly lit gypsy's store, their coupling reflected in the misty glass of that silent crystal ball, the black cat meandering by, its red eyes turned away from the king and queen as they tried to forget the past, fight back the future, pretend this wasn't the present . . . the perfect present.

She had cried as they came, climaxing together in time, his seed filling her again, his mouth smothering hers, his hands claiming every part of her naked curves, his need merging with hers in the cloud of that crystal ball. Then minutes later she pulled at the ring again, her tear-streaked face going red with effort until he stopped her once more.

"You don't understand," she said as she flung her hands down to her lap in frustration. "There's just stuff you don't know. Stuff even I don't know. Stuff I don't understand. Things that don't make sense, Rahaan!"

"Then we must grasp at the things that do make sense," he had whispered. "And if anything makes sense, it is this! It is us! Us in the flesh, the physical, us together."

"But we're *not* together," she'd shouted, pushing him away like she was forcing herself to do it, pulling at that ring like it burned her flesh. "How can we be together?"

"You said you had the same dream," he said quietly.

She had looked at him, alarm racing across her face as she blinked and looked away. "I don't know what I was saying, Rahaan. I was lost in the moment. I think I just meant this whole thing feels like a dream.'

He had pulled back away from her finally, sighing and staring up at the ceiling, hands on his hips, chest heaving as he tried to calm himself down. "OK," he had said. "If you will not be honest with me, then at least sit quietly and allow me to be honest with you. Yes?"

She'd nodded, pulling a red-and-black shawl around

her bare shoulders as she sank into her chair and looked up at him. "Yes," she said softly.

The Sheikh had taken a breath and then begun. He told her of his teenage dream, the vision that had haunted him for two decades, raising questions he didn't even want to ask let alone know how to answer. He told her of the coincidence that brought him down to Albuquerque, brought him through that door, brought him into her life. And then he told her of the dream, the two of them together, three dreams in one, three women in one, three of them in one, all of time itself as one, one moment, one event, one life, one love.

"You said you had a dream," the Sheikh said again, searching her expression that seemed bordering on catatonic, like she had checked out, didn't want to process what he was saying, didn't even want to listen. What the hell was she hiding? "Was it the same dream? Three dreams mixed together? The two of us in—"

"You need to go," she had said, deadpan and cold, like a wall had come down in her, shutting her off from him, perhaps shutting her off from herself.

"What are you not telling me?" he asked. "Tell me, Hilda. I have told you everything, at the risk of sounding like a goddamn lunatic. But you are holding back. You are holding something back. My instinct tells me you are—"

"You need to go," she said, fumbling with that ring again as tears rolled down her round cheeks. "Please. I'm seriously at the end of my rope here, and . . . and . . . damn this ring! What the—"

"I think it wants to stay with you," the Sheikh had said gruffly, feeling himself close up too as he buttoned his shirt and shrugged. Bloody hell, he'd exposed himself as a weak-minded fool swayed by dreams and visions, and if she was not going to respond, if she was going to simply shut down after opening herself to him physically in a way that could not have been fake, was absolutely genuine, then . . . then to hell with her! "Diamonds are forever, as the advertising slogan goes. So perhaps when you wake up tomorrow and try to convince yourself that none of this happened, that none of it is real, that you or I or what we have shared are figments of your imagination, then perhaps this diamond will remind you that at least some of it was real, that you do not get to choose what is real and what is not."

"Rahaan, wait," she had said, still pulling at that ring. "I can't keep this—"

"Then throw it in the trash," he said as he turned to go. "And since you have made it abundantly clear that what we just shared means nothing, then all I have to say to you now—if you will pardon my crudeness—is thanks for the fuck."

"Screw you!" she had screamed as he slammed the

door and walked out into the street, his mind swirling in raw confusion as he tried to understand what in bloody hell had just happened, where in Allah's name all this inexplicable emotion was coming from.

Prince Alim was still waving his arms and moving his lips when the Sheikh focused back in on the present—or at least what he thought was the present. He did not know which way the arrow of time pointed anymore. After reading *Sideways Through Time* his mind was ricocheting between clarity and confusion, understanding and insanity, delight and despair. A lot of what Norm and Di wrote made sense at an intuitive level, but he was damned if he could understand it logically.

Emotion is the wild-card, the joker, the secret ingredient, the connective tissue, the book had said towards the end. *If consciousness is the only thing consistent across the infinite past, present, and parallel lives we lead, then emotion is its foil, the lump in the pudding, the devil in the detail. Strong, unresolved emotions ripple through lives, bleeding through dreams and realities, merging possible worlds, smashing together strands of consciousness in ways that can lead to madness and despair one moment, elation and celebration the next, death without mourning, new life without warning.*

New life, thought the Sheikh as he blinked hard and tried to think back to those three dreams. What was the defining emotion in those dreams, he asked

himself. Yes, there was sex, there was love, there was
. . . Ya Allah, there was new life!

A child, it hit him, as a strange clarity smashed its way into his consciousness, like those strands were suddenly pulled together in his mind, like he could see it clearly, see what was hidden, what Hilda was hiding, what she was keeping secret.

27

"A secret baby," Hilda said to Sabbath as the cat rubbed against her bare ankles. "So instead of a fake marriage story, I'm now in a secret baby romance. Maybe the lamest of them all. I mean, why the hell would you keep a baby secret from the father unless you don't want the guy in your life at all, ever. And if he's so horrible that you don't want him in your life, why the hell do you want to have his child?! Hello?! Common sense, anyone?"

Sabbath glanced up at her with his red eyes that Hilda had pretty much just accepted now. She'd done some research and decided that cats' eyes were weird and they could look different as the critters got older. Cataracts can form, mucus membranes can burst, other shit can happen to make the light reflect off its retinas in different ways, making the color look different. It was even possible Hilda herself was going color blind. Perhaps she should poll her customers about Sabbath's eyes.

"What color are my cat's eyes?" she said out loud, nodding very seriously at an imaginary person in her living room. She sat up straight on her couch, facing the blank television screen as she tried to keep a straight face. "No, I'm not crazy. What's that? Green? So I'm the only one seeing red? Great."

We're all very good at seeing what we want to see and blocking out everything else, Norm and Di had written in their book, which Hilda had been reading feverishly over the past two days as she'd been trying very hard not to open the bottle of wine she'd found behind the television set. *Which explains why we can easily explain away or simply dismiss evidence that a shift between parallel realities has occurred. Most of the time the shift appears consistent enough to provide a cause-and-effect relationship that seems reasonable. For example, things like sudden weight fluctuations or hair loss can be explained away. But how do you explain something that's "scientifically" impossible? How do you explain, say, a certifiably blind man waking up to fully restored vision? How about an irreversibly paralyzed woman walking again? See, we explain those away too as "medical miracles" or "wonders of the human body." But what do we say when a woman without a left leg wakes up and wiggles all ten toes when she was sure she went to bed with just five little piggies? Humans can't regrow limbs. We aren't lizards or worms. So what do we do when faced with something biologically or physically impossible? We ignore it. We simply tell ourselves it didn't happen. And you know what? Eventually the brain simply adapts to that new belief, and life goes on as usual. A self-induced hallucination that lasts the rest of your life. Photographic evidence, video recordings, eyewitness testimony . . . all of it is regularly ignored by normal, intelligent people. It's how the brain works. It's an adaptive, survival mechanism. We see what we want to see. We create this hallucination called reality, this dream called life.*

So what happens if we allow ourselves to wake up?

28

"**W**ake up before you drown," Norm said through her dream, and Di sputtered to life, spitting out soapy water as her mouth went under for a moment.

"Shit," she gasped, rising up out of the tub and grabbing the towel Norm was holding out for her. "I fell asleep. I can't believe I—"

"The entire bottle of wine, Di? That's not like you. Besides, I thought you weren't supposed to drink with the fertility drugs. Are you all right, love? Here, let me—"

"I'm fine," Di said, blinking away the confusion and covering her naked body as if she didn't want Norm looking at her. "I'm not drunk."

"Yeah, right," said Norm. "One look in the mirror should dispel that claim."

"Why?" Di said, frowning as she wrapped the towel around her breasts and allowed Norm to help her out of the tub. "What's wrong? Did I shave my eyebrows or something?"

"Thankfully, no," said Norm, wiping away the condensation from the mirror. "But three hours ago you were a redhead. And now you're blonde down to the roots. Damn, that's some quick-drying color."

"What? Oh, my God. Oh, my fucking God! Move, Norm. Move!"

Di burst out of the bathroom, towel falling away as she ran to the desk near the hotel room window. She grabbed the hotel stationery and began to write, muttering excitedly as she tried to get everything down before it vanished from memory.

"What's going on, Di?" Norm said, hurrying out of the bathroom and staring at his naked wife like she was insane. "What're you writing, hon?"

"The dream I just had," she said without looking up, a smile of excitement breaking on her face. She thought for a moment, wrote a bit more, and then put the pencil down and stumbled to the bed, collapsing on the sheets and staring up at the ceiling.

"What dream?" Norm said, sitting on the second double-bed, his soft body sinking into the even-softer mattress as he frowned and touched his nose. "Honey, what's going on?"

"I don't know yet. I mean, I can't be sure. But if this isn't hair-color," said Di, standing up again and walking to the full-length mirror against the closet. She examined her golden hair and tried to control her breathing, holding back the involuntary panic at looking at someone who was drastically different. Then she glanced down at her full reflection, her breath catching in her throat when she looked between her legs and realized that no, this wasn't fucking hair-dye. "If this isn't hair-dye—and I don't think it is," she whispered as she turned and saw Norm's eyes go wide when he glanced at the triangle beneath her flat belly. "Then shit is about to get very, very strange."

29

That is exceedingly strange, the Sheikh thought as he stood in front of the mirror and gazed at his reflection. Not just strange, but bloody impossible! Ya Allah, how could it be? How in God's name could it be?

He turned from the mirror and raised his arm, staring at the faded black tattoo on the inside of his right bicep. No, he was not going blind. He'd had this tattoo for almost two decades and he rarely looked closely at it anymore, but he certainly remembered getting it done that night in London during his college days. Yes, he certainly remembered the arrogance of his youth, when he had "*Dayimaan Almalik*" tattooed in Arabic along his arm.

"Always a King," it had said when he got it done. And it had said that every moment afterward too. That was how a tattoo worked—it was permanent. It would always say "Always a King." Except now it didn't say anything. It was not even Arabic, perhaps not even words! Just symbols—and not even coherent symbols. Gibberish! The scribbles of a child at best!

"By Allah," he said out loud as he stood there naked, not sure if the excitement raging through his hard body was elation or panic, confusion or clarity, disbelief or dread.

His thoughts raced as the world spun around him. He reached for his phone and pulled up Hilda's number. But then he stopped and took a breath, looking at his tattoo and then up at the ceiling. Finally he looked back at his phone, scrolling through until he found the text message with Di's number on it.

30

"**N**othing that I can think of. I mean, nothing that I've noticed," Hilda said as she glanced once again at Di's luscious new locks. Even the texture seemed different, Hilda thought, glancing at Rahaan now, thinking of the strange tattoo he'd shown her—along with photos of that same tattoo a few months ago: the same tattoo that was also a different tattoo.

"So there's nothing different about your life? Eyes, hair, nails? Something else about your body perhaps?" Di said, frowning and narrowing her eyes as she searched Hilda's face for perhaps a mole with a smiley face on it. "Nothing strange that's showed up over the past few days, weeks, maybe even months?"

"Just you two," Hilda said firmly, crossing her arms over her breasts as she heard Sabbath lapping at his water bowl against the side wall of the store. She remembered seeing Rahaan's tattoo the other day when they were in the café with Norm and Di. Those symbols were there then, weren't they? Yes, and photographs could be faked, so there was no real proof that the Sheikh's tattoo had ever been different.

As for Di's hair? Please. Yeah, it looks different in texture and volume, but it's a woman's hair, for God's sake. People have been working magic with women's hair for a thousand years now.

Hilda shifted in her chair as she stared over her wooden desk at the Sheikh and Di sitting before her, their faces in shadow because of the light pouring in from the front door and store window. Things felt so goddamn weird right now, she thought as she glanced down at the flat wood of the desk, thinking of what had gone down on it just a few days ago. Shit, even that felt like a dream now, didn't it? So faraway. So out of place. So . . .

Stop it, she told herself, forcing herself to stay focused instead of letting her thoughts drift back to him, to what they'd shared, to what felt so damn real—both in the dream and right here in her store. Hilda balled her fists beneath the table, realizing she still had that damn ring on. She'd tried to get it off with dish soap, but it seriously would not budge. Finally she'd given up, figuring that the stress was making her retain water or swell up or something, and perhaps she just needed to relax. Maybe even exercise. Hah!

But now Rahaan and Di were here, unannounced and excited, like there was something to actually be excited about. Had they been together the past few days concocting this scheme? The guy was a billionaire from the Middle East, for God's sake. Who the hell knew what got him off! Maybe he was still pissed about the twenty grand. Maybe the baby wasn't real, the doctor had been bribed, all the drugstores had been bought out and restocked with fake pregnancy tests, her water-supply had been messed with to give her morning sickness. Yes, this was all some elaborate scheme to destroy her totally and completely, mentally and emotionally, turn her into a walking joke with stars in her eyes before pulling the curtain aside so everyone could laugh at the fortune-teller with the fat ass who thinks she's meant to be with a King, carry his heir, ride off in his royal carriage through the mists of time!

He walks in all smooth and seductive, makes up some cheesy fake-marriage plan right out of *Mills and Boon*, puts a goddamn ring on my finger that's probably fake, makes me almost feel like there could be something here. Then the devil kisses me and turns on the charm, and suddenly I'm on my back, moaning like a whore, wailing like a wench, spreading like a slut. Just think for a moment, you dumb cow, she told herself. Is it more likely that there's some magical, pseudo-scientific, past-life, dream-world, parallel universe nonsense going on? Or is it more likely that this is a pissed-off, eccentric Arab billionaire's elaborate scheme to get back at you for humiliating his brother and him? To build you up and break you down just because the sick fuck gets a kick out of it? I mean, you still barely know each other. The sex felt real, but so what? That doesn't mean shit.

Now the wheels started to turn faster, a sort of relief pouring through Hilda as she allowed herself to think of a real-world explanation for what was happening. No magic. No dreams. No past lives. No parallel universes. Earth to Hilda: Come back to us, you stupid weirdo. Use logic and common sense. You're smarter than this. You've read about psychology and the ways in which we can deceive ourselves. Every single thing that's happened has a logical explanation, a simple explanation that doesn't require you to believe in this madness. The thing with the cat's eyes is freakish but it can happen. You've sorta decided that. And the pregnancy . . .

Hilda almost broke down as she realized she'd been trying her damnedest to push that to the back of her mind, perhaps out of her mind, out of her body even, if that were possible. She looked at Rahaan again, and she could see his eyes behind the shadow of his handsome face. He was looking right at her as Di babbled on excitedly to his left. He was looking right at her in absolute stillness, with an expression Hilda couldn't interpret, didn't want to interpret.

"You had the dreams," he said to her quietly. "Three dreams in one."

"Three?" Di said, glancing at Rahaan and cocking

her head. "You had three dreams with you and Hilda? Oh, God, Rahaan, that's significant. That's . . ." She trailed off as she slowly turned to Hilda, and Hilda caught a flash of something in Di's sand-colored eyes, a cloud passing through her, a cloud of emotion, dark emotion, emotion that Hilda swore she could feel even though of course it had to be her own damned imagination. "Listen, Hilda," Di said quietly, swallowing hard as her eyes darted left to right, like she was trying to control some part of her that didn't want to be controlled. "I don't think you realize how big all of this is, how groundbreaking this could be. We have a chance to actually test out the ideas from *Sideways Through Time*, to actually bring a real-life example to—"

"Ah, so that's the end game here," Hilda said abruptly, frowning down her nose at Di. "The book. You maneuver a real-life story into it, and it becomes more than a hypothesis. It goes beyond just the little world of academia. Perhaps they make a movie! You guys get to go to the Oscars! Mingle with the stars! That's stuff that plain old cash can't buy. You guys want the glory, the fame, the—"

"What in Allah's name are you talking about, Hilda?" the Sheikh said, his green eyes narrowing, jaw tightening. "Are you mad? You think this is . . . you think this is a trick? A bloody con?"

I don't know what to think! she wanted to scream,

but she held on, she held back, she held it inside. She told herself she wasn't going to unravel, that she was a match for anyone, that she wasn't going to get sucked into a fake fairy tale where she's the sucker.

"You guys can leave now," she said quietly, a slight tremble in her voice that she hoped wouldn't come across to them. "I'm flattered that you went to these lengths, impressed that you managed to pull sweet Professor Norm into it as well. But I—"

"What are you doing, Hilda?" the Sheikh said, rising and stepping around the table, grabbing her by the arms and leaning close. "You do not believe what you are saying. I know it. I see it. Why, Hilda? Why are you denying this? There is something to what Di is saying, and both of us damn well know it!' He dropped his voice down to a whisper, and Hilda almost melted when she allowed herself to look into his eyes and saw the depth, the sincerity, the urgency, the . . . the love? "There is something here," he whispered. "There is everything here. I cannot understand what you are doing, Hilda. Why are you—"

I can't understand it either, Hilda thought as she held his gaze for as long as she could before blinking and looking away, slowly shaking her head as she tried not to cry.

Di's sharp voice broke through now. "So you actually think the most likely explanation is that Rahaan and I are masterminding some elaborate scheme?

Did you read *Sideways Through Time*? I know you're more than capable of understanding the science in it—Norm convinced me of that. And the science in there is solid, believe me. Norm and I have circulated it to our peers in physics departments at several well-respected universities. Quantum mechanics has long since backed up the parallel universe theory. The only thing missing was how all of it would play out at the level of human experience. And honey, this is how it plays out! With dreams mixing with reality, with sudden physical changes that force us to look beyond the normal explanations, with connections between strangers that are somehow packed with a depth of emotion that doesn't make sense unless you accept that we are connected beyond this one, narrow life. Don't you see it, Hilda? Don't you feel it, Hilda?"

I see it, Hilda said to herself. And I feel it. But I also can't do it. I can't bring myself to admit it out loud, to make that leap, and I don't know why!

Di took a long look at Hilda before glancing at the Sheikh, who had stepped away from the desk and was up near the side wall. He had his back to the two women, and he was staring at a framed photograph on a dark wood shelf.

"This is your cat when he was a kitten?" Rahaan said, holding up the photograph, his face tight, eyes burning right through her. He didn't wait for her to answer. "Yes, it is the same cat. I see the patch on his

Stars for the Sheikh

left flank. I see the way his right ear is slightly misshapen." He placed the photograph on the desk and stood above the two women, crossing his thick, muscular arms over his broad chest. "And I see his eyes, Hilda. Green eyes. Green eyes that I could swear are now red. You lied to us, Hilda. You lied to me, Hilda. You said nothing has changed around you, and it was a lie. So now tell me. What else has changed? About you, Hilda. What has changed about you?"

He glanced at the photograph again, which also had a younger (and thinner . . .) Hilda in it. Then he strode across the room and grabbed a few other photographs that were on that shelf, grunting as he placed them back in their spots. "Nothing external that I can see," he said, turning and looking at Hilda again, accusation in his glare, a strange confidence in his voice, like he knew . . . "So it is something inside, is it not? Something inside you that has changed! Something inside you that is unexpected, inexplicable . . . something new. Something you're not telling me. Something you think you can keep secret."

"Get out!" Hilda shrieked, standing so quickly her hands hit the edge of the desk, her knuckles getting the brunt of it. She winced and rubbed her left hand, and as she did it she realized that holy shit, that immovable ring had twisted around on her finger!

She blinked in confusion as she looked at that diamond, and it looked back at her, its shine a bit duller, its twinkle a bit softer. Slowly she pulled at the ring, feeling a sickening chill as she watched it slide smoothly down her finger until it was all the way off. She could feel the color drain from her face as she stared at the ring, now looking up at Rahaan, finally at Di, who was on her feet as well.

"Your denial is the final bit of proof that all of this is goddamn real," Di said softly, crossing her arms over her tight chest and looking right into Hilda's eyes. "I bet you don't even understand why you're lying to us, why you're hiding whatever it is you're hiding. I had one dream that I believe connects us. But Rahaan said he had three intertwined dreams. I think you had them too, Hilda. And I think your answer lies in the intersection of those dreams."

"The answer to what?" Hilda said, trying to keep her voice steady as she carefully placed the ring on the table, trying even harder to fight the inexplicable feeling of dread that was seeping through her. She could only faintly remember the details of those three dreams from two months ago, and now she almost kicked herself for not writing them down. Yes, the Sheikh was in all of them. But God, she'd just met the guy and she had sensed an attraction between them. He was handsome and exotic, confident and direct. Hell yeah, he stood out. Damn right he was attractive! All of that could easily work its way into a dream. And so what if he dreamed about her as well? A totally reasonable coincidence. Three dreams though . . . yes, it was weird they'd both apparently had three dreams. But were they the same dreams?

"Doesn't matter," Hilda said finally, looking at the Sheikh but unable to hold eye contact for long. She couldn't look at those green eyes that seemed to know her, seemed to actually care. "It's too late now. I don't remember those dreams clearly enough," she said to Di. "And Rahaan doesn't seem the kind of man who keeps a goddamn dream journal, so I doubt he remembers them too well either. He can make up anything and end up convincing both himself and me that we had the same dreams. There's nothing here. A good story, maybe. But nothing else. Nothing real."

"Except our child," the Sheikh said, his voice unsteady with emotion, like he wasn't certain of what he was saying but was somehow compelled to say it. "Except our unborn child, Hilda."

31

The Sheikh couldn't believe his own ears, barely recognized his own voice. A part of him roared that he was mad, that he had crossed the line between imagination and insanity, that he was coming across as precisely that eccentric, insane, Arab billionaire whose head was in the clouds, mind up in the stars, believing things that only happened in fairy tales or in the twisted minds of kings closed off from the real world, living in their own fantasies.

But then the Sheikh saw the answer in Hilda's eyes, and he knew he was not mad even though the truth was dragging him to the edge of insanity. And he stayed still and strong, nodding slowly at the woman who was carrying his child.

"You're pregnant?" Di blurted out, taking a step back in shock as she looked back and forth between Rahaan and Hilda, her voice thick with an emotion that Rahaan couldn't name. "Oh, my God, this is . . . this is . . . oh, God, when I walked in on you two earlier this week . . . tell me that wasn't the first time you had sex! Tell me you two had made love before that . . . before you got pregnant! It wasn't the first time, was it? Oh, God, it was! Oh, this is insane. Hair color changing is one thing. But getting pregnant . . . a new life . . . that's off the charts. Oh, my God. Do you guys realize how . . ." She was sputtering and swaying, her face going red one moment, turning to the color of ash the next.

The Sheikh glanced at Di and saw her eyes cloud over again, and now she looked at him, golden hair fierce like the sun, angry like the wind. Her sand-colored eyes blazed with a darkness, and the Sheikh watched her lips move silently as she backed away from him, those eyes still full of fire, the fire of a woman scorned, of a princess scorned . . .

Now it came rushing back to him, and the Sheikh reeled as the image of Princess Diamante emerged in the theater of his mind, the princess he had rejected in another life, instead choosing his true love in that dream, his true love for whom he had also chosen exile.

Ya Allah, he thought as he watched Di storm out of the store, golden hair flashing in the sun before she was gone. He turned as another flash caught his eye, and it was the diamond ring on the table, twinkling as the sun coming through the slowly-closing front door bounced off its sharp edges, almost blinding him with something brighter than light, a light that seemed to shine from the inside, from inside him, from inside her, from inside time itself.

The Sheikh looked up at Hilda, his eyes narrowing

with a sort of perplexed clarity as something from that book came back to him:

But the reason we titled this book SIDEWAYS Through Time is that even our past lives are actually PARALLEL lives. Those past lives are indeed in the past, but they are also being lived right now in a way, just like your birth event and your death event both exist right now as two different places on the map of time. Which means that somewhere in the cosmos, in those parallel worlds, those past lives are STILL unfolding, with events still in flux, emotions still strong and real, unresolved and raw.

That is the paradox of time, the fight between destiny and free will, a contradiction that can drive us mad if we try to use logic to understand it. Only intuition can explain it. Only instinct can approach it. Only emotion can make sense of it.

And the only way to handle emotions these complex, channel intuition this strong, access instinct this deep is when our own normal consciousness is altered. People reach that altered state in different ways: dreams, drugs, alcohol . . . even sex, which can be the most transcendent of all if a couple can lose themselves in one another with absolute abandon. Yes, transcendent sex can be a path to making sense of the madness. Sadly, not many of us are blessed with such a connection, with a lover who can take us there.

The Sheikh straightened as he looked at Hilda, holding her gaze as he felt a clarity take over his being, like he knew what he needed to do, what they needed to do.

"You are correct," he said quietly as he felt the heat rise in him, sensed an invisible mist begin to swirl around the two of them, like the cosmos was forming a protective cocoon around this couple. "The details of those dreams are hazy, and I cannot be certain if what I recall is memory or imagination. I also believe that you speak the truth about not remembering them. But if the answer lies in those dreams, then we will need to go back there, to that place where our consciousness opens up again, expands again, perhaps breaks down again."

"So a sleeping pill and a dream journal? Sure, Rahaan. That should pop us right back to those dream worlds. Yup, let's just—"

But he was on her before she could finish her sentence, and he shut her damned mouth with a kiss so ferocious she stumbled back, gasping in shock as he grabbed a fistful of her hair and held her steady as he kissed her again, hard and with authority, his heat rising so fast he could barely see.

"Rahaan, stop, you fucking animal! What the hell do you—"

But he kissed her again, holding her head in place by the back of her neck and the roots of her hair, ignoring her as she beat her fists against his hard back, tried to kick at him even as he pinned her tight against the dark red wall with his heavy body. He stayed with the kiss, stayed with it as he felt that surreal mist get stronger, that diamond shine brighter. He stayed with the kiss as she sputtered and whimpered, sobbed and spat. He stayed with the kiss until slowly she went loose, those fists going limp against his back, her fingers slowly sliding into his thick hair as she kissed him back.

"I will take you there," he whispered as he finally pulled away for a moment and looked upon her tear-streaked face, saw the need in her big brown eyes, sensed the desperation in her short, gasping breaths, like she understood how the mind was powerless to make sense of this, that it was time for the body to take over. "I will take you there, Hilda. Back to that place where time and space breaks down, where there is nothing but you and I, nothing but our love, our passion, what is timeless and eternal about us, what connects our bodies to our dreams. I will take you there, my queen. I will take you there and then bring you back again. Now let go. Let go, my love. Let go and ride with me. Let go and run with me. With your king, your prince, your lover, your man. With me."

32

"Ride with me," said the exiled king in her dream as Hilda felt the red walls of the store melt away, a rocky plain opening up before her and the Sheikh, snow-capped mountains in the distance, the snorting of horses heavy in her ears, the smell of crisp mountain air filling her lungs. "Let us ride to the corner of that wood and be alone for a moment, because tomorrow we reach the mountains and then the journey will be slow and hard. Come, my queen. Ride with your king into the warm shade of the forest before we head to the cold of the mountain passes."

"I am the farthest thing from a queen," she said to him, looking into his green eyes that seemed warm as that nearby wood. "And because of me, you will never be king. Because of me, and because of what I carry within me. The fruit of our sin."

"What is done is done," said Rahaan, his gaze unwavering, jaw tight as the wind blew through his long black hair, making his unruly strands look like battle flags against the gray mountains in the background. "A king does not apologize for his actions. And there is no sin when two fated lovers join together and create a new life."

"Fated," Hilda whispered under her breath as she let the long-haired king of her dream lead her to that wood, away from the eyes of their loyal attendants who had joined them in exile. "And is your exile also fated?"

"What is fated is that I am a king," he said smoothly into the wind as he led their horses past the row of dark trees. "And once a king, always a king. Remember that, my queen. Always a king."

33

"I will be king once I claim the throne," he said to her as that carriage bounced through the country road, the horses heaving and pulling as she tried desperately to lace up her bodice and pat down her skirts before they arrived.

She hadn't meant to give herself to him so easily—certainly not in the back of a carriage like some harlot from the rookeries of North London. Of course, she was no whore—though she was not an untouched maiden either. Far from it.

But it is he who was the first. And though I was married once, it is still only he who has truly had me. Yes, only he who has had me, she told herself as she straightened up in her seat and glanced over at his sharp, swarthy profile, his strong jawline peppered with a stubble more befitting a pirate than a king. He is the only man who has had me, even if he does not remember the first time.

Well, certainly he might remember, she told herself as she caught sight of the outskirts of London in the distance, smoke from a thousand chimneys rising up into the blue sky, turning it gray as if reminding her of her deceit, of her sin. Yes, he might remember that night from three years ago. He just doesn't know that it was me that night, my hair hidden beneath a kitchen-maid's bonnet, my mind loose from a surreptitious swig of red wine, my body even looser, my virginity taken quickly and harshly by the Lord's personal guest at the manor—a stranger with broad shoulders and thick arms, a sharp profile and dusky green eyes. A stranger. This stranger.

She closed her eyes as the carriage slowed and took a turn, and she knew they were close now. Eventually he would know she had manipulated her way into crossing paths with him again, allowing him to seduce her again, in a way seducing him with her deception. And then what was to become of her? What was to become of them?

Most importantly, what was to become of the one who was most innocent but yet irrevocably stamped with the mark of sin? What was to become of the child? The child of sin born two years ago, born to her, born in secret.

A secret whose time has come, she thought as the carriage stopped outside the walls of the largest manor in a hamlet just outside of London, this foreign king's temporary residence in England.

"Claim the throne," she said as she watched the footmen step down from the carriage and steady the horses, which seemed a bit nervous, like they could

Stars for the Sheikh

pick up the tension in the air. "But are you not of royal blood? Does that not make the throne your right?"

He smiled as he glanced at his gold pocket watch and then up into her eyes. "In my homeland birthright is not enough to claim the throne, my lady. A bloodline is not enough. Sometimes it takes blood as well."

She paused and looked out the small window of their gold-trimmed wooden carriage. The men were still working on the horses as the manor staff lined up outside and awaited their new master and his lady. She scanned the faces of the staff, squinting to see clearly in the fading light of the day. For a moment she thought she might be safe: there was no one who might recognize her. But then she saw a thick, matronly woman, second-from-last in the line, and she knew she was done for.

She turned back to the Sheikh. Yes, I schemed my way into this carriage, back into his arms. But it started when I saw him at the Wildemeres's Spring Gala, to which I had no invitation! What possessed me to put on my gown and waltz in through the front door, I will never know. But there he was. What a miracle! If that is not fate, then strike me dead, she thought with an inward smile, looking up at his handsome, dark features, the bold line of his jaw, the sharp peak of his nose. She could see the resemblance, and she was certain anyone who'd seen her child would see it too. Dark hair, high cheekbones, green eyes set against olive skin. How could there be any doubt?

Three years it had been. Three years since she'd run back to her village before she began to show. She had the child in secret, her sisters helping her through the birth. She stayed home for almost a year, rarely venturing outside the small grounds of their modest family home, her sisters hiding her and the child as well as they could. But she couldn't stay there forever. Sooner or later the townsfolk would find out, and then she'd be branded a whore, the child labeled a bastard. No, she needed to run, for the child's sake. She needed a new life. A new story.

"My late sister's child," she told the head-of-staff at her first job in over a year. She'd been unable to find work in London proper, finally taking a position at a manor in a small hamlet outside of London. "She died of the pox, and the child is my charge now."

People talked, but the story held, as did her honor and reputation, and a year later she was married to a sweet man of good class and moderate wealth, owner of a modest country estate outside of London. She'd left her job in the hamlet and married him, taking her child and her story with her. The wedding was small and beautiful, and she cried when he kissed her at the altar—tears more of guilt than joy, though certainly she had no doubt what she was doing was best for her and the child. She hoped she might love this man in time, even though the deepest part of her belonged to that mysterious guest of her former employer, that tall, muscular, well-spoken stranger who looked like a pirate but talked like a king, who invited her into his chambers, asked about her life, told her about his land, made her smile, made her laugh, made her blush, made her blink. Soon his deep, exotic voice pulled her in, and before she knew it he was touching her, making her hot, making her wet, making her shiver, making her sigh . . . making her his.

His.

34

"You are mine, Hilda," he whispered as he kissed her neck, his strong hands sliding down along her sides, running down the curves of her hips, fingers pressing into her buttocks as he clawed at the thin cloth of her long, flowing skirt.

She could feel her skirt rising up as he kissed her, and she blinked when she realized she was back in her store. Oh, God, she thought as she recalled the flashes of imagery that had flooded her mind just now. Did I pass out? Was I dreaming? How could I have been awake and still transported in a way that seemed so real?

She breathed deep of his smell as she kissed him back, that now-familiar smell of tobacco leaf and dark sage. Yes, this was the real world, wasn't it? She was in her store, in New Mexico. She was here, with him, up against the red wall, his hands already sliding beneath her skirt, his hardness already pressing against her front. Her body felt loose and open, warm and secure, light and free. But she could feel her mind screaming stop, her common sense shouting cease, her intelligence whispering wait. She could feel the fight between body and mind, sense the struggle between dream and reality, taste the conflict between yes and no.

"Rahaan," she whispered as she felt her skirt rise up over her rear, his fingers pulling at the tight waistband of her panties. "Rahaan, please, I . . . I can't right now. I mean, I want to, but I can't. I'm too turned around, Rahaan. I need to step back and—"

"No," he growled. "This is the way, Hilda. It is the only way."

"The only way to what?" she said, turning her head as he tried to kiss her again. "Rahaan, please. Please!"

He pulled back and looked at her, his body still pressed against hers, hands still on her bottoms, inside her panties, holding her firm. He was hard and hot, she could tell. But he held back, stopping but not retreating. "The only way to find our way out of this without going mad, Hilda," he said. "Di is correct—there is something in those three dreams that has a hold on you, that is the center of this, that has an emotional depth so powerful that it is pulling all of us through time, through space, merging those past and parallel lives into the present. But for some reason the emotional power is concentrated most in you, Hilda. All three of us have experienced physical changes, but not like you. I mean, by Allah, Hilda, you have . . . you are . . ." He paused, momentary disbelief passing through his eyes as he swallowed hard and took a breath, like he himself was fighting to not lose his mind over what was happening. "You are pregnant, are you not? And it happened after we first met, after we had the first dream, before we ever touched each other, yes? And it is not some other man's child, is it? You believe it is my child, do you not? It is my child, is it not? Impossible or not, it is my child! Answer me, Hilda."

She took a breath, a shiver going through her body when she realized she'd never said it to anyone yet, had held it inside for two months, perhaps even denied it—just like Di had said, like how people try to ignore and deny even the most glaring, inexplicable changes in their cozy, private worlds.

"Yes," she said finally, and as she said it she felt a crushing relief, a soaring release, a staggering sensation of something falling into place. She looked into his eyes, those hard green eyes that seemed to say he was with her, that it was him, the same one, the first one, the only one. "Yes, Rahaan," she whispered as the tears rolled. "Yes."

He swallowed hard, making visible effort to keep his voice steady as he nodded. "And so there is something about this child, something about our child. Yours and mine. Ours together."

And she saw the same relief flash in his eyes, the same release rip through him, and he smiled as he said it, bringing forth a smile of her own. Oh, God, something has changed again, she thought as he kissed her gently through their shared joy, a joy that seemed so pure and innocent, light and perfect, simple and direct.

Perhaps because we both said it aloud, she thought as she felt the room swirl around her slowly, pleasantly, lovingly. Perhaps just admitting that the impossible has occurred, that I'm somehow two months pregnant with his child even though our first kiss was just last week, has triggered something. Perhaps that sensible, reasonable, rational part of our brains has just given up, said to hell with logic and reason and stepped away, clearing the path for our emotions to lead the way, lead us out of this maze.

"I know it's impossible," she said, touching his face. "But I also know it's real. Now that I heard myself say it, now that I heard you say it . . . God, Rahaan, what's happening to us?"

"I do not know, Hilda," he said. "But the answer is out there, in those dreams, those parallel worlds, past lives . . . whatever in Allah's name you want to call it. And I think you are the only one who can reach for that answer. I think you are the center of this. You and our child."

"What about you? If it's our child then you're at the center of it too," she said.

"Yes. Of course it is our child, and of course I am

in it with you, all the way, to death and beyond," he said firmly. "But do you see what I mean?"

"No," she said stubbornly, even though her intuition tugged at the corners of her consciousness, like it had something to say, something about a gift, a gift she'd always denied, just like she'd tried to deny this child.

"Just now," the Sheikh said, gently kissing her cheek, moving closer to her warm lips. "Just now, when I was kissing you, when I had you against the wall and the animal in me was bringing out the huntress in you . . . yes, just now, Hilda, your eyes were closed and your eyelids were moving rapidly, like you were dreaming while still awake, lost to the world but still kissing me back, your fingernails digging into my neck, pulling at my hair with a wildness I did not know you had."

Hilda blinked and tried to look away from his strong gaze, but he was too close, his lips already murmuring at hers, sending tingles of raw heat through her body as she felt his fingers squeeze her bottoms beneath her panties.

"Where were you when I was on you like this not ten minutes ago?" he whispered, slowly rolling her panties down over the rounds of her ass. "You were lost, far away from here, with me but somehow also someplace else."

"I . . ." she muttered as she felt her panties move

Stars for the Sheikh

down to mid-thigh as his hands spread her buttcheeks, thick thumbs parting her rear globes as he got hard against her front. "I don't . . . I don't know, Rahaan. I'm not—"

"You do know," he growled as he pushed his hand between her legs from the front, thumb resting on her clit, two long fingers poised lengthwise along her slit, slowly teasing her open as he warmed her with his clean breath against her trembling lips. "You were back there, were you not? Back in those lives, those worlds, those times, those places. Answer me."

"Yes," she muttered as she felt his fingers curl and slowly enter her hot opening. "Oh, God, yes, Rahaan. I was, and—"

"I was lost in the moment too," he whispered as he slowly traced his fingertips around the entry to her slit, bringing forth a wetness that was making her shudder in his arms. "But I was lost in you, Hilda, not my own mind. I could not see those dreams, those images, those lives. I could see only you. Which means I was right. I can take you there and I can bring you back, but I cannot go with you. I do not have the gift you do. I may have hints of it: my childhood dream of the explosion was real, I know, just like the visions I shared with you two months ago. But my intuition tells me that my consciousness only opened up enough to lead me to you, so I could bring us both here, so I could make it clear that I am the one, the only one. You were my destination, Hilda. And I have arrived. I am here. Here to be the foundation on which you must stand to access the full power of your gift."

Her arousal was so strong Hilda wasn't sure if he was speaking out loud or if it was all in her head, and she gaped at him as she felt him stroke her beneath her skirt. Her gift? What . . . how . . .

"There is a photograph on your shelf," he whispered. "Black and white and faded, a boy telling fortunes on the streets of an old city. And now here you are, a woman telling fortunes, seeing the future, reading the past. Perhaps your choice of profession seemed like coincidence before, but does it have meaning now? Does it make you believe now?"

She shuddered as he kissed her neck. "Believe what, Rahaan. God, I'm so lost . . . so . . ."

"Believe in yourself, Hilda," he whispered. "That you have something, a gift that can bring us the clarity we need. You have to go back there, into the depths of your consciousness, find out how those stories end, find out why the ripples through time are so strong, so powerful, so meaningful. Perhaps we need to do this to make sure those stories *do* have an ending! Perhaps the resolution to all these stories can only happen in this world! In this life!"

She moaned as she felt her arousal soar to heights unimaginable, now sink to depths that took her breath, and she could see her own subconscious, a goddess with no eyes, like it was Hilda who needed to give that goddess the gift of sight, Hilda who needed to be the one to see, see herself, her entire self, gifted and glorious, a goddess in her own right, the goddess of second sight.

But I also need the strength and power of my god to get all the way there, she realized. Only he can get me to those heights where my eyes will open and that goddess inside will see across the realm of my consciousness, the map of my soul, the landscape of time.

"OK," she muttered, nodding as he kissed her neck again, feeling herself slip into that waking dream, fear and excitement mixing with the arousal, creating an intoxication that was spiraling her upwards as her man, her king, her lover, her god slowly prepared her secret space. "Take me there. Take me there and bring me back, Rahaan. Take me there."

35

"**T**ake me!" Di screamed, jumping him before he even had a chance to look up from his laptop. "Fuck me, Norm! Goddammit, fuck me!"

Di had stripped topless before she even entered the hotel room, flinging her top and bra down the carpeted hallway, kicking off her shoes at the door, ripping off her jeans and panties as she stumbled towards the bewildered Norm, who was sitting on the bed, squinting at his computer.

"Di? What the . . . Jesus, Di! What's going on? Did you just take your clothes off in the hallway? Did anyone see—"

"Shut up and fuck me!" she howled, slapping him across the face so hard he would have rolled off the bed if Di wasn't straddling him with her strong legs, unbuckling him with her left hand as she pushed three fingers of her right hand into his surprised mouth.

It had taken every ounce of will for Di to get back to the hotel without losing her mind. Something had exploded in her when she realized Hilda was preg-

Stars for the Sheikh

nant, and even though the scientist in her knew what it was, the emotions were too strong to hold back.

That dream had been clear in her head even as she fought with her thoughts on the way back to the hotel. She could feel the anger in Princess Diamante, powerful and raw, unresolved and malignant, rippling across dimensions as surely as the fire-light of a star burns its way across the black abyss of space. Di had felt it during the dream three days ago, sensed the emotional imprint when she awoke. It was strong then, yes, but she could control it. It had excited her more than scared her then, excited the scientist in her: after all, now she could literally observe herself to test out the hypotheses of the book! What an opportunity! Yes, she knew her own theories warned of the danger, foretold the risks of opening up the consciousness before she might be ready. But she had to open herself further, take the risk, ready or not.

But now she felt that intoxicating mix of anger and spite, despair and longing, betrayal and humiliation rip through her just as surely as it had torn Princess Diamante apart. And she tried in desperation to fight back that torrent of emotional energy as she remembered her own words from the book:

. . . the only way to handle emotions of such depth is by reaching an altered state of consciousness . . . people through the ages have been driven to reach for that state with a sometimes uncontrollable desperation, using al-

cohol, drugs, searching their dreams, inducing hallucinations . . . pursuing transcendent sex . . . even descending into uncontrolled violence when all else falls short . . .

Di screamed again as she felt a chasm open up in her psyche, and out of that crevasse peeked the horned twin-heads of sex and violence, fighting each other for primacy in the squirming coil of her mind. She could hear herself sobbing and laughing as Diamante reached across time and pulled her into the abyss, telling her to let go of the person she was pretending to be, coaxing her to come down to that dark cavern with her, that shadowy place where the princess was trapped by her own emotions, where heaven and hell and space and time all danced together in an orgy of sex and violence, birth and death, love and hate, desire and destruction.

Through her manic haze she saw Norm staring at her with fear in his eyes, the man cowering beneath her like a child, a scared animal, a whimpering dog. He does not deserve you, and you do not deserve him, whispered Diamante. You are a princess and you deserve a king, not a dog. Fate may try again and again to saddle us with a lesser man, but destiny is not written in stone. That is the great secret, the dark princess whispered to Di. That we can fix what is broken, change what is written, claim what is forbidden, take what is denied to us again and again. Take it. Take it. Take it!

She looked into the face of the man fate kept putting her together with, and she saw the fear and unworthiness in him like it was reflecting back on her, laughing at her like fate had laughed at her, reminding her that she might be a princess but she never gets to be queen. Di sneered at him and called him a coward as she pulled open his pants and looked down in rage, desperate rage when she saw he wasn't ready for her, wasn't man enough for her, strong enough for her, king enough for her!

"Man up, you loser!" she sobbed as she grabbed him and watched him recoil, his body rejecting her, his eyes closed as he cowered before her. "Oh, no you don't," she spat out through clenched teeth, a sliver of her madness whispering that his insult could not be forgiven, that this lesser man did not have the right to reject her, did not have the option to falter when the princess demanded his strength, demanded proof that she was indeed a queen.

And in that moment Di saw it, the last bit of herself vanishing into the mists of time, and she could see a million Diamantes roll into one, a point of infinite density, the size of a black pea, the size of a gray mole, all of her lives compressed into one, rage and desolation holding hands and dancing across time, those twin heads of sex and violence now merging into one gruesome visage, those horns now a crown, the crown of a queen, the crown of a goddess, roses and thorns, porcupines and worms . . .

Suddenly through her rage she could see blood, she

could taste blood, dark and fresh, and she watched herself as she smashed the edge of that laptop into his face, crushing the bridge of his nose, breaking his cheekbones as he screamed beneath her, choking on his own blood as she kept at it, harder and harder, the violence making her howl with glee as she let the madness take over, the strength of a thousand rejected princesses finally breaking his skull and stilling him, her body still heaving with laughter as she tossed the shattered laptop aside and wiped the blood from her face and neck. A silence descended over the room as Di stared down at the red-streaked bed, her dead husband, her own naked body stained with his blood. It was a heavy silence, punctuated by just her breath. Heavy, but clear. A silence of clarity.

Carefully she cleaned herself, not bothering with the room or his body. She could think clearly, it occurred to her when she realized her mind was racing through real-world considerations of whether anyone had heard and called the police yet, how much time she had to get out of there, how much cash she could get from the bank in the next hour, how long before her passport would be locked and she wouldn't be able to get across the border into Mexico.

Oh God, this is incredible, Di thought when she looked inside herself and realized that the psychological shift had happened in a way no one could have ever predicted. Given the mathematical certainty of parallel worlds, there had always been speculation on how one might move between those worlds—indeed, that was what *Sideways Through Time* was about. But no one could have predicted how parallel personalities might somehow merge, integrating two strands of consciousness into one body, Diamante and Di into one.

Because I can feel her in me, Di thought as she dressed in blue jeans and a black long-sleeved top, grabbing a dark scarf for her blonde hair, putting on sensible shoes. But I can also feel myself in me, still here, the same but different. I should be horrified by what I've done, but I only feel a calmness, a stillness, a coldness that Diamante has opened up in me. Which makes sense, because of course Diamante *is* me. We were one in the subconscious, but now we are one in the ego, the waking consciousness. The power of her unresolved emotions from that life is so strong that my own life's events are running parallel, as if now it's our shared responsibility to resolve all of it in this life, in this world! Together we have a power to change our destiny! I feel it!

And so Hilda must feel it too, this need to direct fate, it occurred to Di as she grabbed her bag and keys, stopping in front of the mirror and smiling thinly at herself, a golden princess with fire in her eyes. Yes, Hilda is at the center of this somehow. Hilda, Rahaan, and their unborn child.

And then Di froze. She understood what she needed to do. She couldn't run to Mexico. No, she had to make sure her path merged with that of Hilda and Rahaan—which wasn't going to happen in freakin' Cancun.

Do I head back to Hilda's store, Di thought. Hotel security hasn't called to check on a disturbance, and clearly the police aren't here yet. Which means nobody heard anything, so I have some time. But there are still things I don't know, don't understand. I can feel Diamante's consciousness merging with mine, rising from my own subconscious and becoming more clear to me, her memories joining with mine. But I need some time to study myself, figure out if I'm insane or if there's a scientific basis for what's happening to me. If this cold calmness I feel is standard dissociation or something else. Either way, I can't just be running around stripping in public and killing people. I need to allow some time for this psychological, perhaps even spiritual integration of two strands of consciousness to take its course. Perhaps I'll eventually get deeper access to Diamante's memories, to find out how her story ends, to see if in this world we can change that ending!

Because that's why this is happening, isn't it? That's why the emotions are so strong that the barriers between worlds are collapsing, why we're all dreaming of each other, why my consciousness opened up and let Diamante in, why I just killed my husband and

Stars for the Sheikh

don't give a shit, why Hilda is miraculously pregnant with the Sheikh's baby.

Now she knew what to do, and she knew where to go. So Di headed out the door and took the elevators to the parking garage, her mind racing again as she calculated how long it would take to drive back to Santa Fe, pick up her passport, stop by the bank and clean out the cash accounts, get a plane ticket, and make it out of the country. The flight would take over twelve hours, she knew, looking at her watch and counting forward. She'd put the "Do Not Disturb" sign on the door before leaving, so hotel housekeeping wouldn't enter the room. And Norm and her weren't due to check out until the end of the week. So yeah, she probably had a solid twenty-four hours, if not more, before they'd find Norm. So she could make it. She could make it out of the country, across Europe, into the Middle East, all the way to Abu Dhabi in the United Arab Emirates. Then she could hire a car and driver to take her across the desert highways to the small, obscure kingdom of Kolah. It sounded insane, but it was her best shot. After all, if Hilda was really pregnant with the Sheikh's child, then eventually the two of them would travel to Kolah, would they not? And hell, once word got out that Norm had been killed and his wife was the prime suspect, perhaps Rahaan would decide to whisk away his fat-assed baby-mama to that fortress in the desert even sooner!

Yes, the Sheikh will want to protect his woman and

his child, and he will take her there, she thought as she drove out of the garage and headed for the highway. After they hear about poor Norm, there will be fear and doubt in those two. Because you know what, maybe the king and his queen didn't get their happy endings in those worlds either!

Oh, God, she thought as she turned onto the open road and hit the gas, driving into a future that was fated but also still being written . . . . perhaps being re-written. Maybe they're trying to change how it ends too!

36

"This ain't gonna end well," Hilda heard the large boy sneer when she closed her eyes and trusted her body to the Sheikh. She could feel her arousal mix with the fear and dread that was coming through time, from that world where a white girl and a brown boy were stealing away into the night, their precious cargo innocent and unborn within her young womb.

"Please," Hilda heard herself say through that girl, who seemed to know the enormous boy who stood in their way. "Don't tell anyone. Not until tomorrow, at least. By then everyone'll know, anyway."

"I know you," said the Sheikh in that world, her young protector who had stepped out in front of her and was standing tall before the other boy. Somehow Hilda could feel her fear recede in that world even as she felt the Sheikh kiss her in this world, and she felt herself smile at him in both worlds. It was so strange to be in two worlds at once, her body alive and electric with both fear and passion, excitement and arousal, her mind somehow expanding to access both realities as her man took her there. "Youse the pastor's boy from the next town. This ain't none of your concern. What're you doin' here in the middle of the night, anyways?"

"I ain't no boy," said Pastor-kid, and Hilda could smell the country liquor on his breath. "And you ain't no man. There's been talk o' the two of youse. And now I seen it, and Pa's gonna hear it." He pointed at Hilda. "My pa, and your pa, little girl."

"People don't know nothing and they just talk," said Rahaan, his body tightening.

"What do they say?" Hilda said, feeling safe behind her man, safe enough to get angry. "Huh? What? Say it if you dare, you bully!"

"Don't," the Sheikh whispered, reaching behind him in that world and touching her side, the touch making her moan and tremble in this world.

"They say you two been sinning," said Pastor-kid. "You been married in secret, in the forest, at midnight, by a . . . by a goat! Yeah, you been sinning, and inside you there's a child now, an unholy child, a bastard that's—"

She screamed in this world and she howled in that one, and the young Sheikh roared as he leapt at Pastor-kid in her dream. Hilda could feel Rahaan's body against hers even as she watched him batter the larger boy with his fists, the two boys shouting as she screamed. The Sheikh was inside her now as the candles flickered to life in the windows of that dark farmhouse in the background, lights and action driving Hilda wild as the young Rahaan broke Pastor-kid's nose in a furious explosion of blood before lowering his blood-red fists and stepping away from the wailing boy.

"Oh, God, Rahaan," she moaned as her eyelids fluttered with the gift of second sight, her mind swirling like a cauldron of bubbling emotion, her body burning with the heat of passion and the flames of fear. She could feel the Sheikh inside her, driving into her, her arousal alive and alert and in control, lighting her consciousness with a dark energy that was somehow fueling her secret sight, bathing her with a cosmic light through which she could see both worlds so clearly, too clearly.

She saw that girl's Pa and Ma step outside the farmhouse gates as more folks gathered, and Pa was shouting as Ma shook her head and sobbed. People were talking and pointing, and the young Rahaan, brown and hard, blood on his shirt, was shouting that she was his wife and they were leaving and no one could stop them.

"You speak like that and I swear to God I'll—" Pa was shouting.

"Don't you think of your family, you wretched girl?" Ma was wailing.

"I am thinking of my family!" Hilda heard herself yell through that pregnant young girl as the Sheikh grunted and flexed inside her, his strong hands holding her firm as her body writhed and flailed beneath his. "The three of us are a family. We're a family now! This is my family! I'm gonna be a mother too, and we're gonna—"

Then in her dream she saw Rahaan's face, his taut brown features going limp for a moment as he looked at her as if to say what have you done, my love. You've finished us. All three of us. We are done.

She moaned and muttered as the Sheikh drove into her, and she could feel herself getting close as he moved on top of her, the weight of his body crushing her as she gasped for breath, the weight of the vision whipping her body as she wailed in both worlds, screamed in both lives, howled in both realms.

She watched her Pa run back into the house as the townsfolk gasped. She watched her Ma tear at her own hair and point to the heavens and then at the hellish truth in her daughter's womb. She heard herself obstinately say no one could stop them and it was God's will, it was fate, it was good, it was right. It was love.

Her orgasm came crashing in as she saw them pull Rahaan away while he fought for his life, her climax ripping through her as saw the men of the town drag her man, her husband, her king away to the dark woods beyond the town well, his green eyes searching for her one last time, green eyes in which she could see despair rising, hope dying, life bleeding, bleeding across time as she wailed and thrashed, tried to go to him in that world even as she came for him in this world, those green eyes finally softening in forgiveness before he was dragged out of her sight.

"Oh, God," she sobbed as she felt her body rock and heave from the force of her emotion, the force of her vision, the force of her climax. "Oh, God, I can't. Bring me back, Rahaan. Please. Now!"

"I am here," he whispered against her as he held her firm. "I am here, Hilda. I am always here, with you, holding you, protecting you. Open your eyes, Hilda. Come. It is I, Rahaan. Come now. You are OK. You are with me."

Finally her eyelids fluttered open and she looked up at him, relief pouring into her throbbing body and swirling mind when she realized she was safe in his arms, that he was safe by her side, the baby safe in her womb. But the despair and helplessness of that girl was too strong, and Hilda could still feel the emotion of that powerless girl watching her boy-king get taken to the dark woods by the men of the town, never to emerge, never to return, never to forget . . .

"Oh, God, Rahaan," she muttered as she forced herself to hold on to the memory. "I saw her. I saw you. And . . . and . . . oh, God, Rahaan."

37

"You think I died in that dream," the Sheikh said, handing her a cup of the hot tea he'd ordered from room service. It was thirty-six hours after he'd brought the almost hysterical Hilda to his hotel suite, leaving the store unattended, sending one of his men back to lock up and bring the cat to the hotel.

He'd calmed her down and then they'd slept in each other's arms, slept all the way through the night. No dreams. No drama. Nothing but a man and a woman. They'd woken up intertwined like they were one person, one body, one soul. They ordered breakfast and fed the cat. They talked and laughed like a familiar old couple. They giggled and flirted like teenagers who'd just told each other their secrets, all the while pushing aside what needed to be talked about.

But it could not be avoided forever, and finally Hilda told the Sheikh what she remembered, what had ripped her consciousness apart in that dream, forced her to reach out and ask him to bring her back to the real world, to the world where he was alive and she was in his strong arms.

"What about the other two dreams?" the Sheikh asked

Hilda exhaled and shook her head. "Just what I told you. There's a great deal of anxiety in both those worlds, an overwhelming sense that things hang in the balance, that it's not clear how things will end."

"They will end the way they started," the Sheikh said firmly, putting his arm around her still-shaking shoulders and pulling her into his broad, warm body. "With you and I together."

"Did you not hear me?" Hilda said, almost spilling the tea as she turned her head. "You die in that world, Rahaan! You die because we're together! That's why there's a part of me that wants to push you away in this world . . . wants to even push the baby away! What if it's a choice I need to make, Rahaan? What if I need to choose walking away from you, from this, from us? What if I need to walk away before . . . before . . . oh, God, I don't even know what I'm saying!"

"You mean walk away before I die," the Sheikh said, frowning as he searched himself for the emotion she spoke of, the despair—perhaps even anger—of a young man torn from his woman because she couldn't hold back their secret. "You believe it is guilt, anguish, the inability to forgive yourself in that world. You think that's why you had this inexplicable urge to keep the baby a secret for two months even though you suspected it was mine? Because revealing that secret led to my death in that parallel world? That's why you were compelled to deny everything to me and Di earlier, even though you knew it was true?"

Hilda took another sip and shrugged. "I think so. God, Rahaan, the emotion was so raw, so intense . . . I can still feel how much that girl hated herself for what she'd done, what she'd said."

The Sheikh forced himself to chuckle as he kissed her gently on her hair. "Well, neither of us is in any danger in this world, Hilda. There is no sin, no shame, no judgment. There are certainly no racist townsfolk ready to drag me into the woods and lynch me or whatever you believe happened. I am sorry you had to live through those powerful, wrenching emotions again, Hilda, but now at least we have an explanation."

"Not really," said Hilda, brushing a strand of hair from her forehead.

"Of course we do. It is clearly the unresolved emotions from that world which have pulled us together, launched us into this parallel world where you are pregnant with my child. It is your yearning for a second chance, *our* yearning for a second chance!"

She nestled into him as he spoke with complete assurance, absolute authority, and he could feel her relax a bit. "So now it's no longer a secret-baby romance but a second-chance romance?" she said finally, a chuckle escaping her lips. "What about the fake-marriage plot twist? That kinda fizzled out before it ever really got going, yeah?"

He grunted. "Yes. You lost the second-chance at your fake-marriage when you took that ring off. And considering the baby is no longer a secret, I believe we are done here, my love. Happy ending achieved! Onward to the epilogue!"

Hilda snorted and playfully smacked his chest. "Speaking of diamonds and second chances, what about Di?"

The Sheikh grunted again. "What of her?"

"Well, if she's Princess Diamante in that parallel world, then she's got some pretty strong emotions to resolve as well. Emotions that involve you, my dear king!"

"Ah, I will just sleep with her and that should take care of it. Happily ever after for everyone, yes?"

Hilda swatted at him again, this time significantly harder as her face scrunched up with shocked indignation even though she was holding back a smile. "OK, that's so not appropriate! You think an orgasm can fix anything, don't you! God! Typical romance-novel hero with his mighty cock. Please note the eye-roll."

He studied her slow-motion eye-roll with a raised eyebrow. Then he kissed her on the nose. "I do not think Di will be a problem. She is interested in this for her book, so I imagine she will just get over her jealousy or whatever and appreciate this from a scientific standpoint. It might actually be fun to talk it out. Perhaps we all go on television! One of those daytime talk shows!"

"No, Rahaan. I'm kinda serious. The dream with Diamante is the most unclear, the most unresolved. And that's the one with all three of us in it! So if we've been pulled back to those parallel lives to fix what broke for us, then Di probably feels the urge to fix what broke for her too. And like I said, *you* are the missing piece in her story! Maybe she wants her happy ending too!"

The Sheikh sighed as he glanced at his private cell phone, which had just lit up with an incoming call. "So what do you want me to do, Hilda?"

"The problem isn't what I want. It's what she wants."

"But you said nothing ever happened between me and Di—Diamante—in that parallel world. So her need to be with me cannot be that strong."

"Strong enough to turn her goddamn hair blonde!"

"Well, I certainly feel no need to be with her, Hilda. So it is a non-starter. Ya Allah, forget Di!"

"I can't, Rahaan. And you know that," Hilda said, sighing and nuzzling back into him. "I don't have a complete picture of that world in which all three of us are connected. But judging by the way Di's expression changed before she ran from the store earlier, I think there's a chance she will have the full picture before I do! The emotional ripples are clearly very strong for her too, albeit in a different way. There's something more than just jealousy going on in Di's story, and we can't just forget about her until we understand what she wants, how she wants the story to end!"

The Sheikh grinned, turning to her and shrugging. "Well then, my time-traveling queen. Let us find out how that story ends. Yes? Come, I think it is time for your romance hero's mighty cock to take you back there. For scientific research purposes, of course. Purely a clinical study. Here, let me get that bra off."

She laughed and pushed him away as the phone buzzed again. The Sheikh ignored it once more, his attention now on her pesky bra. But Hilda ran and grabbed the phone and tossed it to him, sticking her tongue out before skipping away to check on Sabbath, who'd taken up refuge in the suite's bedroom.

The Sheikh answered even as he watched her butt bounce in a way that made him feel faint as she left the room. But then he tensed up when the caller identified himself.

"Albuquerque police department," came the voice over the phone. "We'd like to ask you a few questions."

38

"**D**i left her phone in the hotel room," the Sheikh explained to the wide-eyed Hilda, who was sitting cross-legged on the couch, cat between the two of them, everything and everyone on high alert as the television blared in the distance, reports of Norm's brutal murder all over the local news. "They unlocked it and found my number in the logs from the last few days. So they called."

Hilda nodded as she glanced at the TV. Di's photograph was all over—photos of her as a redhead, of course.

"You told them she's a blonde now, yeah?" said Hilda, still mesmerized by the television, her right hand absentmindedly stroking Sabbath, her body rocking gently back and forth like she was in a trance. "Oh, God," she said for the hundredth time, it seemed. "Norm . . . oh, my God, Norm! I can't even . . ."

The Sheikh held her close as Sabbath looked up at the two of them before lazily getting off the couch and slinking away to explore a new corner of the large hotel suite. "She left her phone . . ." he said, thinking aloud. "Was that intentional or not?"

Hilda frowned. "What difference? She's clearly lost it, either way. Lost her mind, I mean—not the damn phone."

"It does make a difference," Rahaan said grimly. "If it was intentional, it means she was thinking rationally. She knew she could be tracked using her phone, so she left it."

Hilda swallowed hard, trying to hold on to her own damn rationality. "OK. So then she's on the run. Either way, she's unhinged, Rahaan. She won't get far."

"Cash withdrawn from her bank yesterday afternoon in Santa Fe," Rahaan said, reading aloud as he scrolled through the breaking news updates on his phone. "And they've just gotten word from sources at the airport that her name showed up on a flight manifest. She apparently flew to Houston yesterday, and then—"

"London," said Hilda, turning up the volume on the TV. "It's on the main news now. Shit, they missed her in London. But they've tracked her connection to . . ." She trailed off as the news anchor delivered the update with relish.

"Abu Dhabi," the Sheikh repeated, partly in disbelief as Hilda felt the cosmos closing in on her once again. "Ya Allah, what in God's eternal name . . ."

"Oh, God, Rahaan," she whispered. "She had too much of a head-start for them to intercept her at the airports. The flight landed in Abu Dhabi six hours ago, and she's already cleared customs and immigration there." Hilda swallowed hard. "Rahaan, why in God's name would she go to the Middle East?"

"Kolah is a four-hour drive from Abu Dhabi," the Sheikh said softly, looking at his phone and reading a message that had just come in, his face all business, serious as all hell. "Three hours if she gets a driver who knows how to cut through the southern part of the Great Southern Desert."

"Would she be able to get across the border, though?" Hilda asked. "Aren't there guards or some kind of checkpoints? Even if she got there before the news hit, doesn't she need a visa or something? Can't you alert your—"

"*La ymkn 'an takun,*" Rahaan muttered, standing bolt upright and staring at his phone, the color draining from his face so fast Hilda rose to her feet and grabbed his arm. "*La ymkn 'an takun!*" he said again.

"What is it, Rahaan? What's going on?"

But the Sheikh just stumbled across the room like he was drunk, shaking his head like a dog with earworms, muttering in Arabic, blinking rapidly, muttering again. Finally he stopped and turned to her, his green eyes narrowed to slits, like he'd just figured out what was going on and it was bad. Really goddamn bad.

"In your dream Diamante marries the younger brother," he said, his voice almost a whisper. "The young prince who is set to be king because his older brother has chosen exile, because the older brother removed himself from the line by choosing a woman that disqualifies him from the throne. That was the dream, yes?"

"I . . . I think so," Hilda said, frowning. "I mean, that part was clearer in the dream from two months ago so I can't be certain. But yes, I felt the undercurrent of it when I returned there yesterday." Her frown cut deeper as she stared at the fearsome look on the Sheikh's face. "Wait, you have a younger brother," she said as he glanced at her and then back at his phone, half-nodding, half-shaking his head in confusion. "But he's not involved, and Di doesn't even know him. So why are you asking? Oh, God, Rahaan. What's happened?!"

The Sheikh spoke slowly, carefully, his face so serious Hilda almost dropped to her knees when she heard him speak. "Di entered my kingdom of Kolah almost two hours ago. She was not detained."

Hilda went quiet even as the craziest thought began to take form in her mind. "She wasn't detained at your border because . . ." she said hoarsely.

"Because she was accompanied by the crown-prince of Kolah. As his wife. Di has entered my kingdom as my brother's *wife*, Hilda! Somehow, someway, my younger brother, to whom I have just abdicated the throne as a result of my fake marriage to you, is married to Diamante!"

Hilda collapsed into the couch as the room began to spin. An older brother giving up the throne for a woman. A rejected princess marrying a prince she did not choose. But how . . .

"But how, Rahaan? They don't even know each other, do they? How could they have met and gotten engaged overnight? It's . . . it's impossible, Rahaan!"

"So is this," said the Sheikh, pulling her close and placing a hand gently on the round of her belly. "This is impossible too, is it not? Hilda, *we* were impossible up until the moment that . . ."

"Until the moment we weren't. It was impossible until it happened. Until we happened. Until this happened," said Hilda as clarity hit her like bag of sandstone bricks. "And it happened overnight, before we even knew each other. Oh, God, Rahaan. That's what's happened, isn't it? Di has somehow, someway pulled all of us into a new parallel world! Her world this time."

39

Di smiled at Alim as the young prince waited for her to step out of the silver Range Rover that had stopped outside the side entrance to the Royal Palace of Kolah. She gazed up at the red sandstone pillars gracing the facade, gasped when she took in the sheer immensity of the great white marble dome in the center, squinted as she glanced up at the towering gold minarets rising from the palace's four corners, pointing up at the stars, the heavens, perhaps the future.

Diamante's memories had poured into Di's mind as she tossed and turned during the long, restless flight from Houston to London. She clearly saw Diamante's motives in that parallel world, understood why she'd agreed to marry the younger brother in that world. Di realized that it was no longer about Diamante getting the man she wanted. It wasn't about petty jealousy. It wasn't about a man at all. It was about a woman. The ambition of a woman.

After the rejection, Diamante had decided she didn't want the exiled king anymore. She didn't want the king to love her. She didn't want the king to marry her. She didn't want the king at all. Diamante wanted the kingdom! She wanted to be Queen! A queen with no king! That was her endgame! She'd channeled the anger and humiliation from her rejection into something grander, a burning desire for power over not just the man who'd rejected her but over his family, his people, his land, his future! Those were the emotions that collapsed her parallel worlds, creating a bridge across time, merging Diamante's reality with Di's!

The realization had blasted through Di's consciousness at the tail end of her journey, when she'd fallen into a deep sleep on the flight to Abu Dhabi. She'd seen the worlds merging as Diamante's humiliation transformed to ambition, her need for revenge moving beyond just the man himself, a twisted transformation of emotion, a sense that if she couldn't possess the man, she'd possess everything else—his kingdom, his land, his people, and his family. Starting with his brother. The younger brother. The weaker, unprepared younger brother. Easily manipulated. Easily overshadowed. And when his purpose was served and she was queen, easily eliminated.

Di had awoken with a start when they landed in Abu Dhabi, her body burning with a fever as her mind buzzed with images and memories. She could feel things being rearranged within her own mind, and she shuddered and shivered as she tried desperately to separate dream from fantasy, reality from imagination, this world from that world, herself from Diamante. She needed her wits about her when she got off the plane, she knew. Had they found Norm's body yet? Had they already tracked her name on the flight manifests? Would armed guards storm the plane and escort her away? Would Interpol be waiting to pick her up? Would the goddamn CIA put a bag over her head and shove her into a white van with a painted logo that read, "Creamy Instant Arugula"?

But as the plane slowly taxied to the gate, Di felt Diamante in the background, and she got a strange sense that something significant had happened. Something else changed while you were dreaming, she realized. And this time it was you who forced the change, yes? It was you this time, not Hilda. You've opened your consciousness to Diamante so completely that her emotions are coming through with a power that's causing a shift in the timeline, pulling together past and future, parallel and present. The physics says that is indeed possible, that it indeed can happen. And now your emotions say that it has happened! Something has changed in a way that helps me. But what?!

Your memories have not re-aligned yet, so you don't know what's changed yet. No, you don't know what has changed yet, so be alert, she'd told herself as the plane finally got to the gate and passengers started disembarking. Be alert and ready to roll with whatever new event has been pulled into your world. It could be something in the news. It could be an incident at the airport. It could even be a person or people. Keep alert and have faith. There will be a sign.

A sign, she thought, almost laughing in gleeful shock when she walked into the airport lobby and saw a white-clad Arab holding up her name on an ornate . . . sign! His uniform bore the seal of the Kingdom of Kolah, and two veiled female attendants stood with him as if ready to serve a member of the royal family. The realization took a moment to register, and when it did, Di almost buckled at the knees when she understood the power of Diamante's emotions, understood her determination, the sheer intensity of her will to possess and destroy.

Oh, God, Di thought as she followed the silent train of attendants out to the front of the airport, right past customs and immigration, directly to where a silver Range Rover flanked by two black Range Rovers was waiting. Waiting for her. Waiting for the . . . princess? The queen?

"I still cannot get over the sheer genius of this idea, Di," said the young crown-prince of Kolah, the narrow-shouldered Alim, when Di got into the large backseat. "And it has worked out brilliantly. This is a scheme worthy of my brother, the great dealmaker himself! Ya Allah, when all is said and done, perhaps Rahaan will even be impressed with me! Yes, I think so. He will be impressed. Once he gets over his anger and humiliation at what we have done, of course."

Stars for the Sheikh

Di straightened her hair and swallowed hard as she tried to put the pieces together. She searched her memories as the heavy car pulled away from the airport and Alim gave his driver instructions in Arabic. Slowly she found what she was looking for, those rearranged memories that explained what the hell was going on in this parallel world she'd pulled herself into.

"You think Rahaan will be angry?" she said cautiously as the pieces fell into place, the images of what had happened in this timeline coming to her like a mixture of dream and memory. The Di of this new parallel world had visited New York City and met with Alim, told him she was a professor at UNM and an old friend of Hilda Hogarth's. She'd told him how Hilda had confided in her that this ridiculous Sheikh Rahaan had offered her an obscene amount of money to pretend to be his wife for the next few months—done it just to teach his lazy younger brother something about responsibility!

"Hilda agreed to the deal because she needs the money, but she's apprehensive about traveling to the Middle East alone with your brother," Di remembered explaining to Alim in this new parallel world. "She asked me to come along, and I was like, what the hell. Sure!"

"I suspected Rahaan was up to something," Alim had said. "And when I heard that his mysterious new wife was the very same astrologer who had cheated me out of fifteen thousand dollars two months ago .

. . ya Allah, I had laughed and told him he was a fool to think that I could be so gullible! Of course, I simply assumed all of it was a lie and the Ministry of Elders had never actually been informed. But then he showed me his official letter to the Elders, and I confirmed that it was indeed delivered to the Ministry, informing them that his marriage was official and that he had abdicated the throne and would step down officially in six months. So I backed down again until you showed up and confirmed my earlier suspicion that it is indeed a ruse."

"No marriage certificate, though, right?" Di had asked when they met in New York in this new world. "You should have asked to see one. That would have called his bluff."

"A marriage certificate would not be needed. The Sheikh's written declaration is as good as gospel for the Ministry. So by law they would have to allow the Sheikh to abdicate, forcing me to ascend to the throne."

"Abdicated the throne . . ." Di had mused, trying to beat back the soaring ambition of Diamante, who seemed to want to get to her future with a fearsome desperation. "So technically speaking, you are already king?"

Alim had shrugged his narrow shoulders and scratched his thin neck awkwardly. "Technically, I suppose so. But it will be months before the Ministry goes through the motions of consulting the Council of Clerics, who will then go through the Islamic Holy Calendar and select a suitable time for the actual ascension. The formalities will take about six months, which is why Rahaan has made the deal with Hilda for that long. Of course, I assume that after four or five months Rahaan will go back to the Ministry and declare that his marriage has been voided, and therefore there will be no abdication. Yes, four, maybe five months. Rahaan will watch me squirm and sweat for five months, and then he will pull the plug on it, giving me a fine lecture on growth and maturation, responsibility and the real world. Perhaps a reminder to visit a gymnasium. Ya Allah, I love my brother, but sometimes I wonder about his thought processes."

"There's always one crazy in the family, am I right?" Di had said, looking Alim up and down before glancing around his lavish penthouse in Midtown Manhattan. Video games and glossy magazines, posters of comic book heroes and villains, the lingering smell of pizza and Chinese delivery. It really did seem like an overgrown teenager's place—with a breathtaking view of the New York skyline, of course. "OK, listen, Alim. I came to talk to you because I'm worried about my friend Hilda getting caught up in something bad. But you seem like a decent man, and other than a lot of old pictures of your brother with actresses and supermodels, there aren't any serious red flags I saw when I googled Rahaan. So I think your brother is being honest in this deal." She'd shrugged and given him a look as she prepared her sales pitch. "Honest with Hilda, at least. Not with you."

Alim had laughed and clapped his hands. "By Allah, my brother! Yes, he is a good man. Your friend is not in any danger, if that is what worries you. But regardless, you said you would be accompanying her when Rahaan brings her to Kolah for a visit, yes?"

"Actually, that's what I came to talk to you about," Di had said. "I—"

"Say no more. It is the expense you are concerned about? I will have a jet available for you when the time comes. I myself am scheduled to leave for Kolah tomorrow to meet with the Ministry of Elders, so I will not be able to accompany you on the journey. But no matter. You will arrive in Kolah as my guest!"

"How about I arrive in Kolah as not your guest but . . . your wife," Di had said, swallowing hard before delivering the line. "As your wife, Alim. Do you see?"

A long silence as the young prince looked close to fainting. Then he cleared his throat and blinked. "What do you mean?" he said hoarsely.

Di had shrugged, holding her gaze, playful determination in her eyes. "Instead of waiting five months and then telling Rahaan you knew his marriage was fake all along, why not turn the tables on him. Flip the script, Alim."

"I do not follow," Alim had said, stammering in a

Stars for the Sheikh

way that almost annoyed Di, the fire of Diamante briefly rising as if that princess was being reminded once again how fate had insisted on pairing her with a man way below her level.

"Rahaan is faking a marriage because the laws of your kingdom stipulate that if the Sheikh marries a woman who isn't Arabian royalty, then he must abdicate the throne to the next in line, correct?"

"Correct. But I still do not—"

"Just be quiet and listen," Di had snapped, almost losing her cool at the prince's slowness. "Listen and think for a moment, Alim. Now, what would the laws of your kingdom say if even the next in line marries a woman who isn't Arabian royalty?"

It took Alim a moment, but then his face lit up. "Ah, heavens, it would be a mess! There is no precedent! I think . . . I think the Ministry would have no choice but to declare that Rahaan cannot abdicate! There are no other heirs! It is just Rahaan and I, and since he is the older brother, if both of us disqualify ourselves by marrying American women, then Rahaan's brilliant plan is dead in the water and he will have to back down and admit defeat! Yes! Flip the script, like you say! A fake marriage to foil another fake marriage! Ya Allah, it is genius! You deserve that PhD, Ms. Diamond! What is your field again?"

"History," Di had said, smiling as she sat back and exhaled. "History."

Rewriting history is more like it, Di thought now

as she watched the car turn onto the broad, magnificently straight highway that plunged into the endless desert. "Oh, Diamante," she whispered beneath the steady hum of the car's powerful engines, watching as Alim pulled out a red box with her "fake" wedding ring. "We've somehow managed to rewrite our past as we claw our way to the future, haven't we!"

And as the young, clueless prince slipped the ring onto her finger, blushing like a teenager as he did it, Di caught sight of herself in the side mirror, that flaming blonde hair, those sand-colored eyes that seemed dark with determination. And as they passed the rolling dunes of magnificent gold, Di slowly understood just how much of her past she'd managed to rewrite, how much power she might actually have to shape her own future, turning the tables on destiny itself. Perhaps she could indeed rewrite her story, have her own say in what was to come.

40

"Well, what did your brother say?" Hilda asked, her voice peaked with anxiety, her mind still whirling. She'd watched Rahaan call his brother and ask him very politely if he knew that the woman he'd just brought to the Royal Palace of Kolah as his goddamn wife had just brutally murdered her husband with a Samsung laptop. She'd listened as Rahaan switched to Arabic, pacing the hotel suite as he ran his fingers through his thick black hair, his voice deep and calm even though his eyes told a different story.

The Sheikh was still on the phone and he didn't answer her, and so Hilda sighed and turned back to the TV to see if there was anything new about poor Norm and his fugitive wife. There was a commercial on, and Hilda poured out two cups of milky sweet tea as she wondered what would happen after Rahaan got his palace guards to detain Di and hold her while they figured out what came next.

"Well, we'd obviously call the local police first and tell them Di's being held in Kolah," Hilda reasoned, talking out loud to Sabbath, who'd finally emerged from the far side of the suite, nonchalant and disinterested as usual. "Then they'd get in touch with the FBI? No, the FBI is just for domestic stuff. They'd have to get the CIA to pick up Di and have her shipped back! Wow! Maybe Professor Di gets to visit Gitmo for free along the way, yes? What do you think about all this, Sabbath? Come. Come hither, Sabbath. Come!"

Sabbath came, reluctantly at first before purring in approval when Hilda lifted him up onto her lap. Then she almost flung the poor critter across the couch when she looked into his eyes.

"Oh, God," she cried, placing a hand over her chest as she tried to slow her heartrate. "And just when I was getting used to those red eyes of yours, Sabbath!"

She tried to smile as she looked at the cat's eyes once again to make sure. Yup. Dark yellow. Not green. Not red. Yellow. Yellow like sand. Yellow like . . . like Di's new hair.

So she's managed to pull Alim and even my little Sabbath into this new parallel world, Hilda thought. What else has Di and Diamante managed to pull into our shared reality along with your yellow eyes, Sabbath?

Hilda glanced at the TV again and frowned. The news was back on but it was just a local reporter covering some mild graffiti at a church or something. Strange. She flipped to another channel, then another, finally tossing the remote and grabbing her phone and pulling up the news.

Stars for the Sheikh

The realization hit her just as Rahaan tossed his phone onto the carpet and shouted in anger, turning to her with the same realization in his steely green eyes.

"She has somehow changed her past," he muttered in disbelief as he stood before her, rubbing his chin furiously. "She has pulled all of us into her reality, a parallel world where she did not kill Norm, where—"

"Where she never even married Norm!" Hilda cried out as she feverishly read through the faculty bios on the UNM website. "This is insane, Rahaan! How could she have changed her past like that?"

The Sheikh shook his head as he thought. "Remember what Di and Norm wrote in the book. It is not a matter of changing her past. The parallel world in which she murdered Norm still exists, but it is no longer in our current timeline. Di has pulled us all into a parallel timeline. Ya Allah, that is . . ."

"It's terrifying, is what it is, Rahaan!" Hilda shrieked. "She's no longer a criminal, which means . . ."

"Which means we have to take care of this ourselves," the Sheikh growled, grabbing his phone again and barking out orders in Arabic, then switching to English just long enough for her to catch something about getting a private jet ready. "It is just us now, Hilda. I hope your cat likes airplanes, sand dunes, and camel milk."

41

Hilda watched the coastline of America fade away beneath them as the silver jet headed into the thick cloud cover. She couldn't see the ocean beneath her, couldn't see the sky beyond. It was just white mist outside the windows, and then the plane broke through the clouds and ascended into the thin air of cruising altitude, the cloud cover forming a thick layer of white beneath them as if to remind her that she wasn't grounded on Earth but wasn't quite in heaven yet either.

They'd talked themselves hoarse for the past three hours as they tried to understand what the hell was going on, how Di had managed to pull herself—and the rest of them—into a parallel world in which so much of Di's past timeline was different. At one point Hilda wondered if Di had managed to change everyone else's past that dramatically too, and she almost panicked when it struck her that ohmygod was she even pregnant anymore?!

Of course, then she'd looked up and seen the Sheikh sitting across from her, dark and handsome, calm and composed even though he had to be anxious for his brother's safety. No, Hilda had thought as she felt herself share in his strange calmness. His child is still in me. I can feel it. No one and nothing can change that, no matter how crazy everything gets. This is something I know. Not Di, not Diamante, not the Demon-goddess herself can change this part of our past. This is our past! Mine and his! Our emotions control this! Our love protects this! Our strength drives this!

But she is strong too, Hilda thought as she watched the clouds drift by. And she understands so much more of the mechanics of how this works, perhaps even more about the psychology of it. Perhaps Di is combining her own conscious will-power with Diamante's emotional intensity to drive things to the future she wants.

So maybe that's what I'll have to do as well, Hilda thought as she smiled at Rahaan, who'd gone silent and thoughtful. Perhaps I'll have to find the will power in myself to fight for the future I want. I don't know how—or even where—I'll need to fight: dreams, parallel worlds, in the women's room of the Abu Dhabi airport . . . but I'll have to figure it out pretty damned quick. And I'll have to be ready, just like she's ready.

Hilda watched Rahaan quietly, an overwhelming feeling of love swelling in her breast. She could feel the depth of their connection again, like she'd felt when they made love, when he held her in his powerful grip and took her to that place in her consciousness where things all made sense, where logic and timelines didn't matter, where past and present and parallel were all one and the same, one beautiful, playful, magical moment that contained all of time within it.

"What're you thinking?" she asked him softly.

He smiled and blinked as he slowly looked away from the window and into her eyes. "The past. Family. My mind was wandering."

"Take me along," she said. "Take me where your mind is wandering, Rahaan. Tell me about your family. I know your parents died when you were young. What happened, exactly?"

The Sheikh sighed and reclined his seat, raising his long legs and resting them on the empty seat next to Hilda in the secluded seating area. She smiled and placed a hand on his heavy legs, feeling his muscular calves beneath his smooth trousers, stroking him gently and listening as the Sheikh began to tell of his past, his own timeline, his own story.

"My father had been very excited about this new state-of-the-art oil rig being built by his newly-formed Royal Corps of Engineers. You see, building an offshore oil rig is so complex that there are only a handful of engineering companies with the know-how and staff to do it. None of the smaller Sheikdoms of the Arabian Peninsula have a domestic engineering corps that can pull off something like that, and many other Sheikhs had told my father it would never be completed on time, that it was an impossible task, that he should concede defeat and simply hire the Saudi Arabian engineers like everyone else did."

"And he refused, I gather," Hilda said, as if she knew Rahaan's father would have been as stubborn and determined as the son, as convinced of his own power to build or fix anything, take care of anything.

The Sheikh nodded. "He set a date for when the rig would begin pumping, announced it to the kingdom as well as the entire region. He said the entire Royal Family would attend the opening ceremony, and he invited several other Sheikhs and Sheikhas to attend." Rahaan paused and shook his head. "Of course, the date he set was actually two months ahead of schedule. My father was always a believer in setting aggressive deadlines. He used to say there is a kind of magic to setting a deadline, that when you set a deadline—no matter how impossible—strong people will rise to the occasion and deliver the goods, accomplish the mission, save the day."

Hilda squeezed his leg as she felt him tense up. "So the engineers were rushed, and they made a mistake? Or was it something else?"

Rahaan shook his head and shrugged. "Nobody knows exactly what happened. I mean, there was no indication of a bomb or anything like that. No evidence of sabotage—though it is quite difficult to retrieve already-shattered evidence from the bottom of the Arabian Sea."

"Oh, God, no—I wasn't implying there was anything nefarious. Do you believe there was? Did your father have any enemies?"

Rahaan snorted. "A rich, proud king who always gets his way? Such a man makes enemies without even realizing it." He smiled and shook his head. "But no. Kolah has been a nation of peace for almost forty years, as have most of our close neighbors. The rivalries have always been there, but just in the form of ego and showmanship."

"My rig is bigger than yours," said Hilda, snorting as she saw Rahaan's face light up with surprised laughter. God, they needed a moment of lightness, didn't they? Especially now that somehow, as crazy as it sounded, sweet professor Norm was back in Santa Fe, preparing for summer classes, oblivious to that entire thread where he got beaten to death by his psycho wife!

"Something like that," the Sheikh said, laughing heartily as he reached across the seats and unbuckled her seatbelt. "Come. Sit by me. Sit by your husband."

"Oh, that's right," Hilda said, feigning an epic eye-roll as she got pulled across the seats and plunked down squarely on the Sheikh's lap like she was light as a feather. "I forgot about the fake marriage. Are we still doing that?"

"We absolutely are still doing it. Now that my brother has got a fake American wife, I must prove that my fake marriage is more fake than his!"

"Wait, what?" said Hilda, scrunching up her face. "For one fake marriage to be more fake than another fake marriage, doesn't it actually need to be more *real* than the other?"

"Please do not attempt to use logic at this point in our fake lives, woman," the Sheikh said sternly. "It could very well drive us both over the edge."

She laughed as he leaned in and kissed her, his hands caressing her thighs as she snuggled into him. They kissed again, and she felt secure in his arms, confident against his mass, happy against his body. She touched his hard chest, looking upwards to receive his warm lips again. But then she stopped.

"You just went all serious again," she whispered. "What happened? Where's that mind of yours wandering now? Come back to me. I want you here with me now. Body and mind, Rahaan."

He nodded and took a breath, kissing her gently once before exhaling. "I am sorry. Yes, I was wandering again. Thinking of what you asked me about my father having enemies."

Hilda took a deep breath and looked up at the ceiling. She was starting to get hot and bothered under his touch, and she wanted him back now. "I shouldn't have asked you about that. I'm—"

But the Sheikh's mind was off again, even though

he pulled her against his body as he spoke. "And the truth is, he didn't have any real enemies as far as I can remember. I've spoken to older attendants, his personal guard, some of the older ministers who knew him well, and they barely even mentioned him having any serious disagreements with other Sheikhs or ministers within Kolah. Father was an outspoken, immovable man, but he also had a way with people, with diplomacy. In fact, the only time I ever heard my father seriously angry with someone, it was . . ."

"You, for being a brat?" Hilda said, looking up at him hopefully as she wriggled her bottom on his lap. What was wrong with her, she wondered when she realized she was getting hot and was so not into talking anymore.

"Well, if we are counting that, then my father was angry a lot," he said with a half-grin. "But no. It was actually with the head of the Royal Engineers. A man called Yezid Mohammed Iqbal. I remember my father summoning him to our private day-chambers, and they had a heated discussion about the progress of the oil rig."

"Wait, what? So that's significant, right? I mean, if the head engineer was saying the deadline was too aggressive, perhaps he sabotaged something just to prove himself right?"

Rahaan shook his head and smiled. "Ah, you give me a run for my money when it comes to paranoid thoughts, my little con-artist wife. And yes, I thought of that. It might have actually made sense too—if not for the simple fact that Yezid Iqbal himself died in the explosion along with my father and the queens. And suicide-bomber stereotypes aside, I do not think Yezid Iqbal was the type."

Hilda nodded as the Sheikh went quiet, and she kissed his cheek and touched his chest as she tried to understand what he was feeling.

"Yezid had a son," the Sheikh muttered, almost to himself as his body tensed up for a moment before his grip tightened on her thighs, his touch making her gasp. He smiled, face turned towards hers now, like he had finally decided to pay some attention to her. "A son around my age. He is also an engineer."

42

The thought came through just as the Sheikh kissed Hilda hard on the lips, his body stiffening with a quickness that surprised him. Now he was suddenly conscious of how Hilda's soft bottom was moving slowly on his lap, how her breathing had slowed to a deep, steady rhythm. Ya Allah, she was hot, was she not? And by God, so was he!

Somehow the thoughts kept coming as he clawed at her ample thighs through her jeans, unbuckling his seatbelt as he turned her and made her straddle him full. God, he wanted this right now. He wanted it with a goddamn vengeance!

His body stiffened as thoughts ebbed and flowed, and instead of trying to empty his mind he simply allowed it wander as his hands wandered all over her curves. He was intensely aware of Hilda, his body deeply connected to hers as he kissed her lips, squeezed her boobs, clawed at her ass as she bounced her heavy body on his rising erection.

Rahaan hadn't been oblivious to the dark irony of his own involvement with Yusuf Iqbal. In a way that meeting a couple of weeks earlier had motivated the Sheikh to fly down to Albuquerque the next day with the fake marriage proposal. Of course, the moment he walked into that store and back into Hilda's life, the Sheikh hadn't had the time or space to think back to the meeting with Iqbal. But now ... now it occurred to him how ridiculously strange that meeting had been. Was this also something to do with parallel worlds and unresolved emotions reaching across dimensions? Was it two fatherless sons subconsciously trying to recreate the most traumatic events in their own lives? Or was it just meaningless, everyday coincidence?

Logic would dictate it was the latter, would it not? After all, many sons choose to enter the professions of their fathers. Yusuf was a talented engineer—indeed, he would not have risen up the ranks of the Royal Engineers without talent. As for Rahaan's own insistence that the new oil rig be complete in two months? Perhaps it was a son's unconscious repetition of the way his father set aggressive deadlines. And besides, the oil-rig project was already way behind schedule, so it was not like the Sheikh was being overly aggressive. Who knew. Who the hell knew!

Rationality, logic, trauma, parallel lives ... ya Allah, I have had enough! I need to relax, because there will be much to deal with when I confront Alim and the woman who is spinning this latest web of madness. I need to relax and lose myself for a moment. Lose myself in my woman. Let myself be spun away in her magical web. Trust myself to her healing touch.

After all, it is she who is the center of it, is it not, he thought as he pressed her breasts so hard she moaned, her pretty round face twisted in a grimace of pure arousal as she rose and descended upon him.

Yes, she is the key to it all, he thought as he removed her loose black top, grasping her heavy breasts and pushing up her white satin bra. He groaned in pleasure as her boobs popped into view, and he sucked her swollen nipples until they were stiff and tight, the pink tips dark red and pebbled as he hungrily pulled on them with his lips and teeth.

"I need you, Hilda," he muttered as she reached down and undid his belt, rubbing his hard cock through his trousers in a way that made him dizzy. "Oh, bloody hell, I need you in a way that frightens me! By God, I need this right now!"

"What do you need?" she whispered, her voice low and husky, eyes narrowing as she backed up off his lap and stood before him, her gaze dropping to the tremendous peak in his unbuttoned trousers. "What do you need, my king? Tell me what you need."

"On your knees," he growled, the words coming out so quick he wasn't sure if he said them. "Now. I need a release, and I need it now. Now!"

He saw a glint of surprise, perhaps even fear whip past her eyes, but in a moment she was there with him, on her knees before him, obedient when he needed her to obey, submitting to him when he needed her to submit.

"Undo my pants," he said, removing his white linen shirt and tossing it across the cabin as he stretched his body on the double seat. He raised his tight buttocks off the seat so Hilda could slide his trousers down past his hips, and then he watched as she released his cock and sat back on her haunches, her eyes going wide when she saw how hard he was, how monstrous his need had grown.

"Stroke me," he ordered, and she rose to her knees, her naked breasts swinging forward as she reached for his massive erection.

"Oh, God, Rahaan," she whispered as her fingers closed around his girth, her grip barely going all the way around, he was so damn swollen and hard.

"Silence," he commanded. "Stroke me. Slowly, in rhythm. Ah, yes, like that. Again. A bit faster now." His breath caught as she grasped his shaft with two hands, coating his cock with his own oozing pre-cum, her nimble fingers rubbing his dark red cock-head and gathering his sticky juice as she slicked him up in a way that made him feel so damn aggressive he wasn't sure if he should let himself go any further.

He leaned forward, pushing his cock against her naked breasts, smearing her pert nipples with his oozing tip as she lowered her head and tried to suck him.

"Not yet," he growled. "Suck your fingers first. Taste

me from what you have gathered on your fingers. Do it now."

She gasped as she looked up at him, and then she looked down at herself. Her breasts glistened from the pre-cum he'd rubbed all over her, and she gathered the fresh flow from her nipples and sucked her fingers.

He watched her do as he said, and then finally he rose, his hands grasping her head, fingers sliding into her thick brown hair. His arousal was so strong he could barely see straight. All he could feel were her hands on his body, soft hands stroking his throbbing cock, massaging his heavy balls, caressing his thighs as her breasts rubbed against his bare legs. She was on her knees before him yet as much by his side as any woman could ever be. She was powerless in his viselike grip but as powerful as any woman he'd ever known. She was strong. She was beautiful. She was his.

She looked up from her knees as if she could read his mind, and he smiled down at her, his lips parting as he spoke the words that he knew were true but had not been uttered in this world.

"I love you," he groaned as he looked into her big brown eyes, his fingers tightening their grip in her hair, pulling at the roots as he struggled to hold himself back out of fear of hurting her. "By God, I love you, Hilda."

He waited for her response, groaning again as she

jerked him back and forth, massaging his balls and rubbing his shaft. Then she looked up from her knees, her head held firm in his grip. She looked up at him and said, "I know."

"I know," she said again with a smile. Then she opened her mouth wide and took him in, all the way in, all the goddamn way.

43

She starting sucking him immediately, reveling in the way he pulled at her hair from the roots, his entire body tensed up, brown muscles hard and rigid as she went back and forth over his beast of a cock, massaging his balls as he pumped into her. Slowly they got into a feverish rhythm, his grip on her head so tight she couldn't even turn an inch, his girth filling her mouth to the point where she could feel her lips straining from how wide she was stretched. Her breath came in short, heaving spurts through her nose, her breasts rising and falling as she sucked her king towards the release he needed.

Her own arousal was strong but she was completely focused on him. She could sense his desperate need, feel how badly his body needed that primal release. His taste and aroma surrounded her, invaded her, overwhelmed her, its clean, heavy musk intoxicating her as she tasted his juice, rolled her tongue along his throbbing shaft, swallowed her own saliva mixed with his clear pre-cum as he flexed and groaned, pumped and thrust, driving deep into her mouth, into her open throat as she struggled to stay on her knees and control his power.

Hilda could feel the wetness dripping out the sides of her mouth as she sucked, and she pressed her lips down hard against his cock to make the seal tighter so she could suck him harder, like a king should be sucked when he asks for it.

"Ya Allah!" he roared as she clamped her lips tighter around his cock, her jaw in agony from how wide she was forced to make her mouth. "By God, I am mad with lust, insane with arousal, delirious with desire! What are you doing to me, Hilda. What are you doing!"

He shouted the last word out, and just then she felt his balls seize and tighten in her hands. His cock flexed inside her mouth, and he let out a deep, guttural sound as he pulled her hair so hard her eyes went wide. Then he pushed himself into her mouth as deep as he could go, until his balls were against her chin, her throat wide open for his swollen head, ready to receive his warm load.

And then he came.

He came, he came, he came, the explosion surreal and slow, like a fresh geyser blasting up from the ocean floor, flooding the calmness with a violent injection of heat.

"Ya Allah!" he roared as he poured his semen down her throat, the entire airplane seeming to vibrate with the force of his orgasm, the intensity of his release, the power of his desire.

See, I can take you there too, my king, she thought as her entire body rocked back and forth as she squatted before him and took everything he had to give, swallowing his seed as he emptied himself down her throat, his balls seizing and clenching again and again as he poured fresh spurts of semen into her.

He came for almost a full minute, perhaps longer, and then finally he was done, groaning one last time as he squeezed out his final discharge into her mouth before collapsing into the seat, his cock springing out past her lips as he released her.

Hilda fell back on her haunches and almost shrieked as she swallowed massive breaths of fresh air. She was dizzy from the exertion, wired from the experience, buzzing with both arousal and a strange sense of pride, an odd glow that seemed almost at odds with the primal, visceral scene. She could feel herself smile wide as semen and saliva trickled down the side of her mouth, and she licked her lips and started to laugh when she looked down at her bare breasts, sticky with semen, glistening with glory, shining with his seed.

"By God, I think you just merged a billion parallel worlds with your lips," he muttered, reaching for her even though he looked spent and worn from what she'd done to him, where she'd taken him.

"If that's your way of saying thank you," she whispered, clambering to her feet and dropping her half-clothed self into the seat next to him. "Then you're welcome."

"It is my way of saying I damn well love you," said the Sheikh, turning towards her and reaching between her legs, rubbing her mound through her half-buttoned jeans before she grabbed his hand and stopped him.

"I'm OK," she whispered, even though she could feel her own wetness still fresh and flowing inside her panties. A part of her wanted to feel his strong fingers enter her, his heavy thumb flicking her clit as he curled his fingers and brought her to climax. But another part of her was whispering for her to hold back, to hold it in, to let it build . . . let that climax build, build, build towards the end, the end for which she'd need to fight, fight on a battleground that was between body and spirit, between this world and the next, between this world and all other worlds. "I'm OK," she said again, nodding and smiling into his weary eyes. "Let's get some rest, yeah? We've got a world of trouble to deal with when we land."

44

"You are in for a world of trouble," Rahaan said slowly and carefully to the royal couple sitting before him. "Alim, you do not know this woman like we do. You cannot even begin to understand what she is capable of doing! What she has already done!"

It was just past noon, and the four of them were having a remarkably civilized showdown in an open courtyard within the walls of the Royal Palace of Kolah. Surrounding the courtyard were broad corridors lined with heavy sandstone pillars, dividing the massive open space into four perfect quadrangles, like a giant four-square court. Each quadrangle had a center fountain, black marble and magnificent, and the ground was unfinished sandstone speckled with old cobblestones that gave the area a strangely Mediterranean feel to it.

They were sitting beneath a shaded gazebo, the two couples seated on hand-carved, jewel-studded benches made of fine Burma teak, facing each other, a low wooden table laden with a silver tea-set and bowls of dates, almonds, and fruit separating the two warring factions.

Stars for the Sheikh

Hilda studied Di's expression when Rahaan spoke. The woman barely even flinched, and Hilda couldn't be certain if it was because she didn't remember beating her husband to death, or if she just didn't care.

Well, as far as this world goes, Di didn't kill anyone, Hilda reminded herself as she tried to keep her head straight lest the contradictions drive her insane.

"Hi, Hilda," Di said abruptly, waving cheekily across the table as a desert crow glanced at the four of them from its perch on a nearby date-palm. "How was the flight? Get any sleep? Pleasant dreams, I trust?"

"Oh, you psychotic bitch," Hilda snarled, almost biting her tongue when she realized that Di was clearly trying to get Hilda to look like the psychotic bitch in front of Alim, who was the wildcard in this scenario. After all, how the hell were they going to even begin to explain to the simple young man that he might be a prince on paper but was a pawn in this game. And pawns get sacrificed, don't they . . .

Alim glanced at Hilda, blinking and quickly looking away when she turned towards him. The boy doesn't stand a chance, she thought as she reminded herself to shut the hell up and let the Sheikh handle his brother for now.

"OK, yes, well," said Alim, clearing his throat and not making eye contact with anyone. "There seem to be a lot of accusations of psychosis being tossed around. That is the word you used when we spoke on the telephone, yes, Rahaan? When you explained to me that my wife has very recently . . . ah, what is the polite word . . ."

"Murdered? Beaten to death? Bludgeoned to a bloody pulp?" Hilda offered, throwing in an eye-roll with it.

"Hilda, I will lead this conversation with my brother," said Rahaan smoothly as he reached over and placed his hand on her arm. "Yes?"

But Hilda couldn't hold back, even though she'd told herself she would. "You killed him, Di! Do you even realize . . . can you even . . . oh, God, Rahaan! Can't you just order her to be seized and locked up in some goddamn dungeon! You're the supreme Sheikh, aren't you? Now that he's pretending to be married to an American too, you're the supreme Sheikh again, yes? You can just command for her to be—"

"Actually, it is by no means clear who the supreme Sheikh of Kolah is right now," said Alim somewhat jovially, glancing at his brother like a child expecting to be congratulated by his father for doing something precocious but clever. "The Ministry of Elders is somewhat flummoxed right now, it appears."

"Well, un-flummox them, Rahaan!" Hilda shouted, realizing she sounded like a spoiled child but not giving a damn. "And then lock up this blonde witch while you make Alim understand what the hell is going on."

"That's it, isn't it," whispered Di from across the table. "You hate the fact that I'm the blonde in this story."

Hilda closed her eyes tight and willed herself to wake up from this dream that was part horror, part slapstick. She could feel her fingernails digging into her palms as she clenched her fists and tried counting to ten backwards. She got there, but it didn't seem to help, and it was finally the Sheikh's steady grip on her arm that got her to stay put and not leap across the table and punch the murdering bitch's lights out.

"Is she all right?" Alim asked the Sheikh with some caution, glancing fearfully towards Hilda and then back up at his brother.

I'm right here so why don't you ask me, Hilda wanted to growl, but there was too much wired energy in her system right now. Maybe she shouldn't have pulled Rahaan back from getting her to climax on the flight. Maybe then she wouldn't be the only one acting unhinged in this freakishly civilized setting in a bizarro world where truth and lies and dreams were all interchangeable.

"Yes," said Rahaan quickly. "It has been a long flight, and there have been some events that have been trying for all of us. I would try to explain it all, but I do not think you will understand."

"I will not understand, or I will not believe?" Alim said, his eyes narrowing momentarily, making him look older. "I am just the simpleton kid brother, yes? Unable to understand the complicated matters that my brother the great Sheikh deals with all the time."

"No, Alim," Rahaan said, his hand leaving Hilda's

arm as he looked with concern at the angry Alim. "It is not that. Brother, I do not think even I fully understand the events of the past two months, and so I do not know how to start making you understand!"

"It is not a question of understanding, Rahaan. Not anymore. It is a question of trust!"

"You do not trust that I unconditionally want what is best for you?"

Alim exhaled and folded his arms over his black *sherwani* coat that he wore over his traditional white robes. "Of course I trust you at that fundamental level, brother. It is just that . . . I mean, by Allah, Rahaan, you must admit that from my perspective your behavior over the past two months has been extremely . . . odd."

Rahaan sighed and looked away for a moment before nodding. "Perhaps. But still I must ask you to trust me right now."

"How can I, Rahaan! First you concoct this elaborate scheme of faking a marriage just to put me in the hotseat by making me believe I would suddenly need to take over as Sheikh. Then I find out that the woman you have married is the very same astrologer who cheated me out of fifteen thousand dollars! Now this madness about Di murdering a man who is verifiably alive and well in Santa Fe!" He paused and glanced furtively over at Hilda once again before lowering his voice, as if she couldn't hear him. "Rahaan, what am I supposed to think? I trust in your love for me, yes. But at this point I am not sure if I can trust in your . . . in your sanity!"

"My sanity," Rahaan repeated, swallowing hard, his thick Adam's apple bulging as he leaned his head back and swallowed again. "Ya Allah, so this is where we are right now." He shook his head and looked down, smiling and then nodding. "By God, Alim. If I even tried to explain what is happening here, it would only make you doubt my sanity even more!"

The Sheikh spread his arms out wide and laughed, shaking his head wildly, his thick black hair opening up like a lion's mane. Hilda hugged herself as she felt his frustration, and she couldn't even bring herself to look at Di. Instead she looked back over at Alim, who was squinting and frowning, like he was perplexed by something he'd seen.

Suddenly Alim leaned over and grabbed the Sheikh by the arm, twisting Rahaan's muscular forearm and pushing the half-sleeve of his linen shirt up over his bicep.

"*Hal 'araa al'ashya'a?*" said Alim, the color rushing from his face as his frown deepened. "Am I the one going mad now? Or has this old tattoo somehow been changed?"

Rahaan froze, looking up at his brother before slowly glancing at Di and then Hilda. "Come," he said carefully and clearly, masking his relief from everyone but Hilda. "Walk with me. I think perhaps I will be able to make you understand after all."

45

The Sheikh caught the flinch in Di's expression and posture when Alim stood and prepared to step away, and that told him everything he needed to know about Di. She was very much aware of what she'd done to Norm—even though in this world she hadn't actually done it. Rahaan also knew that he was taking a gamble right now by pulling Alim aside like this. After all, neither he nor Hilda were clear on Di's ultimate motive, Diamante's endgame, which meant that if Di panicked and thought the game was up, it might force her hand to do something drastic. And, by Allah, they knew how drastic she was capable of getting!

Still, it was a risk he had to take. The Sheikh was at an information disadvantage here, and as a dealmaker and negotiator he knew that the best way to play that hand is to bluff. Bluff with everything you've got, and trust you have the balls to stick it out until your opponent folds under the pressure.

"Alim," said the Sheikh when they were out of earshot. "Alim, look at me."

"Yes, brother. Speak. Please, I am all ears. I am

desperate to understand what is happening. We are sitting here like cartoon characters with fake wives and a game of musical thrones—and somehow that is the least confusing and alarming part of all this! Please, Rahaan. If there was ever a time I was ready to hear a lecture, it is now."

The Sheikh nodded. "First, I need to ask. Have you had any strange or particularly memorable dreams over the past two months? Especially over the past few weeks, leading up to the time Di contacted you in New York."

Alim blinked and furrowed his brow. Then he shook his head slowly. "No, brother. Nothing that stands out."

Rahaan sighed. "What about any physical changes in yourself. Your hair and eyes are the same, but it could be something else. Anything?"

Alim frowned and rubbed his eyes. "You mean like . . . like have I grown a tail? Is there a strange new mole on my left buttock? Do I have an extra testicle? I do not even understand your question, Rahaan! Is there some health risk in the air? What physical changes do you mean?"

"I mean like this!" the Sheikh snapped, holding up his arm and showing him the tattoo, those childlike scribbles that were once Arabic letters that said, "Always a King."

Alim squinted and cautiously touched the black

tattoo on his brother's arm. "How in Allah's name did you get this done? A removal and then another tattoo? Or did they modify the original? And what is this gibberish, anyway? It makes no sense to me."

"No, it does not make sense," Rahaan said, sighing when he realized his frustration was mostly to do with my own inability to explain the madness of what had brought all of them to this point. "And it will make less sense if I attempt to explain it. But Alim, look at me. I am not insane. There is something happening here that defies logic and reason but is real as the sun and the moon, real as flesh and bone, real as these sandstone pillars and marble domes. You have been pulled into it unwittingly, and I am sorry it has happened. But I need your help to find our way out. I need your help, and your trust."

Alim was quiet for a moment, and then he nodded, his face glowing, as if he was delighted that Rahaan was looking to him for help. "Of course, Rahaan. I was foolish to question you. Anything. I trust you completely. You know it."

"OK," said the Sheikh, glancing towards the two benches in the distance. Hilda had stepped away, it seemed—which was good, Rahaan thought: Hilda had sensed she needed to back off and disengage from Di. Yes, although the Sheikh hadn't said a word to her about what he was planning, she seemed to pick up on how to best let it play out. Ya Allah, she is a sharp one, is she not? She will make a fine queen, will she not?

Suddenly it hit Rahaan that, by God, she was his queen, was she not? In all this fake marriage and parallel lives chaos, their bond had only grown stronger even as their hold on reality felt weaker. She was pregnant with his child. She was wearing the ring he gave her. By Allah, this fake marriage was more real than anything else in this mixed up world, was it not?

The Sheikh heard his brother call his name, but his mind was spinning as back-and-forth feelings of Hilda and Di, himself and Alim, joy and apprehension, optimism and dread, panic and peace whipped through him as he considered his options. He could see that the wheels were turning in Di's head too right now, and the Sheikh was reminded again that he was at a disadvantage against her because he still did not grasp her deeper motive beyond just jealousy or some misplaced desire to be with him.

He thought about it for a moment, and soon it occurred to Rahaan that Di's reaction to his presence was dramatically different now as compared to their first meeting at the café, when he was certain she was going to jump him right there at the table, in front of her damn husband. Yes, she had been shamelessly flirting with him then, almost like she couldn't help herself. But now . . . now his presence seemed to barely register on her, like he was no longer an object of desire, perhaps not even an object of focused anger or scorn. Instead she'd looked at him like he was just another pawn in her game . . . her own game. But what game? If not love and passion, then what else is there?

Power.

By God, that is it, yes? Rahaan thought as he watched Di's lips move as she muttered something to herself in the distance. The rejection, the arranged marriage to the lesser prince . . . all of that had been subsumed and consumed by the soaring ambition of Princess Diamante. She no longer wanted the king. She wanted the kingdom! His kingdom! She wanted to be queen! By God, they were *all* pawns, were they not? Pawns to the one who would be queen! After all, in chess the most dangerous piece is not the king but the queen, is it not?

And by Allah, the chessboard is set up just right for her to become queen, the Sheikh realized almost immediately as he thought of the odd political situation in Kolah. The Ministry of Elders still needs to formally reverse the decision that I forced them into last week when I sent them official word of my marriage to Hilda. So right now it is still actually Alim who is Sheikh, in some sense! Of course, Alim's own fake marriage will now force the Ministry to reverse themselves again and put me back on the throne, but the formal decision will still take a few weeks, given the pace at which the Elders work.

Which means that if . . . he started to think as he caught Di finally look over towards him, her eyes cold, face calm, like she had thought through it already, perhaps gotten there already.

By Allah, he realized. Could that woman possibly be so far gone that she'd consider it? Consider the unthinkable? Why not? Although Professor Norm was alive and well in this world, the fact remained that the woman sitting calmly on that old wooden bench had very much murdered him, in flesh and blood, in a world as real as any other. And that was a man she must have actually cared about! The three of us mean nothing to her, yes? Alim, Hilda, myself . . . just pawns, ready to be sacrificed so the dark mare with the golden hair can be crowned queen!

Yes, it could play out in her favor with terrifying simplicity, the Sheikh thought. She is technically the wife of the Sheikh of Kolah right now, albeit temporarily. But if I were eliminated before the Elders formally reverse their decision, then Alim would remain Sheikh, which would mean Di would indeed be just one step away from being the sole and supreme ruler of Kolah! Of course, Alim would immediately void his marriage. But what if he does not get the chance? If I am dead and if Alim dies before he annuls his marriage . . . then the game is hers, the throne is hers, everything is hers! Ya Allah, she is two royal deaths away from giving Princess Diamante the ending for which she has reached across time!

And so Hilda is in danger too, the Sheikh thought. Because Hilda carries my heir. Yes, even if both Alim and myself are somehow killed while Alim is still Sheikh, the Elders may consider Hilda to be the rightful queen simply because she carries a child of royal blood, the last of the Royal Kolah bloodline! It is not clear because there is no precedent for such a complex situation, but all the more reason to leave no doubt, yes? So yes, if I were Di, if I were Diamante, if I were playing this game with all the seriousness of the universe, then I would take out all three pawns and clear the path, would I not? Has she thought this far? Is she capable of it? Can she pull it off?

I cannot take the risk, the Sheikh thought as he caught sight of Hilda emerging from the palace, her pretty round face glowing as she stopped to talk to one of the attendants, who was so shocked and pleased he almost swooned at her graciousness. No, I cannot take the risk. In all likelihood Di thought this far ahead before she even got in touch with Alim. After all, her marriage to Alim was pitched as a way to actually remove him from the throne, yes? Which means that if becoming sole queen is indeed her endgame, then she would have realized she only has a short window of opportunity to clear her pathway to power. By God, she may already have a plan to eliminate all three of us! I must order Di to be detained immediately! Then I must convince Alim to void his marriage and support my decision to imprison Di and not overrule it as Sheikh. In a sense that is unjust, because Di has not legally done anything wrong in this world! I would be detaining her immorally, perhaps even illegally! But what else can I do?

You can trust her, came a whisper from inside him as the Sheikh watched Hilda stop in the wide corridor to admire a portrait of Rahaan's mother, the painting completed just three days before the old queen's death in that fated oil rig disaster.

Trust her to finish it, came that whisper again, and the Sheikh almost turned to see if someone else was around. But no, the voice had come from inside somewhere, perhaps from across somewhere . . .

Rahaan stared at Hilda, blinking as a new idea began to form, an idea that chilled him to the core, burned him up inside, made his hands clench into fists, turned his eyes to green stone. He looked at Di now, then back at Hilda. Back and forth once more, and then he knew what had to be done. It was reckless. It was dangerous. It was bloody insane! But that was about par for the course, was it not?

He turned to Alim and spoke quickly, with authority, making sure he said the words before he had a chance to question his own decision.

"You know what, Alim? This is over," he said. "You have won. Your fake marriage has out-faked my fake marriage, and I will accept defeat in our little private game of passing-the-throne. In a week or two the Elders will finally emerge from their lumbering deliberations and announce that Rahaan is Sheikh again and Alim is demoted back to Prince, and then life will return to normal. In a sense you have learned something, I suppose, yes? And so have I. It is done."

Alim blinked and stared at his brother as if wondering if Rahaan was serious. The Sheikh held his sincere, relaxed expression, and Alim finally exhaled and clapped his hands in relief. "Ya Allah, brother! Thank God! I was seriously beginning to question whether we had all ingested the hallucinogenic desert root of the Bedouin gypsies! Wonderful. Come, let us go back to our pretend-wives and tell them the news, yes? Perhaps we celebrate for a week! Shall we organize camel races for the people? A street festival of kebabs and Arabian sweetmeats? Traditional dance shows? Demonstrations of tapestry-weaving?"

The Sheikh shook his head and squeezed his brother's shoulder. "I am afraid not. In a week I need to be back in New York, and so while I am in the Middle East I want to oversee the finalization of this new oil rig. I want the opening ceremony to occur on the full moon of this month, I have decided."

Alim frowned. "That is in five days, Rahaan! I thought you gave them another six weeks! How can they possibly—"

"Father used to say that if you set an impossible deadline, the strong ones will rise to the challenge. Hilda and I will stay in the royal quarters on the oil rig itself. That should add some fuel to Yusuf Iqbal's flame. Five days, Alim. And then you will join me and Hilda on the rig. As you may have guessed, Hilda and I are starting to enjoy one another's company. I think you will like her too when you spend a little time with us. Come at sunrise on the fifth day for the opening ceremony. It will be fun. The three of us!"

"Three? What about my fake wife, Rahaan?" Alim said with a snort.

The Sheikh shrugged. "Oh, well, of course you can bring her if she wants to join. I assumed that since the game has been played out, she might simply choose to return to the United States. But please do inform her of our plans so she can decide for herself."

Now you have done it, Rahaan, the Sheikh told himself as he patted Alim on the arm and walked over to where Hilda still stared into his dead mother's painted eyes.

Yes, now you have done it. You have set up yourself, Hilda, and Alim as bait, laid the trap, presented Di with a mouth-watering opportunity to take care of all three of us with one strike, one blow, one boom!

"Boo," he whispered into Hilda's ear as he came up behind her and slid his arms around her waist. He kissed her cheek as she pushed her soft body back against his hard frame, and he thought once more about what he'd just done, what he was about to ask Hilda to do, what he was trusting Hilda could in fact do.

46

"You want me to do what?"

Hilda stood with her back to the portrait of the old queen, her brown eyes blazing as she glared at Rahaan. They were too far for Di and Alim to hear—which was good, because Hilda was pretty close to the boil.

"It is the only way, Hilda," the Sheikh said. "We have to force her hand. Just like in war, there are times for diplomacy and maneuvering, trickery and negotiation. But sometimes the best strategy is to clearly set a date, choose a battlefield, and engage the enemy."

"Engage the enemy," Hilda repeated, running her fingers through her hair as she felt the desert heat rising up around her in a way she hadn't noticed earlier. "You mean Di."

The Sheikh nodded. "Hilda, the woman was able to pull all of us into a parallel world in which she changed some major events in her own past. She has merged the emotional energy of Diamante with her own scientific knowledge of the mechanism of time travel. We are at a severe disadvantage if we try to engage her face-to-face in this world. The rules no longer apply. Even if I order her locked up right now, who is to say if she can somehow intentionally change her timeline again, just like she did with Norm and Alim! We could lock her up a hundred times, but what if she could undo it all just like she has somehow un-murdered Norm! I do not know how much control and power she has, but clearly it is considerable. More than us, unless we pull her into a battlefield where you have the power to face her." He took a breath and rubbed his forehead. "Hilda, for all my wealth and authority, my stubbornness and strength, I am still powerless if whatever I do gets undone by Diamante pulling us into another parallel world."

"But I don't understand what you want me to do," Hilda said. She could see the strain behind those steady green eyes of his. He was terrified for her safety, she could tell. But at the same time he was conceding that he needed her help, needed her gift, needed her strength. "How do I engage with Di? Where? What battleground?" she asked, the answer already clear in her mind even as the Sheikh spoke.

"The battleground of your dreams, Hilda. Our shared dreams. Di may have found a way to merge her consciousness with Diamante's. But that is just one of the parallel threads of our shared love. You have the power to access all three of those parallel lives. You are more powerful, whether you believe it or not. I do not think Di has the gift you do, Hilda. You can go back there and—"

"And do what? Di isn't even part of two of those lives, yeah? How am I supposed to engage her?!"

"You don't engage Di. You engage yourself, Hilda! That is how you strip away her power! So far when you accessed those parallel lives in your dream state, you were merely an observer, were you not? You could feel the emotions, witness the events, bring back the story. But you were still just part of the audience. Now you need to take it a step further, Hilda. You must use your strength, your power, your goddamn will to write the endings to those stories, to step out of the audience and join in the play, step into those women's minds, their bodies, their very souls . . . those women who are all you, Hilda! Take your gift, take what you know, take my love and strength and unwavering support, and finish this for us!"

Hilda sighed as she understood. She touched his face and took a breath. "Step out of the audience and into the play, huh? All right. I can do drama." She feigned an over-the-top look of anguish, clutching the sandstone pillar and reaching towards the imaginary stars. "You're our only hope . . ." she cried dramatically.

She swatted at Rahaan when it was clear he didn't get the *Star Wars* reference. "Don't you know anything about American mythology?" she teased.

"Oh, I got it," he said very seriously, feigning an over-the-top frown. "But I could not laugh because it reminded me of how you Han-Solo'd me on the plane when I told you I loved you. Who replies to an I love you by saying I know?!"

"Oh, was that a real I love you?" she asked, matching his frown and touching her lip. "It's so hard for me to tell what's real these days, what with two fake marriages, one imaginary murder, our immaculate conception, and you setting up some cosmic trap on an oil-rig in which we are bait. And why the oil rig, anyway?"

The Sheikh didn't answer, and Hilda immediately saw that he couldn't really answer. Not in a way that made logical sense. Not in a way that would sound even remotely rational. And as she stared into his eyes she thought she saw stars, as if the universe was winking at her through those green orbs of his, reminding her that just because something cannot be explained does not mean it isn't real. And by definition a mystery is something that cannot be explained, yes?

But Hilda tried anyway, mysterious universe be damned. "It's because of the oil-rig explosion that killed your father and his queens. You think that's the missing piece, don't you? That by gathering all of us at a re-creation of this one event, you'll be able to tap into your own unresolved emotions. You'll access your own emotional power. Perhaps somehow combine it with mine? You're risking it all for a chance to give me your strength as well."

The Sheikh narrowed his eyes dreamily, sighing and then slowly nodding. "Yes. I think so. And I also think Yusuf Iqbal is the key to bringing Di into it, dragging her into this battlefield even if she suspects that it is a set-up of sorts. His involvement in all of this is what makes me believe that I am right in forcing the issue on this oil-rig."

Hilda blinked and shook her head. "I don't completely understand. You think he's going to actually set up an explosion? To . . . what, avenge his father's death or something?"

"It does not matter, actually. It does not even matter what Di does. It only matters that Yusuf Iqbal has unresolved emotions that I believe Di will somehow tap into and connect with, pulling both her and him into a new parallel world, a world in which they work together to arrange an accident at the oil rig. That work might happen in this parallel world or the next. It may get pulled into our timeline today or in five days. It is hard to understand without falling into paradoxes and contradictions. But it will happen. Either way, it will happen. Di's emotional energy will make it happen. I always thought Iqbal had a role to play in this, and this is his role. To set up the battlefield."

Hilda had to close her eyes tight for a moment. Eventually she nodded. "So you think Yusuf Iqbal in our current timeline wouldn't do anything as ridiculous as killing his Sheikh or anyone else. But you also believe he still holds onto strong emotions that might somehow pull Di and him together in some other parallel world where Yusuf Iqbal is a little on the unhinged side? And then Di and Diamante could pull that parallel world into this timeline?"

"Perhaps you should have finished that physics major in college," said the Sheikh very seriously. "Because I think that was a bloody brilliant explanation. Ya Allah, quick. Let us draw a diagram!"

Hilda laughed. "I guess it shows how messed up things are if the convoluted nonsense I just spouted is the best explanation we have!" But she understood what the Sheikh meant, and she realized that he was right. The details didn't matter as far as what Di or Yusuf Iqbal was planning. Because the Sheikh, in his own way, with the brute force of his real-world intelligence, had pulled everyone into a timeline where something was going to happen in five days, on that oil-rig, on that final stage, with every player present, every parallel life in balance.

And then it would be Diamante against Hilda. A race against time. A race across time. Who gets there first? Who gets to keep the world she wants? Who gets the ending she writes? Who gets the ending she deserves?

"Say it," he said suddenly, his voice cutting through her haze.

"What?" she said, frowning and then melting when

she saw the warmth in his eyes, like he was reminding her what this was all about, what they were all about.

"You know what," he whispered, kissing her gently on the side of the mouth. "Say it, my starry eyed soothsayer. Say it for me. Say it like you mean it."

And then she remembered what she was fighting for, she remembered who she was fighting with, she remembered why this would all be worth it in the end. So she looked up into his eyes, and she said it. In this world, in that world, in every world. She said it like she'd said it a million times, always and forever.

"I love you."

47
FOUR DAYS LATER

Hilda watched the dolphins ride the surf of the deep blue waters, three of them playing together, their sleek gray bodies rising and falling with the waves. She'd seen these dolphins for three days already, and today was the fourth day. She waved to them from her perch on a metal observation deck on the western side of the oil rig, a spot she'd been coming to every evening to watch the sun set over the horizon.

She waved once more at the dolphins, wondering if they were really the same ones she'd seen every day. Then she smiled and sighed, stretching her bare arms out wide and raising her face towards the setting sun, trying to catch the last of its golden warmth before the cool night breeze flowed in over the Arabian Sea.

The past four days on the oil rig had been the most surreally peaceful time Hilda had ever experienced. Around them it was chaos: engineers and workmen working every second of the day, worklights and blowtorches illuminating the black of night, the screech of cranes, the thunder of metal beams being lowered into place, the rumble of the massive diamond-tipped drill being overworked in preparation for the ceremonial opening that was scheduled for sunrise the next morning.

Yes, chaos all around her, but calm and silence inside her. In a way it felt like the Sheikh and she were all alone on an island, surrounded by the blue Arabian Sea, no one but the dolphins and the occasional seagull even aware of their existence. Rahaan was right, Hilda had realized once he brought her here on his thirty-foot boat and showed her the small but lavish quarters they'd be sharing. This was about them, and their focus needed to be on each other, on the internal and not the external, their own emotions and not the schemes and machinations of anyone else.

Yes, Rahaan was right in that it didn't matter what Di and Yusuf Iqbal might or might not be planning. That was Di and Diamante's world, a world pulled into existence by the darkness of their despair, the fire of their ambition, the twisted transformation of an emotion that had started as simple jealousy and humiliation and was now leading to the attempted assassination of a king, a prince, and an astrologer. You couldn't write a romance more convoluted than this, she thought. Fake marriages, secret babies, time travel, evil princesses, and . . .

And happy endings, Hilda thought with a shiver

as the sun began to slip beneath the dark blue of the horizon, its fierce gold morphing into a dull red glow, slowly bleeding into the indigo of the approaching night. Yes, happy endings. The happy ending that she would need to fight for.

They had held back from making love the past four days, even though Hilda could tell how badly the Sheikh wanted it, how badly he wanted her. But although her arousal and need was strong too, there was a serenity in the way she exercised self-control, a deep peace in knowing that she was preparing herself to fight for her dreams, her ending, her birthright. It still sounds ludicrous, she thought as her mind drifted for a moment and she wondered what Di was doing. It's like the evening before a battle, isn't it? This is how armies used to do it in the old world, soldiers camped on opposite sides of the battlefield the night before, campfires burning bright, the sounds of men feasting and talking, the underlying tension palpable but somehow tempered by a calmness, perhaps even an excitement. After all, it was all a play at some level, wasn't it? It was all drama. Actors on a stage, using emotions as their weapons, faith taking the place of the shield, someone's hatred powering the arrow, another's love sharpening the point of the spear.

I really must be insane, she thought as she watched the sun finally disappear as those three dolphins rose and dived for the last time before night swooped down. I am seriously sitting here, the night before some kind of assassination attempt is likely to kill all of us in the middle of the ocean, preparing myself to take on a cosmic adversary, do battle in the realm of the psyche, in the depths of the subconscious, the heights of the dream-space, the underworld between timelines.

But somehow it felt sane, even though it sounded mad. Yes, she thought as she heard the Sheikh step onto the metal deck behind her, his familiar, masculine scent swirling through the air and awakening her body as if to remind her that the body is the house of the consciousness, the body is as spiritual as the soul, the body is still made of stardust, just like the body of the goddess, the body of the universe.

Stars and stardust, she thought as she rose to her feet and let the Sheikh pull her into his body. The cool night breeze was coming in, and the waters of the sea looked black as the night sky as they stood there together. For a moment Hilda felt a panic rise up when she realized the sky was shockingly black, with no stars, no moon even. Her breathing picked up as she felt her brain trying to kick down the door she had bolted shut in her mind, the door behind which she had locked up logic and reason, common sense and rational thought, those voices that wanted to slap her upside the head and scream that the only thing more far-fetched than believing someone's planning to kill you, your man, and your child tomorrow is believing that you can stop it by stepping into a goddamn dream!

The panic almost had her, the darkness almost took her, the self-doubt almost broke her. But then she saw the twinkle of Venus, the first star of the evening, and soon Venus was joined by her sisters, ten of them, a hundred now, millions suddenly popping into the sky like diamonds, the eyes of the goddess reminding her that she would not be sent into battle alone and unarmed, that she had the strength of her man behind her, the blessing of a child inside her, the gift of the divine within her.

But she would still need to fight for her ending, she knew. And when she saw the full moon glowing through the mist of a cloud, she understood that yes, the stars were indeed shining, but it was up to Hilda whether she could reach the stars when it counted, when the time came.

"Just before sunrise," the Sheikh whispered against her neck. "When the night is darkest and the stars are brightest. That is the chosen time. And when the heat of the sun flows across the cool waters, it will be over, one way or the other. Come. Let us go inside, my love. Let us prepare to greet the sun."

48

Di watched the sun rise over the desert. She'd returned to the United States and was back in New Mexico. Day was just breaking over the badlands. She'd driven out here alone, to a spot she'd come to a long time ago, when she was a teenager with fake dreadlocks and way too many beads around her neck. She'd camped out here with three friends, one of whom had just been through a vision quest ceremony where she'd taken peyote under the supervision of a Native American shaman. Of course, the three girls just had a box of cheap wine and some weed with them that night, but Di remembered the stories of that vision quest: Images of other worlds, the supreme sense of meaning, the overwhelming feeling of being poised above reality somehow, looking down on life like one could see all the events taking place, all of time laid out as if on a map. Deep wisdom. Divine focus. Open consciousness.

The only way to harness that deep wisdom, focus those powerful emotions, make sense of the connections between parallel worlds, is by reaching an altered state of consciousness, like people have done for centuries on vision quests . . . shamans who claim to see all the mysteries of the universe in their travels, able to reach across space and time in their visions, to come back with stories of their journey, stories of their adventures, stories of their future, a future they claim to be able to rewrite . . .

"Well, Diamante, here's where our story gets rewritten," Di said out loud as she looked down at the three button-shaped pieces of the peyote cactus she'd gotten from a colleague in the anthropology department. "Shaman or psycho, we're doing this. You and me, girl. We were powerful enough to change our timeline and get this far. Can we change it once again, like we did to bring Alim into the picture? Can we bring another pawn into our game, pull ourselves into a parallel world where something happens on that oil-rig where all three of them are going to be gathered when the sun rises over the Arabian Sea?"

She glanced at her watch and sighed as she did the time-zone math. The kingdom of Kolah was almost twelve hours ahead of the Western United States, which meant that the sun had just set in the Middle East. And since it was just about sunrise in New Mexico, it meant that they were almost precisely at opposite ends of the cycle. Shortly after the sun set over the New Mexico desert, it would begin to rise over the Arabian Sea.

Di thought through her plan again. She needed

to go into her altered state about three hours before sunset, just to make sure she was deep into her trance by then, her consciousness opened wide before her. After that . . . who the hell knew! She'd have to follow the breadcrumbs left by her emotions, find a psychic bridge to a parallel world where she could find someone to sabotage the oil-rig or plant a bomb or something. Di didn't know who it would be, but she knew there would be someone whose emotions were strong enough for her to connect with—connect with and then manipulate, just like she'd done with Alim.

Yes, there will be someone, she thought. And the irony—or the madness, rather—is that Rahaan knows who that someone is! That's why he's planned this oil-rig event, a re-creation of the event that killed his father and mother, a tragedy surrounded by strong, unresolved emotions for both him as well as many others who lost loved ones. Rahaan is setting the stage, is he not? He's setting up the battlefield, tempting me to step in and see if I can take what I want, conquer him and Hilda, claim my throne, claim the ending that I want! And he knows that I will answer the call, because he knows that the fire and ambition of Diamante is within me, integrated and alive. He knows that I will not try something as stupid as attempting to kill anyone myself—certainly not a heavily guarded Sheikh and Prince! He knows that I will take the bait even though I know it is bait. I will take the bait and accept the invitation to battle, because I know I have a chance to win. And he knows it too. He has forced my hand, but I have forced his hand too. Just like I cannot defeat him alone in this world, he cannot face me alone in that world. It will be Hilda who must do it.

Because the battle will happen in the dream world, in the open space within time, the grand hallways of eternity, a world where you cannot get to yourself, great Sheikh. Do you have that much faith in your woman, you arrogant Sheikh? So much faith that you are willing to risk it all by sending her to meet me on this cosmic battleground? You believe your shared love is more powerful than the ambition of a scorned woman who was denied her due? You believe Hilda is powerful enough to seize her happy ending from the warrior-grip of Diamante? You think you and Hilda together is enough of a match for me and Diamante put together?

We shall see, won't we. We shall see.

49

"See who it is," whispered Hilda from the bedroom of the royal quarters on the rig. After pacing and trying her best to calm down, she'd finally gotten under the silk covers to ready herself for the night. But then someone had pounded on the metal door past the anteroom of their chambers, and Rahaan had angrily shaken his head and muttered something about telling his guards he did not want to be disturbed.

"I do not care who it is," the Sheikh growled. "I gave orders, and my orders are final. I was not to be disturbed. I will have my guards thrown to the sharks if that knock comes again."

The knock came again, more urgent this time, and Hilda finally let out a giggle as she watched her king flex his arms and turn towards the door. "There aren't any sharks here, just dolphins. Just see who it is, Rahaan. It sounds urgent."

"Everything is urgent it seems," the Sheikh rasped as he finally strode out of the bedroom. Hilda heard him yank open the door even as a sudden panic rose up in her as she worried that oh God, what if this is the assassination attempt?! What if the guards are lying in pools of their own blood outside, the rig has been cleared, Alim's throat has been slit, and—

Just then the Sheikh walked back into the bedroom and Hilda sighed and clamped her eyes shut tight as she forced herself to try and relax again. But one look at Rahaan's tight jaw and she knew she needed to ask.

"What?" she said, almost afraid to hear the answer. The stillness of the past few days seemed long gone, and the uneasiness of being in a place where seemingly anything could happen was rising up in her again. "Who was it?"

"Yusuf Iqbal," said the Sheikh quietly. "He was in a bad state. I could literally see the conflict all over his face. He was almost begging me to relieve him of the pressure of whatever he has planned. To free him of the conflict."

"What did he say?"

Rahaan shook his head. "He was rambling. But mostly it was something about calling off the opening ceremony. Like he was giving me one last chance."

"To what? Back off? Was it a warning? A threat?" said Hilda.

The Sheikh took a breath and sat down on the side of the king-sized bed, his weight causing Hilda to almost roll towards him. "It wasn't a threat. Not intentionally, at least. It was strange, like he was confused. Perhaps confused about what he is planning—whatever that might be."

Hilda nodded and placed her hand on Rahaan's

broad back. "Which means you were right. He has been pulled into this, but it is into Di's world, a world where he is just a side player, a pawn."

The Sheikh nodded, but then he shook his head. "Or maybe it wasn't him giving me one last chance to back off. In a way it was me pulling at him. My conflict."

"I don't understand."

Rahaan turned on the bed, and she could see the struggle on his face. "I think this last-minute conflict is because it is my emotional needs that are pulling him away. I am struggling with the decision of sending you, my woman, alone into battle on a battleground I cannot enter. A part of me still wants to resolve this in my world. In the here and now, even though I know that my physical strength, my wealth, my willpower . . . none of it can be relied on in this realm of shifting timelines. It is that sense of powerlessness that is tearing me apart. That sense of being vulnerable in a way I have never experienced."

Hilda took a breath and closed her eyes once more. He was right. But he was also wrong. "You're not sending me into battle alone," she whispered, pulling at his flowing tunic and forcing him to turn once more to her. "You'll be my foundation. My source of strength. The arms holding me upright. The horse I ride upon. This is our story, Rahaan." She looked down at her pregnant belly and into his concerned eyes. "It is our family. You were right when you said that it's my unresolved emotions about this child in those three worlds that's causing all of this, which means only I can resolve it. I have to see those stories through to the end." She paused and swallowed hard as a moment of doubt rose up and then subsided. "And I have to make sure they end the way I want. For us. All three of us."

The Sheikh nodded as an awful thought passed through Hilda's mind. *God, what if deep down I don't want them to end as a fairy tale! What if some part of me believes that I don't deserve the happy ending? What if something inside me feels guilty, unworthy, unsure of myself to the point where I can't summon up the emotional strength to counter Diamante? Is it right for me to go on? Or do I tell him I'm scared and we need to call this off and get the hell off this oil rig! Oh, shit, I don't know. I don't know!*

But then it hit her, and just like that Hilda could feel a blanket of serenity drop down over her. It hit her that *this is it, isn't it? This is where the battle is truly fought: within myself. Parallel worlds, angry princesses, vengeful engineers . . . all of it might as well be illusion, props and backdrop in the grand play. The problem isn't solved "out there" somewhere. It's handled in here. In me.*

She pulled him to her as he smiled and pressed his weight upon her. She looked into his eyes and nodded as if to say yes. She opened her mouth and waited for his kiss.

And it came, swift as the waves upon the silent sea, it came. His kiss. His strength. His faith. His love.

50

"But I love him!" screamed the girl from the attic, tearing herself away from her mother and rushing toward the darkness of the wood where the townsfolk had dragged her man, her boy-king, her secret husband.

"You know nothing about love," roared her mother, who watched as the women of the town grabbed her daughter and held her firm. "You're just a silly, sinful, awful girl."

"I'm a queen!" she spat, her eyes narrow like twin daggers. "And you'll all burn for this."

"No, you'll burn for what you're carrying within ya," shouted her father. "You'll burn in hell. You know what, give her to me. Let me take her back there. Let her watch her n*gger pay for her sins. Maybe then—"

"Don't call him that. He's a king!" she shrieked as her father grabbed her hair and arm and dragged her toward the wood. "He said he was!"

Her father ignored her screams and he pulled her past the line of trees, to where the men would be stringing the boy up already. But when they got to the clearing beneath the hangman's tree, the noose was empty and the townsmen were gathered around and talking loudly, arguing with each other and an older couple.

Hilda could feel Rahaan's kisses in the "real" world, and she could sense his touch starting to give her the power she needed to truly enter this parallel world. She could feel the emotions of this girl, but she still felt like an observer, like she was still in the audience and not yet on the stage.

"More," she heard herself whisper as she felt the Sheikh undress her, his strong hands clasping her naked breasts, thick thumbs pressing down on her nipples, causing them to stiffen like a cold breeze had blown upon them. "More," she groaned as she felt her passion soar, the sense of danger in the little girl's world mixing with her arousal in an intoxicating blend. "Oh, yes, like that!"

Now she felt him lift her gown, and she could smell her own arousal along with the freshly crushed twigs and leaves of the forest floor beneath her father's feet. She could hear her own cries of ecstasy as she listened to the defiant sniffles of the little girl. And then, almost without realizing it, Hilda sensed that those sniffles were coming from within, and just like that she was there, in the scene, no longer an observer but a participant.

The change almost took her breath away, and the

sudden in-rush of the most visceral anger, peaked fear, and heightened awareness of the young pregnant girl was almost too overwhelming to handle.

She is me, Hilda found herself saying. I need to trust that she is me, and I must let go of Hilda Hogarth for now. Trust that your Sheikh's strength will sustain you, and go ahead and let go of that world so all your power can awaken in this girl's world. Step fully into your dream and make her dream come true! Make this little girl's dream come true!

And what is her dream, Hilda wondered as she felt the Sheikh melt away into the background even as she felt his skin against her nakedness. What does a poor farmgirl in Middle America dream about?

"I'm a queen!" squealed the girl once more, but no one gave any notice. They were all focused on the older couple in the middle of the gathering.

Those are the boy's parents, Hilda realized as the girl's words rippled through her consciousness. I'm a queen! I'm a queen! I'm a queen! Of course that's what a poor farmgirl in Middle America dreams about! How else does an uneducated girl translate her powerlessness into a dream of supreme power? A queen has the power to make everything right, doesn't she? Doesn't she?

Hilda felt a shiver somewhere deep within her, like something was shifting, moving into place, the carousel of time turning, events moving around as the gods and goddesses watched in glee. Hilda watched as the parents of the boy held up a long sheaf of leather-mounted paper. And she watched as the townsfolk listened to the schoolteacher (the only one who could read) speak as he furrowed his brow and scratched his bald-spot and slowly explained what was written.

"The boy is from the Ojaanawe tribe," said the schoolteacher as he held up a lantern to the leathery scroll. "His newborn hand-prints are placed in elk's blood as proof. His name is Dancing Thunder, and he is from the royal line of the vanquished Ojaanawe Indians, a child given to the white man for safekeeping, destined to lead the survivors of the Ojaanawe tribe in the new world of America."

There was confused silence as the illiterate townsfolk looked at one another and then at the schoolteacher. "Wha . . . whas that mean?" asked one of them finally, his voice shaking.

The schoolteacher was quiet for a moment, his pasty face orange and saggy in the lamplight. Then he sighed and looked at the boy's parents, handing the document back to them before turning to the crowd. "Royal line. It means . . . well, I think . . . I guess . . . yea, I guess it means he's a king or something. A king."

Hilda felt herself merge fully with the little girl, and she felt her heart leap as the townsfolk began to argue again, some of them saying it didn't matter, that nothing excused what he'd done, that he'd hang for

Stars for the Sheikh

what he'd done and who gave a crap about some Indian tribe. But others shook their heads, doubt in their simple eyes, hesitation in their expressions. Soon the tide appeared to turn, and slowly the townsfolk began to back away as some of the older men decided they'd need to at least talk about things with clearer heads in the morning, that perhaps it was best if they backed off for now, that no one was getting lynched tonight. Certainly not a . . . king?!

Did I do that? Hilda wondered as she felt the delight and relief in the little girl, sensed her crushing joy in seeing her boy-king released. Did I do that or was it always going to play out that way? Did I change this couple's timeline? Did I pull them into a new parallel world where somehow this brown-skinned adopted boy was really a king of some kind?

"I really am a queen," the little girl whispered, as if only to herself and those that might be listening. "I knew it, I knew it, I knew it!"

Who knows, Hilda thought as she felt herself drifting away from that world. Who knows if I did anything, if any of this is real, if it's even a dream or just a fantasy.

But she did know, and she'd always known, it seemed, Hilda thought as images of the Sheikh began to push their way into her vision as she felt his body against hers again. She allowed herself to bask in the soaring emotions of that little girl one last time, smiling as she felt the girl resolve to leave this town with her king and their child, to start her new family on her terms, to leave her parents who no longer meant anything to her, who were no longer relevant in her timeline, in her life. The girl was a woman now. The girl was a queen now.

51

"Am I queen now?" rasped Di as she trampled on a patch of desert ragweed, stomping and spitting as she paced in manic circles. She'd been throwing up and choking on the bitter peyote for at least an hour now, it seemed, and after an initial period where she was sure she was about to die, she'd found herself spiraling up and up and up and then crashing down and down and down in a maddening roller-coaster of visions and flashes, uncontrollable and indecipherable sights and sounds, smells and signs.

She had no idea where she was, no clue who she was. There were vague memories of . . . of something . . . something she needed to do, someplace she needed to go.

"Am I queen now?" she gurgled as bits and pieces joined together in her fractured mind before pulling apart and spinning away. "Am I queen now!?"

She stumbled beneath the fading evening light of the New Mexico desert, clueless and hoarse, until slowly Di felt something shift within her, like a steadying force had grabbed her hand, helping her see straight, think straight, fight straight.

You are me, whispered Diamante through the peyote haze as Di gagged and went to her knees, her eyes rolling up in her head as a burst of overwhelming clarity racked her body. Focus with me. Join with me. Come with me. If we get there before she does, we can control our story. We must get there before she does.

52

"Did you get there?" the Sheikh was saying when Hilda blinked through what seemed like a hundred different worlds before she found herself back in her king's strong arms, the two of them naked and warm in bed, the clean salty smell of the ocean rolling in through the portholes of the rig's royal bedroom.

"I . . . I think so," Hilda whispered as she looked up breathless, feeling a smile plastered on her face. The joy of that young girl had come back with her, and Hilda somehow felt more complete, more composed, more confident, more real. "Oh, Rahaan, if only you were there to see it, to feel it!"

"I was," he whispered, kissing her gently as he moved his body over hers. "I know I was. I do not have the memory, but Hilda, I feel the energy. By Allah, I feel it! What happened with Princess Diamante? How did that story end? Did—"

The Sheikh's expression grew grim when Hilda shook her head and told him no, she'd only gone back to one of those worlds. "Rahaan, I think there's a sequence to this. I had to go there first. There didn't seem to be a choice. I think it's because in my last dream you were already so close to death in that world, so I was pulled there first because of the urgency."

"There is no first and last," said the Sheikh, his voice betraying his own sense of urgency. "We must get to the world in which Diamante exists. That is where you'll have to face her. You understand, don't you?"

Hilda nodded, smiling as she reached up and touched his face. "I understand more than I thought I ever could, Rahaan. And I understand that although you're right and there is no first and last, there is indeed an order, a method, a sequence of some kind. God, Rahaan, I think I gained something from stepping into that girl's world. Some kind of strength or emotional energy that I think I'll need to finish the job. I don't know how to explain it, but—"

"Then don't explain it," said the Sheikh. "Just do it. Just be it. Come on. What do you need for me to send you back, my love. Are you ready to—"

"Not yet," Hilda whispered, suddenly aware of how aroused she was, how wet she was, how ready she was. But a part of her said hold on, let it build and build, let her king control her arousal, sustain her need, give her that foundation of divine energy from which she could launch herself once more into the stars, merge with starlight, dance in stardust. "Take me there and hold me there, but don't let me go over the edge. Not yet. Can you do that?"

The Sheikh raised an eyebrow and nodded. "Now we are talking about things within my power, my queen."

And he kissed her ferociously as he pressed his hardness against her warm, wet mound, making her moan. She arched her neck back as she felt the ecstasy take her back to that place beyond, and with her newfound strength, her seemingly enhanced vision, she surveyed the multicolored rings circling the cosmos, the realms of consciousness, the lands of dream and fantasy, searching for that woman from the carriage, the second of the trio, the next world where a secret child threatened to destroy everything.

53

"What do you mean by they'll destroy you?" she asked him in the privacy of her chambers. "Who? Your enemies?"

He sighed as he looked upon her, smiled as he took her soft white hand in his rough, meaty paws. She looked down and gasped when she saw the scars on his forearms. Long, ugly scars. Some of them old and dark, some newer, like not long ago those lines were red and bloody, raw and ripped open.

"What . . ." she stammered, running her finger along a scar too straight to be from anything other than a knife—a really big knife!

"A duel," he said quietly, his expression hardening as he looked away and past her, his dark face clouding over. Then he blinked and forced a smile. "But I am here and my challenger is not. A happy ending, yes?"

"Heavens," she whispered, touching his scar again. "Challenger for what?" she asked, the thought of two men fighting over some exotic woman coming to mind and making her jealous in a way that almost embarrassed her.

He grinned that devilish grin, like he'd seen her

thoughts written on her expression. "Rest easy, my lady. A challenge to my claim of succession. My third cousin, young and overconfident. I warned him to back down. In fact I refused to fight him at first. But the laws of my land are . . . well, let us say they have not been updated for centuries."

"Old laws," she said. "Oh, God. How horrible! So you . . . you . . ."

"Ah, we are not to talk of such things. Especially not when I am in my lady's private chambers after dark. Come. Come to me."

Hilda felt the Sheikh's hot breath against her neck, his hardness grinding against her soaked panties as Rahaan kissed her feverishly, his lips and mouth exploring every inch of her skin, moving down to her chest, her naked breasts, ravaging those tight red nipples as she moaned out loud.

"More," she groaned as she watched the scene unfold in this second world. "I'm too far away. Still just watching. I need to get closer. More, my king."

"More," whispered that dark rogue as he watched his lady slowly reveal her naked shoulders, the corset beneath her gown still tight around her. "I want it all."

"It is all yours to have," she whispered, and now Hilda was close, getting closer, almost there. "All yours," she heard herself say as Rahaan pulled her panties off in his world and pressed his hand full against her naked heat.

Now Hilda was pushed into this woman's mind

and body in a way that felt so physical she almost choked. Everything came flying at her at once: memories and emotions, fears and fantasies, mind-games and machinations. The feeling was shockingly different from the innocence of that teenage girl, and it almost sickened Hilda for a moment when she realized how convoluted this woman was inside, that this was not a light and happy woman, not innocent by any means—at least not in the way Hilda wanted to believe she was. Who is this woman?

She is me, Hilda reminded herself. She is me in another time and place, doing what she had to do to survive, doing what was in her power to advance. But she does love him, and there is an innocence to her somewhere inside, is there not? She was just a girl too when she allowed this man to take her virginity. Yes, she manipulated her way back into his arms, but certainly this man was no fool. Even if he did not recognize her, it still—

"I knew it was you the moment our eyes met across that ballroom floor," he muttered as he undid her corset, and Hilda felt her heart flutter and she knew this woman loved him even though she barely knew him. Hilda settled in and tried to focus her energy, to advance the story, to figure out what the hell was going on in the first place. She could feel the woman's need in this world, but Hilda also carried with her the Sheikh's sense of urgency, that she needed to take care of business and move on, as oddly efficient as that sounded. This wasn't the time to revel in a cosmic lovemaking session in nineteenth-century England, however romantic that might be!

"You knew? You know?" she whispered as she grasped his hands to slow the rate at which she was being undressed. "Why did you not say it then?"

"Why did you not say it? Why did you present me with a different name?" He grinned again, white teeth shining in the candle-flames as panic raced through her system, like she was horrified that her deception was in the open.

"You do not even remember the name I gave you when we first met," she stammered, touching her hair and looking away. "So how would you even—"

He laughed. "It is true. I do not." His expression softened, but with a seriousness that betrayed a depth of emotion that made her skip a breath. "But, my lady, I remember everything else about you. Everything. Every word you said. Every moment we shared." He kissed her and she let him. "Every kiss. Every touch. The beginning to the end. Again and again." He kissed her again and she let go of his hands as the need weakened her resolve. "Why do you think I returned to England?"

"What?" she muttered as she forced herself to draw back from the kiss. "I do not understand."

"I do not either, in some way," he said, taking a

breath and suddenly standing up. He straightened to full height, undoing his heavy white henley at the collar and beginning to pace as if in the grip of some force.

Oh, God, is it . . . could it be . . . is Rahaan somehow forcing his way into this world with me, Hilda thought in both worlds at once. I mean, yeah, this is Rahaan, but his consciousness isn't focused in this world in the same way mine is. But that was really strange how this man suddenly backed away and stood up, as if Rahaan really is trying to push his way in and take control!

Hilda almost laughed with surprised glee when she saw something change in this dark man's eyes, a glimmer of recognition, a twinkle of awareness. It was fleeting, but it was real.

He is with me, Hilda told herself. He is here to help me finish this story.

Thoughts raced through Hilda's mind as she tried to sort through memories and connections in this woman's frazzled brain. But it was too much, and Hilda just grabbed the last question that seemed important and blurted it out:

"Who is trying to destroy you?" she said. "More cousins? What is this claim of succession, and why is your family killing each other? Isn't there—"

The dark king spoke quickly, like he was been impelled from within by Rahaan's urgency. "The king of

Stars for the Sheikh

my land never married and never fathered an heir. He was a warrior-monk of sorts, you could say. He took a vow of celibacy as a young man, and was a believer that a king should prove himself and should not be simply granted the throne based on lineage. In fact he did away with the royal bloodline over the years." He snorted and shook his head. "Ended the bloodline with blood. At least he thought he did."

Hilda took a breath and kept pushing. She wasn't sure if the Sheikh's consciousness was fully present in this man, but it didn't matter. She knew she had to keep going. She'd learned from her experience with the girl from the attic that once she figured out the solution, she could pull them all into a new parallel world, change this couple's timeline, fix things and then fly off like a fairy godmother!

"Go on," she said almost matter-of-factly. "So the king wiped out his own family over the years?"

He nodded. "His own brothers and sisters. His cousins, uncles, aunts. I believe that if his own parents were alive, he would have executed them as well, he was so committed to his goal of having the throne pass down to the one who is most able."

Hilda frowned as she glanced down at her half-open corset. Well, she certainly had the same boobs in this world. She found herself drifting and wondering how that little girl would "blossom" over the years, but then quickly chastised herself and got back to the moment, only briefly noticing how chilling it was that this woman seemed unfazed by talk of such brutality. "And how would he decide who was most able? That's the old laws you mention?"

He laughed and nodded. "Yes. The laws of nature. That is what I meant, my lady. The king decided there are no laws greater that the natural law."

"Which means what?" said Hilda, impatient almost. "So who becomes the next king? Who gets the throne?"

The man stood broad and tall and looked past her for a moment before focusing his green eyes on her. "The man who takes it. Simple as that."

54

"I can't take it," Di gurgled as she doubled over and coughed and finally curled up in the fetal position as she stared with bleary eyes at the red glow of the sun as it began to kiss the horizon. "Wake me up."

You are awake, came the answer from Diamante. We are both awake. Truly awake. Come with me. Let go of your hold on this world. The pain is because you are trying to hold on to what you think is real. You must let go and walk with me across the bridge of time.

"I don't know how," Di gasped as she tried to stand. "I can't even sit up. How can I walk?"

You do not need your legs, Princess, whispered Diamante. You do not need your body. Let go of the illusion that your "real" self is in the New Mexico desert. Merge with me and we will fly together. Give yourself to me and we will have the power to walk anywhere, anytime, anyhow.

Somehow the words in her head registered, and Di began to laugh hysterically when she realized that of course she didn't need to stand up and physically walk anywhere! That was the whole point! Time travel wasn't about transporting your body! She knew that!

Go with her, Di told herself as she felt a mystical calmness envelope her. She could felt herself soar, a part of her rising up in a way that terrified her at first and then sent exhilaration rushing through her like the swift desert wind. Suddenly the landscape changed, and Di knew she was back in her dream, back in that place, walking with Diamante.

Go with her, was the last thought of Di as she saw a woman with flaming yellow hair riding with a hundred men across the plains, toward the mountains, in hot pursuit of an exiled king and his commoner bride.

Go with her because you are her, whispered Di into the sand as New Mexico faded and the sun touched the horizon. You are her, and this is your story now.

55

An inexplicable sense of dread seeped into Hilda's world as she tried desperately to stumble through this world and into the next. Or the previous. Or the third. Whichever. It was all so messed up. So turned around.

You are this woman but don't get dragged too far into her short-term needs. She doesn't know what you know. Not in the same sense. She's still marveling at how she ran into the father of her child again seemingly by coincidence at that ball. Now she's wondering if this man engineered that meeting. Perhaps it was magic, she's thinking. Was it black witchcraft, it occurs to her next. Had God forsaken her for sinning with this foreigner, with a heathen, bearing his child and lusting for him even while married to another? Was Satan leading her to his lair now? Was this dark, devilishly handsome man with long scars on his arms speaking the truth or was he telling her the lies of the devil? Did she even care? What other options did she have? The last of her money was spent on these clothes to get to that ball. And so what if he was a liar? So was she! She'd lied so much over the years her tongue might well be black! But still, had he really come back for her? Why?

It doesn't matter, Hilda tried to convey to the woman—and to herself. Coincidence or not, it doesn't matter. It's not surprising that you two met again. It makes perfect sense that you were drawn to each other. Shut your trap, you silly woman in your corset! Put your boobs away and let me speak!

"I bore your child," Hilda blurted out, taking over but still using this woman's emotions to power her words. "Your son. He is with my sisters in my village. I told him of his father. I told him his father was a king, and that you would return for us and take us to your castle. I told him I was a queen, that he was a prince, but that it was a secret. He is two years old so he cannot understand, of course. But I told him anyway. Perhaps I needed to tell it to myself. Perhaps it was the only way to—"

He took a step back and then a step forward as all the color drained from his face before rushing back in. He blinked three times and then held her gaze, searching her expression.

"Do you speak truth? About the child? A son?" he said, his voice low and hoarse. "Speak quickly, my lady. Do you—"

"Yes!" Hilda shouted as she felt the Sheikh's urgency in the other world, an urgency combined with that unmistakable sense of dread coming across time, like although time was an illusion, she was still running out of it! "Yes!" she screamed again, and now the pieces suddenly fit like when a jigsaw becomes clear and you rush through it with delight, snapping the squiggly bits into place as the picture comes to life. Saying all that was the missing piece, and it pulled everything into perspective. That was this woman's dream, was it not? This fake lady's fantasy. This lying wench's childish dream. She told herself the story of bearing a king's heir in secret, of herself being a queen in secret, of their tryst being more than a Lord having his way with a kitchen maid. She had the same dream as the girl from the attic. Of course she did. It was the same dream, the same woman, the same man. The girl from the attic. The woman from the carriage. And the astrologer from Albuquerque.

Finish it, Hilda thought as she felt that shift somewhere deep inside her consciousness, the sign that parallel worlds were aligned according to her will, her power, her gift.

"That is my dream," she said confidently, wondering how she was thinking in modern American but speaking like an English woman who probably couldn't read. "And I will have it. I will have my dream."

56

The Sheikh groaned as he kissed Hilda's smooth bare stomach, his face dangerously close to her hips. He could smell her clean feminine scent, and his need was so strong he could barely see straight. He wanted to bury his face between her legs, feel her wet pubic curls in his mouth, drive his tongue through her warm forest and taste her. He wanted to hear her scream as she came for him, howl as she bucked her hips into his face, moan as her orgasms rolled in. Then he wanted to flip her over and raise her magnificent buttocks, kiss her smooth rear and spread her wide from behind, grasp his throbbing manhood and guide it close, touch the massive head of his cock to her perfect pink rear pucker, slide his fingers into her cunt and push himself into her dark—

"Enough," he grunted into her skin as he forced himself to get back in control. She needed him to hold her in this state, which couldn't happen if he allowed himself the release he desperately wanted. Did their fate truly depend on whether or not he could control his own swinging balls?! Were the gods that trivial? That cruel? That sadistic?!

I am going mad, he decided as he heard her moan and saw her eyelids flutter as he forced himself away from the intoxicating smell of her cunt and back up along her naked, glistening body. They were both soaked with sweat, and although the night was cool, their bed was ablaze with the heat from their combined fever.

Yes, I am going mad, he decided when he thought back to the moment where he felt he had managed to slip into that dream with Hilda, where he was there with her. But he hadn't been able to hold himself there, and now he wondered if that had been real or not.

Hilda moaned again, and she was writhing beneath him, deep in an erotic trance but somehow restless, he could sense.

"What is it, my queen?" he said as he drew his head back but kept his body close. "What do you need?"

"I need help," she muttered. "It is taking too long. There is too much . . . too much to work out still. I need . . ."

She trailed off, and the Sheikh looked down at her, confused for a moment. Help? Was she in danger? No, she said it was taking too long, Rahaan reminded himself. And by Allah, it is. I feel it too. My intuition tells me we are running out of time, that Diamante is moving faster than we are, that if she shifts her story too far in that world, it is all over.

He glanced over at the dark porthole. The stars

were still out, but he knew the sun would begin its ascent soon. He had no idea why sunrise was somehow a deadline, but it felt like it was. Yes, the opening ceremony would happen shortly after sunrise, and along with it the assassination attempt. But it was more than logic telling him to hurry. It was instinct, his goddamn gut.

My gut, he thought. My instincts. My . . . gift?

Bloody hell, Rahaan thought now. I may not have the gift my woman does, but I have some of it, do I not? And I do believe I broke through into the world Hilda's in right now, albeit briefly. Can I do that once again? Is that what she needs? Can I do it? Will it help?

The Sheikh took a breath as he wondered how, but of course he knew. It was time to give in to what he needed. To use some of that pent-up energy. To step into his woman's world. To advance. To go forth. To enter.

He looked down as her shimmering body, her white skin looking silver in the starlight. Did she know what he was capable of in bed? Did she know how rough he could be, how hard he could be, how desperately he wanted to spank her buttocks red, lick her rear hole pink, enter her every which way and claim her for all of time. Ya Allah, there is still so much we need to learn about each other in this world! Will she handle the man I truly am?

He touched her brown curls gently, bringing forth a moan as he parted her dark nether lips. He gasped at the sight of her open vagina, bright and beckoning, red and glistening. And then he got on top of her and spread her wide, grunting as he entered, inch by inch, pushing himself into her as he felt his consciousness soar and spin, twirl and curl, rise above them both and then dive deep within itself as he drove himself all the way in, all the way down, all the way deep.

"I will finish it," he gasped as he felt his consciousness leave him as her warm valley cradled his heat. "I don't know how, but I will finish it. Even if it kills me, I will finish it."

57

Hilda heard herself scream as she watched her man bleed into the dark sand of the arena as cheers rose up around them. She stood there with her son, forcing the child to watch and not bury his face into her skirts.

My God, she thought, still reeling. It seemed like a moment ago she was in her chambers on the outskirts of London, this man excitedly telling her about the reason he'd come to England to find her, that she'd been his first and only.

"I was secretly raised to be the next warrior-monk king of my land," he had told her. "Celibate and chaste, in the mold of the king. You see, my mother believed she was part of the king's bloodline, the bastard daughter of the king's murdered cousin. She'd decided that when the time came for a new king, the people would stand behind a man who lived his life according to the philosophy of the king but also shared his blood. She thought that although the people liked the idea of a king proving himself on merit, there was also the romanticism associated with a royal bloodline, hearkening back to the days where people liked to believe their rulers were somehow connected to the gods in a way a commoner could never be simply by virtue of blood."

She'd stared at him as he spoke, wondering if somehow they'd been pulled into a new parallel world where they'd never made love before. Hilda searched the memories of that woman she was, but the memories of that night three years earlier were still clear and fresh, just like the memory of the two of them in the carriage just the day before, just like the certainty that their son was very real and very much alive.

"I do not understand," she'd said. "Even if what you say is true, that I was your first and only, it means you are no longer chaste. Does that not disqualify you from the throne?"

He had smiled and shaken his head. "My lady, it in fact qualifies me for the throne in a way nothing else can!"

Hilda watched as her man spun away from what would have been a fatal blow to the head, grasping his curved blade from where it had fallen. She did her best not to scream again, and she held her son tight as she reminded herself that she was a queen and her son was a prince and this brutality was the price they paid for who they were, for who they wanted to be. Strangely enough, she wasn't scared. And as sick as it sounded, she was almost enjoying this. What kind of a woman was she in this world! What kind of a man was this lying rogue?

The man had gone on: "One year ago it was discovered that our great and honorable monk-king was in fact human, suffering from human desires and needs," he told her with not a small amount of amusement in his tone as he glanced her up and down in her corset. "Desires and needs that I know only too well can sway even the most chaste and cherubic of us."

"You seemed to know your way around a lady quite well, I would say," she'd said. "It was hardly your first time. You can't convince me I was the first."

"Believe what you want," he'd said, almost gruffly before smiling. "It is no matter. See, once word spread about the great king's transgressions, the public began clamoring for a return to the old laws, to the royal bloodline. They forgave their king—indeed, the only violation he'd committed was towards his own sworn philosophy—and they asked him to give them an heir, to revive the royal line, to make sure the kingdom would have a ruler for the next generation."

Hilda had nodded. "And?"

He took a breath and shook his head. "The king admitted that he'd sired many bastards over the years." He paused. "And put each one to the sword, in keeping with his oath to end ascendancy by blood."

"Oh, God in heaven!" she'd said, closing her eyes tight as a chill whipped through her. Immediately she made the connection that if this man before her was of royal blood, then his bastard son was of royal blood, which meant that—

"So what does it mean for . . . for our son? Is he in danger?" she'd asked slowly. "No. Because you did not know until I just told you. And so . . . and so I still do not understand why you came back."

"I came back for my queen," he'd said firmly. "The old king cannot father an heir now, and so this is my chance. That is why I came back for you. Because you were my first, and I carry with me the idea that for each man there can be only one woman. If I stake my claim with a queen at my side, the people will stand firm with me against my challengers. And now, with a child, a son, an heir . . . by God, woman, it is magic, destiny, fate, a miracle! You were my first, woman! And although I am a pretender and a rogue at many levels, in this one thing I am true. This one feeling of mine is pure. When I return I will make my blood-claim to the throne, make it in public. My mother married a wealthy merchant when I was a child, and my family is well-known and well-respected for our charity and honorable business dealings. The people will stand with me. Public opinion will be in my favor." He'd paused. "If the people stand with me in overwhelming majority, by the old laws very few will have the right to challenge my claim. There is maybe just one who can challenge my claim. Perhaps no one will challenge my claim! Our claim!"

Hilda had shaken her head as she felt that urgency

rise up again. She needed to move all of this to a new parallel world, resolve this before time ran out. In fact, it should have moved to a new world by now, given that the solution appeared to be in sight. Why had it been so easy with the teenage girl and not with this woman, this version of Hilda? What was different?

She does not believe, came the answer from Hilda's subconscious. Remember, this woman isn't just a bystander. It is still her story! That girl from the attic at some level truly believed she was a queen, in the innocent way a child can make herself believe anything! But this woman has suffered years of indignities and hardships, insults and injustices. She has made mistakes, compromises, small decisions that have chipped away at her sense of self-worth. She may dream of being a queen, but can she actually get herself to believe it? That's what's preventing me from taking this to a new parallel world even though the solution is in sight. Her negative emotions are holding us back.

I don't have the time to coax and coddle you, Hilda had thought as she watched the conversation go on, somehow firmly within the woman but also above her and able to think in parallel. It could take days or weeks for this man to convince you that you deserve to be a queen. I need to short-circuit this story, force this dark king to stake his claim in the quickest way possible and make you a queen, whether you believe in yourself or not. And to do that, I need to bring *my* king into it.

And that's when she'd reached out to him, to her king, her Sheikh, her Rahaan. I need help, she'd said, somehow knowing he'd hear her. I need help, she thought again, a strange feeling that perhaps this was an important part of the sequence, that perhaps this was training in a sense, that she needed to figure out how to bring in Rahaan because although she might eventually work her way through this story on her own, she'd need all the help she could get in the next one, the final chapter.

58

The Sheikh stared at the long, twisted cut on his right arm. Blood flowed like a river as he spun around and grabbed his curved sword, standing back up and taking a stance that seemed natural, like he'd been trained in the art of the scimitar! By Allah, where was he? Who was he?

He glanced over at his opponent, a bearded man who stood almost a foot taller than the Sheikh. He was not as broad though, and Rahaan decided that this needed to become a close-quarters battle to take advantage of his own size. The thought came to him naturally, adding to that sense of wonder the Sheikh was feeling—wonder at how he was himself but also someone else, like in that half-dream state where you're aware of the dream world and the real world at the same time.

Ya Allah, but which is the real world, because this feels bloody real, Rahaan thought as the pain shot through his arm while he reflexively raised his sword and repelled a swift attack from his opponent. Can I die here? What happens if I die?

Stars for the Sheikh

The thought occurred to him even as he instinctively looked toward the crowd, and immediately he locked eyes with her—his woman, his wife, his queen, his lover. His Hilda. She looked different, darker, not as confident. But it was her, he knew. And the boy with her . . . was that his—

Just then a new sliver of pain ripped through the Sheikh, and he realized he'd been slashed again, this time across his chest. The cut was deep enough that it immediately began to bleed, drawing a gasp from the crowd as Rahaan grunted and tore off his tunic. What in God's name is happening, he wondered as he faced his opponent again, wondering if this was some completely different timeline where he was a gladiator or something ridiculous like that.

No, this is the same world where she and I made love in the carriage, where I returned to England on a quest to find her—to find her for no other reason than I wanted her and no one else! Why—I do not know. I barely knew her except for that one night. But somehow I was compelled to return, and somehow it was so easy to find her, and somehow—

"Focus!" the Sheikh said out loud, gritting his teeth as he tried to push away the thoughts of the man he was in this world. It took him a moment to realize that they were the same person, but still separate strands of consciousness. The Sheikh had some access to this man's thoughts and emotions, but certainly not all of it. This man was a shadowy figure to the Sheikh, like it was the darker part of him.

The Sheikh circled away from his opponent as he pieced together the sequence of events. We've jumped from England to wherever this is—somewhere hot and sandy: maybe North Africa, Morocco, or even Egypt. But who pulled us here? Hilda? Me? The two of us combined? And why in Allah's name am I fighting for my goddamn life here?! Why would I or Hilda pull this event into our timeline?!

He parried another blow and circled again, and then he saw her: a flash of golden hair in the crowd, a look in those sand-colored eyes that chilled the Sheikh to the bone as he bled and sweated in the arena. Instantly he knew he was running out of time, perhaps was already out of time. Time! Hah! What did the word even mean now!

But how do we get out of this world and into that third dream when I have no idea what in Allah's name is happening here! Or do Hilda and I not need to move to that world anymore? Is Diamante here with us now? Is this the new battlefield? Ya Allah, I am going mad trying to use logic even though I know it does not work when dealing with the paradoxes of time. Focus!

He glanced quickly at Hilda and then over at Diamante again—or at least to where he swore he'd seen Diamante. But the golden-haired princess was gone.

Stars for the Sheikh

Had she ever been here? Was it his imagination? Was it a dream within a dream? By Allah, am I truly unhinged in space and time?!

He looked over at Hilda again, and she was staring calmly at him, one arm around her son, holding the boy facing forward so he could see his father. It seemed strange to subject a child to the gruesome sight of his father bleeding in what certainly appeared to be a fight to the death. Why am I fighting? Why are they watching?

It does not matter, came the answer suddenly. How the hell does it matter? What matters is that you are in a fight! Save the questions for later, you fool! Your job is simple and straightforward: There is a man who has cut you and slashed you and clearly wants to kill you. Still your mind and stop him. How can there be any other objective for you? Just win the goddamn fight! Your answer lies in the physical. The flesh, the bone, the goddamn blood!

Now clarity rushed through the Sheikh even as he felt the warm blood on his body, took in the stench of his opponent's sweat, tasted the salt from his own sweat on his lips. And all those questions dissolved into the ether as Rahaan felt himself take over this body, pouring in his own will and combining it with the training and instincts of the man he was in this world.

He held his ground and crouched as his opponent

came in, scimitar flashing in the sun. The man was quick, but Rahaan was feeling a new energy, an invincibility almost, and he dropped to the ground and raised his own sword, fending off his opponent's swipe and simultaneously striking at the taller man's knee with his free left hand.

The bearded man's knee-joint snapped and with a scream he went down. The Sheikh swiveled his body around, a smooth, natural motion driven by years of training. He watched his own arm wield that curved sword, bringing it down swift and silent, cutting the man's throat wide open like it was nothing. And just like that it was over.

What in Allah's name is happening, thought the Sheikh, wanting to feel horror but feeling nothing but the adrenaline throbbing through his veins. The blood pounded in his ears as he stood and raised his arms, the blood still flowing down his bare torso as he took in the crowd, listening to their cries. They were calling his name. They were calling him . . . king. King?

What in bloody hell is happening, the Sheikh thought when he saw Hilda smile at him, relief apparent in her expression. But it was more than just relief he saw in her eyes when he went close to her. There was triumph. There was excitement. There was . . . an apology?!

59

"Oh, God, I'm sorry, Rahaan," she sobbed as the Sheikh pulled out of her and lay flat on his back by her side on the soaked sheets. His massive chest was furiously rising and falling and he breathed hard and heavy, muttering in Arabic as he rubbed his head. "I didn't know what else to do!"

She waited as the Sheikh caught his breath, until he exhaled hard and finally turned to her. "What did you do? What did I do? I do not understand. I do not think even the man of that world understood. Did you pull a new parallel world into that timeline? It was all you?"

"I . . . I guess so. I think so," she whispered, looking at his smooth brown chest as she thought back to that sword slashing him in her dream. "I just tried to focus all my will on finding the fastest way to resolve our story in that world, to get to a point where you were king and I was your queen and our son was with us. I mean, I didn't know it would play out like that, with you having to kill . . . to kill . . ."

"It is all right," the Sheikh said, pulling her close.

"It is all right. Whatever I did had its place in that world, I suppose. The man I was in that world seemed to know what to do, and he did not hesitate to finish his opponent. And so . . . hold on, what is it, Hilda? Why are you looking at me like that?"

"You don't remember?" Hilda said, blinking and looking away. She swallowed hard before summoning up the courage to face him again. "I guess you didn't get a clear picture of all the memories and feelings of the man you are in that world. Probably for the best, I suppose."

"Why? What is it? No, I thought the man in that world was as confused as I about how he got to be in that arena, fighting some bearded goon."

Hilda sighed and shook her head. "No, it wasn't that. The man you were knew what he was doing. He knew what he was fighting for, and he knew who he was fighting. I didn't know it would play out that way, but I guess that was the shortest path to being king and so that's the parallel world I must have pulled into that timeline, to claim the throne. You'd said there might be one more challenger, but I didn't think . . . oh, God, Rahaan, I didn't think . . ." She paused and took another breath, wondering if perhaps she'd unwittingly made a mistake, that she'd lost her nerve and sent them down a dark path. "It was his brother, Rahaan. The man in that world killed his own brother. Without remorse. Without hesitation. While I watched. While our son watched."

60

"How can this be right? How can that life of ours be defined by me cutting my own brother's throat while my woman and child watch?" the Sheikh asked her, sitting up against the heavy wooden backboard of the oversized bed. Outside the porthole the sky was turning from black to a deep blue, and soon hints of orange would flicker at the horizon. They were running out of time, though perhaps it no longer mattered.

"I don't know," Hilda whispered, pushing herself up alongside him and covering her bare breasts with the sheets. "Perhaps it's a flaw within me. Perhaps there's some kind of darkness in me that pulled that event into that couple's timeline. Perhaps I'm so desperate to get my happy ending that I don't care how I get to it! Oh, Rahaan, what kind of a person am I! It's—"

"It was not you," he said suddenly, cutting her off as he turned to her with a look of shock, his eyes widening as if he'd just remembered something. "I saw her, Hilda. She was there. It was just for a moment, but she was there. Diamante. Di. Both of them. I don't know. But she's the one who did it. It has to be." He looked full upon her face, smiling and shaking his head as he reached out and touched her chin. "Hey, I know you. I know you in at least four lives, flaws and all. You did not do this. You did not engineer this. It was her."

"But how? Diamante was never in that world with us when I dreamt about it before—at least not in any meaningful way," Hilda said, blinking and shaking her head as she tried to make sense of it. "But you're right. The shift to a new parallel world did occur almost too suddenly, like maybe Di's emotional energy reached across somehow? God, I don't even know what I'm saying!"

Rahaan nodded as he turned to her. "No, you are correct, I think. Somehow she reached across from that third world into the second one. That is why I saw her briefly. Perhaps she wasn't meaning to do that, but it just happened. A side-effect of the force of her will, her dark emotional energy. After all, these worlds are connected—we already know that. Her power wasn't enough to stop us getting the ending we wanted: Me, you, and our child together, the royal family. But . . ."

"But she managed to infect those lives by twisting the path we took to get our ending in that world. She made it hollow, meaningless, dark," Hilda said as that sense of dread began to rise up in her again. "And so if she was able to exert so much power in a world where she didn't have a major role to begin with, it could mean . . ."

Stars for the Sheikh

"It could mean she's firmly in control of the third world right now, that she's already changing the timeline to get her ending," said the Sheikh. He took a breath. "Which means we have to get there now." He glanced out the porthole and then back at Hilda.

She nodded and then shook her head. "I don't know if I can, Rahaan. I feel drained. I mean, how do I get back in . . . um, in the mood, I guess! I'm way too wired, too worked up. How can I relax enough to get back to the place I need to be? Rahaan, I . . . wait, why are you smiling?"

The Sheikh was suddenly looking exceptionally relaxed, his hands lazily propping his head up as he glanced at her. He held her gaze and he held his smile until finally she understood that he was taking over, taking control, showing her that he was indeed a king in this world, that she should follow his lead and trust in him.

"OK," she said, trying to match his calmness as she forced a smile and tried to pretend they were two lovers who were in bed together, nothing more, nothing less.

They both stayed silent for a long moment, listening to the waves lap against the metal frame of the oil rig. The gulls that had taken up residence on the rig were waking up, and the looming dawn was undeniable. Outside preparations would soon begin for the opening ceremony of the rig, the closing ceremony of their lives. Hilda could feel herself losing her nerve, and she opened her mouth to speak and say it was no use. But the Sheikh spoke first, his voice smooth and deep, graceful and resonant.

"You know, Hilda," he said in that Arabian accent. "In all of this it occurs to me that I have not heard about Hilda Hogarth's dreams. Not her dreams of other worlds and other lives. Her dreams of this world and this life. What did little Hilda dream about when she was alone in her room? What did—"

"Magic," Hilda said without thinking, and now the smile on her face came from the unconscious as she felt the Sheikh pull her close and listen. "When I was a kid I dreamed I was magic."

"You mean you dreamed you had magical powers? Like a witch or wizard?" the Sheikh asked as his soft stubble brushed against her cheek, making her shiver.

"No," she whispered as she felt herself warming again, opening up again. "I dreamed I *was* magic! I don't know how to explain it. I mean, I was a . . . oh, God, Rahaan, OK, although I'm pretty comfortable with it now, I really struggled with my weight as a girl. But the weird thing is I never really dreamed of being thin or skinny or even really losing weight. I dreamt about being . . . I dunno . . . light as a feather, airy and free. I always pictured myself as sort of the same shape and size, but somehow weightless! And that would be magic, to be the same size and shape but also weightless, yeah? So I guess I imagined that my body was made out of magical things, magical dust. I imagined that I was magic." She gasped as she felt the Sheikh pull the sheets away from her breasts and gently begin to kiss her bare chest. "Are you even listening?" she said, covering her nipples with her hands.

"Your body *is* made of magical things," he grunted as he forced her hands away and glanced intently at her bare breasts. "And I am looking at two of them right now. Keep your hands off your breasts, woman. They belong to me now."

She giggled and swatted at him, then gasped when his warm lips closed around her right nipple. He sucked hard, again and again, moving to her left breast while pinching her swollen, glistening right nipple. Soon she was moaning uncontrollably beneath his hot, heavy body, and before she knew it her eyes were closed and the Sheikh was beneath the covers, his face between her legs, his tongue pushing its way into her as she cried out in ecstasy.

"Light as a feather," he gasped from between her thighs, kissing her pussy once more and then rising to his knees and rolling off the bed. He stood there for a moment, naked and hard, every muscle in his body peaked and shining with the effort of the night. Then he leaned over and lifted her in his arms, like she weighed nothing.

She squealed in surprise at being carried like that,

and then she gasped at his strength as he walked with her across the room, crossing the threshold and stepping onto the private metal balcony overlooking the dark waters of the Arabian Sea. The gulls were awake, the sun's glow lighting the horizon. But the sun was not up yet, and as the Sheikh pushed her against the warm wooden top of the railing, she glanced up and gasped at the sight of a million stars, still bright even though morning approached.

I *am* made of stardust, she thought as she looked into the diamond-studded sky. I am magic. And this is my night.

And as she drifted away, light as a feather, in the arms of her king, in the dark waters those three dolphins swam silently by, three bodies writhing against one another, three souls intertwined.

61

"It is just the three of us now," Diamante said through the night sky.

Hilda came to with a gasp, the now-familiar inrush of a new woman's emotions and memories still hitting her so hard she almost passed out. For a moment she wanted to leave this world, to go back to her Sheikh, to be in his arms, death be damned. But she couldn't, she knew. The previous world had been a training ground, she realized. Both for her and Rahaan. Was he here with her? Where was she, anyway?

She was seated on a wooden chair, her robes filthy and worn, chains around her ankles, irons holding her wrists firm. Her body hurt. Her heart pounded. Her vision was blurry. Now the memories came rushing in: The band of exiles set upon by a hundred armed horsemen, Princess Diamante at the helm on her black mare. Every man and woman was cut down, leaving just the exiled king and his commoner bride, Rahaan and Hilda.

But where was Rahaan? Hilda squinted as she tried to remember. Yes, he'd fought like a madman, trying to protect her while also doing his best to save his loyal followers. He'd been struck in the thigh by an archer, and when he fell from his steed he'd been subdued and bound. Was he alive? Probably. Diamante had said something about being just the three of them now, yes?

Hilda looked around as she took deep breaths, allowing herself to get accustomed to the woman she was in this world. The practice she'd gotten from the last two dream-worlds had paid off, and she knew she was fully within this woman here, fully in control. In control of her senses at least—not so much the situation, it seemed.

She was indoors, that much she knew. The walls were stone, with long, narrow windows cut in the shapes of what Hilda swore were the outlines of coffins. *Am I in a cemetery church? Is the dark princess going to sacrifice me to her guardian demon?*

Hilda looked at Diamante, almost with curiosity. The woman was beautiful, with sharp features and sand-colored eyes that seemed as wise as wicked. Diamante met her gaze with confidence, and the two women shared a long moment of silence.

"You said it's the three of us," Hilda said finally, breaking the silence but not averting her eyes. She'd be damned if she was going to back down from a staring contest with this witch. "Where is he?"

"Rahaan? He's alive, but nowhere close. I don't

want him popping in and interrupting, you know?" said Diamante, smiling and nonchalantly looking past Hilda to break the eye-contact deadlock.

A shiver passed through Hilda when it occurred to her that wait, did she just say "Rahaan?" Did she just say his name?

"Di?" Hilda said cautiously, squinting again as if trying to look within Diamante. "Are you . . ."

"Am I in here?" said the princess, smiling and shrugging. "Honey, I am her. I've learned a few things too, while you and your Sheikh were off gallivanting in nineteenth century England. Nice job working things out in that world, by the way. Making him kill his brother was a nice ending. Definitely king-worthy. The crowd loved it, so that's something." She paused. "And you know what? You loved it too, my innocent, cherubic fortune-teller. We're not always the person we like to think we are, yeah?"

"I didn't like it, and I didn't make him do anything. You pulled that into our timeline, Di. It was your darkness that pulled us down that path. I wasn't ready to counter it there. But it's not going to happen here."

Di laughed. "My darkness? Hilda, I only got a fleeting glimpse at that world. I didn't have a role to play in that world—I never did. I was there for a flash, almost by accident. But it was long enough to see that you knew exactly what was happening there. Both of you did!"

"Yes, but only after it had already happened! I didn't—"

"You did. You wanted it so bad you didn't care how you got it. You can't admit it to Rahaan, and maybe you won't even admit it to yourself. But you can't hide it from me." Di shrugged as she gathered her purple skirts and began to pace the cold, barren room. "Nothing to be ashamed about. Every woman wants her happy ending, and most women will take it no matter who gets hurt along the way. Men don't understand that we're actually the more ruthless of the genders."

"Speak for yourself," Hilda muttered, telling herself not to get pulled into Di's nonsense. Maybe some of what she said was true, but it didn't matter. Hilda was good enough. She was pure enough. She was . . . dark enough? Willing to do whatever it took? Maybe. "Now, where's Rahaan. I want to see him."

"I told you he's alive, but far from here. It's just the three of us here."

"Three?" Hilda said before the realization hit her and she instinctively clutched her belly. But how would Diamante even know she was pregnant? No one in this world knew!

Oh God, the Diamante of this world wouldn't know. But the Di of the modern world would have guessed that I was pregnant in this world—indeed, that a child is part of each of those conflicted worlds.

"What do you want?" Hilda whispered as she closed her eyes and tried to will herself to a new parallel world where a raven flew in through that coffin-shaped window and gobbled up Di's eyeballs. She opened her eyes and looked around, suddenly feeling powerless and foolish when she saw that nothing had changed. Who was she kidding?

Help, she thought now. Rahaan, I need you. I need more. I need something. Help!

Hilda tried to focus, to reach out to her man across time, to harness the power generated by their intertwined bodies on that secluded balcony overlooking the dark Arabian Sea. But she couldn't get there, and now she began to panic. Oh, God, what if there is no "real" world left! What if the explosion or the assassination or whatever has already happened?! What if this is it, this world is the only world left?! Does that even make sense? Am I alone here?

"What do you want?" Hilda asked again, pushing away the panic before it took her spiraling downwards to the point of no return. "You're already in line to be queen. Your children will be princes and princesses. What more do you want? You want to watch me suffer? You want to kill Rahaan for some imagined rejection when he didn't even know you? You want to—"

"I want you to see," Di said quietly, stopping in the middle of the room and putting her hands on her slim hips. "I want you to see that you're no different from me when you have to make the hard choices. I want you to see yourself. Yourself in me."

"I don't understand," Hilda said, frowning.

Di began to pace again, her boots clicking against the cold stone floor. "Hilda, in our modern world I suggested that there was something about your child in each of these dream-worlds that was causing a conflict."

"What conflict?" Hilda said in a low voice, a sinking feeling entering her as she clutched her belly again. No. Please, no! "Not even you can kill a child, Di."

Di laughed and shrugged. "Well, your child would be the first of the next generation, and he or she would always have a rightful claim to the throne, regardless of whether the father dies in exile. And if I were to never bear an heir, then . . ."

She trailed off, and Hilda saw something in her expression that made her realize that *God, Di is living through her own unresolved conflicts, isn't she . . . conflicts she perhaps doesn't completely understand herself. I don't know what her situation with children was in the real world, but she didn't have any and maybe she . . . couldn't? Is that one of the things holding her here? Yes, the ambition was always there. But also the yearning to have what she can't? Is that part of what's bringing her back? Joining her to me, the woman who has a different sort of conflict with pregnancy and children?*

"Oh, God," Hilda blurted out as it hit her. "You're barren. You can't bear the king's brother an heir, and so you . . . you want . . ." Hilda swallowed hard as she met Di's gaze. "You don't want to *kill* my child. You *want* my child! You want to raise my child as your own, pretend it came from you, all the while knowing it carries the blood of the king. You sick bitch!"

Di stayed silent as a chilly breeze wafted in through those coffin-shaped windows and across the barren floor. Now everything looked cold and sterile, like all of it was a reflection of Di, of Diamante, of her world, her emptiness. It terrified Hilda, and she felt lost, defeated, alone. What could she do? She could feel the power draining from her as she looked away from Di and down at herself. She felt heavy, unable to move.

Now's the time, she managed to think as the world began to spin and that sickening dread got heavier. Now's the time, honey. She's winning. She's pulling me into her world, her cold, sterile, barren world which feels like death to me. I need your warmth, Rahaan. I need your heat, my Sheikh. I need your strength, my King. I don't know how you can come here, since Diamante has made sure you are not in the room with us, but I need your help. Help me save our child, my king. Help me fight for our happy ending.

62

She needs me but I do not know how to get back there, thought the Sheikh as he watched her eyelids flutter and her lips mouth silent words he could not hear but somehow understood. What am I missing? How do I take myself there again? How did I get there the last time, in the last world?

The fight, thought the Sheikh as he looked down at his woman. Hilda was pressed up against him, the two of them naked as babes, the dark sky and the silent waters the only witnesses. He'd been careful with her, controlling his arousal yet again even as he controlled hers. He'd been tempted to take it to the level his need demanded, but he'd held back, telling himself she had entrusted herself to him and he could not take advantage, could not push it too far.

But by Allah, it has been hours without release, hours in this suspended state. And now she needs her man, he thought as a darkness fell upon him as if a cloud was passing over the two of them. She needs him to find his own source of power, a source which she does not have access to. A source that he has kept hidden so far. A source that is deeply mas-

Stars for the Sheikh

culine, primal, animalistic and beastly. Is that what she needs? Does she need her man to be a man right now? An animal who takes what he wants?

The fight . . . the arena . . . came the thought again as the Sheikh felt a strange energy rise in him. Adrenaline, blood, violence . . . is that not the arena where the men of history exercise their power? Perhaps there was a lesson in that previous world, the world where I cut my brother's throat to get the ending I wanted, to *take* the ending I wanted! Was it right? Of course not—not according to the man I am in the here and now. But it felt like nothing to the man I was in that world. And although Hilda was distraught when we returned to this world, the woman whose eyes I looked into in that world was unmoved to a degree, yes? She stood there strong, holding our son's head up high as his father did what the time and place dictated. Is that the lesson? That we are all composites, all of us with dark and light within us, all of it fighting for primacy as the universe continues its merry dance of push and pull?

After all, the Sheikh thought as he looked down at his woman, this astrologer from Albuquerque . . . yes, after all, the two of us have not led perfectly honorable lives in this world, have we? I have manipulated people for both profit and entertainment, and she has done the same. Does that make us "bad" human beings? Or does it just make us . . . human?

Adrenaline, violence, sex, came the thoughts again

as he looked down at his sweet, soft, light-as-a-feather, magical woman made of stardust and starlight. "Hilda," he whispered. "Hilda!"

But she was deep in a trance, a restless but somehow lumbering trance, like she was freezing to death somewhere out there. She needed his heat, it occurred to him. She needed his fire.

Now the circle of the sun showed itself on the horizon, and Rahaan swore he smelled the pungent aroma of gasoline cut through the salty ocean air. They were minutes away from all of it being over, he thought. All of it.

"No," he said resolutely as he shook Hilda to her senses and looked her in the eye. "What do you need, Hilda? What do you need!"

Her eyes flickered open but he could see the mist and haze in them, the cool glimmer of defeat. She smiled weakly at him, and he shook her again, finally grabbing her hair and pulling it as his temper flared. "You are not going to back down now, my queen," he said to her. "Tell me what you need to fight and I will—"

"You know what I need!" she suddenly screamed, her eyes opening wide, her voice almost shocking him. It was deeper, stronger, yet more feminine, more vulnerable. He didn't know what she was going through in this third world with Diamante, but the Sheikh sensed that perhaps she was coming to the same realization as he, that part of all this was a manifestation of the sliver of darkness that lived within the two of them. It was not as simple as them versus Diamante, good versus evil, the pure versus the filthy, the dark versus the light. In a sense Diamante was the darkness in the two of them, and perhaps it was not so much eliminating the darkness as simply consuming it, taking it in, granting it a place within them without allowing it to corrupt them. Perhaps at the end of it all, after time travel and magic and dreamworlds, the point remained that it was the flesh and bone that was real, the physical that was the truth, the gritty truth that humans will always have one foot in the dirt, one hand in the grime. Perhaps that was the sublime secret of the universe, the cosmic joke of life. Indeed, perhaps that *was* life!

"You know what I need," she gurgled as she grinned up at him from wherever she was. "Take me, Rahaan. Take me hard, the way you want, the way the beast inside you wants. The way the animal inside me wants. Take me like a man takes a woman. Make me feel your flesh. Make me burn from your heat. Make me scream from your strength. That's what I need to finish this, Rahaan. The physical. The flesh. The violence. Now take me, my King. Take me there."

63

The burst of adrenaline woke her so fast she almost fell off the chair. It was clarity, heat, and raw, visceral energy all rolled into one. She could feel the Sheikh pounding into her in that world, grunting and roaring as he let himself go, pulling her hair, turning her and pushing her against the railing as he took what he wanted, how he wanted, hard and desperate, hot and wild, hands around her throat, fingers groping and pinching, slapping and slamming, pushing hard, driving deep, violence merging with lust, dark merging with light.

Now the heat was palpable, real, burning within her breast even as she felt a wetness between her legs in this world. It was sick, but she feel the power it gave her. Pure physical power.

She took deep breaths as she watched Diamante pace that barren stone-walled room in her purple skirts and black leather boots. She smiled as she felt herself float up like a feather, a cloud of stardust, weightless magic. She gasped when she saw in her mind's eye that view of the heavens, which was nothing more than all of time, every event, every birth, every death, every man, every woman. She could feel her man taking her in the most physical, filthy, beautiful way on a platform above the Arabian Sea, dolphins calling out, gulls screaming in unison, the sun rising over all of it.

That's the answer, isn't it, she thought as she slowly rose to her feet, only now realizing that those chains were gone, her hands were free, that she and Rahaan had managed to pull her into a slightly different parallel world where she was not bound. God, that's the answer, isn't it?! And I had to go all the way there and back again to figure it out—that there's no escaping the flesh, that all of these connections between worlds and timelines mean nothing without the physical to hold it all together, that the physical *is* the spiritual, that life is flesh and bone and blood and lust as much as it is stardust and magic and heavenly light!

Hilda could feel her climax approaching in the distance, hear herself scream in raw ecstasy as the Sheikh took her to that place only a man can take a woman, that place that can only be reached in the flesh. She smiled and looked down as she felt cold metal on her hand, and lo and behold it was the ring, that platinum banded ring with the diamond the size of Jupiter. Had she always had it on? Was it always this big? Were the edges always this sharp? More importantly, did I always lead with my left?

And as she walked as if in a dream, fist clenching, ring shining with deadly starlight, the voice of all the women inside her whispered that sometimes you just need to stand your ass up and *take* the ending you want! Take it in the physical! Take it with your flesh-and-blood hands! With your goddamn fists!

Diamante turned just in time to catch the full impact of Hilda's swing, and the blow cracked the dark princess's jawbone clean as she went flying across the room in a whirlwind of yellow hair and purple skirts, blood-spatter lining her path as she landed on the cold stone floor in a choking heap.

And as Hilda felt that climax roll in from worlds away, volcanic and violent, her man exploding in her depths and giving her the last of his strength, she took a deep breath and walked over to the fallen princess, raising her bloody left hand once more to finish the job, to finish the story, to protect her happy ending, her child, her dream, her perfect world.

"You were right, Diamante," she whispered as she brought her fist down, wedding ring leading the way. "I am willing to do what it takes to get my ending."

64
THREE YEARS LATER

Hilda smiled at her two-year-old son as he looked up at her with a quizzical expression, as if to say, "Is this OK, Mama?"

"Yes, all right, go ahead," she said, shaking her head as she watched her boy, freshly bathed not ten minutes ago, step into the muddy mess that had been a sand-castle earlier that morning, before the tide started to come in.

She watched as her son got himself covered in golden sand and saltwater grime once again, his face gleaming with delight as he sat plumb in the middle of his destroyed castle and started to rebuild it with his little fingers.

The Sheikh strolled up as she watched him, and he knelt by her side and kissed her on the head.

"Is it done?" Hilda asked, looking up to see if Rahaan looked sad or nostalgic. But he seemed fine. Happy even.

"Signed and sealed. As of now, I have suspended all drilling in the waters controlled by the Kingdom of Kolah, and I have designated the zone as an international sanctuary for . . . dolphins." He frowned and raised an amused eyebrow at his wife and queen.

"What?" she said, giggling already. "You think that's lame?"

He laughed and shook his head. "No, it is fine. I simply think that perhaps someone should inform the dolphins that they have a sanctuary."

"I'm sure they know," Hilda said with a shrug. "They get it. Trust me."

Rahaan laughed again and lay down on the sand, placing his head on Hilda's soft lap. The two of them watched their son make the most intricate designs with his pudgy little fingers: swirls and swishes, circles and waves, splashes and splotches.

"Am I a horrible person," Hilda whispered as she looked down at her husband and then over at her son. "Are we both—"

But she stopped when she saw the Sheikh look up at her with those green eyes of his. They'd talked about this countless times over the years, ever since she'd returned from that last dream, screaming as she climaxed with her man on that balcony, violence and lust somehow seeming beautiful and magical as the sun rose and the moon set and the stars said goodnight. The opening ceremony had passed without incident, and later they realized that neither Alim nor Yusuf Iqbal had any conscious memory of Di or any of the madness. Alim had taken over as Sheikh briefly: just long enough to get a taste of the "real" world . . . and long enough to realize that as ruler he could simply issue an edict that struck away the outdated law about marrying a foreign woman from the code of Kolah. By the time the child was born, Rahaan was Sheikh again and Hilda was his queen, and just like that they were living the dream. The dream that both of them had killed for in other worlds!

How to make sense of it? How to live with it? We all like to think we are models of goodness and purity, shining beacons of light and charity. But just like there is no way to keep my son's feet squeaky clean at all times, no human can be all good, all light, all pure. Perhaps that's the curse of seeing behind the veil, is it not? After all, if all of time was laid bare before us, how many of this world's priests might be another world's predators? Could a previous life of dishonor and violence be the foundation on which a current life of charity and compassion is built? Is the universe not driven by the dance of opposites? And so perhaps it is indeed the burden of someone with our gifts, with our experiences, with our love, to be forced to live with the knowledge that we are many people in one, good and bad in one, light and dark in one. And perhaps that knowledge will lead us to live the best lives we can, raise the best son we can, be the best king and queen we can.

"Anything new from the investigators?" Hilda asked, running her fingers through the Sheikh's thick black hair. "Have they found Di?"

The Sheikh grunted and shook his head. He'd never been particularly interested in tracking down Di, but still hired a team of investigators at Hilda's insistence. There was a part of her that wanted to reach out to Di in this world, strange as that seemed.

Of course, what was stranger was that the University of New Mexico had no record of Di. Norm didn't know who she was. And Hilda didn't know her last name, so couldn't get much further than a description of someone who was either a redhead or a blonde! Were they in a timeline where Di was never born? Was Di born as someone else, with a different name? Different colored hair? Who knew? And that was just one of the many questions they'd had after what happened three years ago . . .

"And still no tattoo," she said, pushing up the Sheikh's sleeve and glancing at the smooth brown skin. The tattoo had disappeared sometime that night on the rig, and they'd never quite figured out why. In fact, they'd never quite figured out why it had changed in the first place, or what the hell those weird childlike squiggles were!

Hilda watched her son play in the sand for several long moments before she felt an excitement bubbling up like the seawater through the rocks.

"Rahaan," she muttered, grabbing a fistful of his hair so hard he grunted and sat up in annoyance. "Rahaan, look!"

He turned to see what she was pointing at, and his frown changed to a look of shared excitement. "By Allah," he said. "That looks familiar."

Now they both crawled over to the sandy masterpiece of finger-painting done by their son, and in an instant they both knew why it looked familiar.

"Take a picture," Hilda said quietly. "And we'll get it tattooed on your arm."

The Sheikh nodded and pulled out his phone and snapped a few images. Then he looked into her eyes, his gaze saying so much. He leaned in and kissed her, and she almost cried in joy.

"It means we still write our own future," she whispered to him. "I'm sure it means that. It's a reminder that although our fates are written in the stars, perhaps it's we that do the writing! That we're in control even though we're not. Does that make sense?"

"Of course not," he grunted. "But it cannot make sense in any ordinary way. That's the reason quantum mechanics is regarded as something mystical even by the most analytical of physicists."

Hilda laughed and leaned her head back as she glanced towards the domes and minarets of Kolah in the distance. The sun was setting. It was time to go home.

"You know," she said as the little royal family gathered their things even as white-clad attendants rushed in to help, "the downside of being in a world where Di and Norm never met is that nobody wrote that time travel book."

The Sheikh shrugged as he hoisted his pup onto his broad shoulders, not caring about the boy's grubby feet smearing sand and salt all over his fine white tunic. "Maybe someone else wrote it." He looked at her and grinned. "Maybe it made its way into a cheesy romance novel, cloaked in fake marriages, secret babies, and second chances. Actually no. It is too complex for the simpleton readers of—"

"OK don't push me," she said, raising a finger as the Sheikh laughed and shut the hell up. Hilda laughed too, shaking her head as the caravan of silver Range Rovers pulled up on the golden sand, ready to take the royal family back to their fairy-tale castle. "It would be a pretty darn convoluted romance novel, I'll give you that. But so long as there's a happy ending, the romance readers will handle it. Don't underestimate them."

"So are we a happy ending?" the Sheikh said as they piled into the sprawling royal car, kid first, wife next, king last.

"This time we are," she whispered to him as the heavy doors shut on the royal family and Sabbath the cat looked over from the front seat, his eyes the color of ____. "This time we are, my love."

∞

EPILOGUE
LOCATION: GUANTANAMO BAY
TIME: WHO THE HELL KNOWS

Agent John Benson, head of the CIA's Dubai Field Office, stared at his secured company cell phone and rubbed his bloodshot eyes. He'd just flown nonstop from Qatar to Cuba after getting a call from Homeland Security that his expertise was needed with a strange situation involving an inmate—an inmate who had seemingly showed up out of nowhere.

"That doesn't make any goddamn sense," Benson had said over the phone, annoyed that he was being asked to travel to Gitmo yet again. "Someone put her in a cell, didn't they? Find out who did it and figure it out yourselves. This doesn't concern me. I got shit to take care of in the Middle East, and—"

But they'd said this did concern the Middle East, and so Benson was forced to listen. Apparently a fire-blonde woman had been found in a solitary cell during the rounds the previous morning. She'd been frantically talking about Sheikhs and Kings, about someone murdering someone else, a Sheikh killing his brother, and on and on. It sounded like gibberish, but she mentioned the name of a Sheikh who was in fact a real person, though not on any CIA or DHS watchlist by any means. Then, when they tried to pull up records on this woman, they found nothing. They ran her prints and found nothing. Facial recognition turned up zilch. The woman was a ghost, they said. Was she CIA full dark, they asked?

"How the hell should I know?" thundered Benson even as he headed for the U.S. Airbase in Qatar to take a military flight to Cuba. "That's the goddamn point of full dark, you fools! We don't know, and if we did, we wouldn't admit it!"

After landing Benson went straight to the interrogation room where the woman was being held. By now she'd calmed down, and in fact she'd clammed up. Gone silent. Not a word. She didn't ask for a lawyer. She didn't proclaim her innocence. She didn't even mention the Sheikh she'd been ranting about earlier.

"So I fly all the way here and you no longer want to talk? Come on. Now I'm curious. What's your story?" Benson said, squinting as he tried to make eye contact with the strikingly beautiful blonde woman with the sharp, sand-colored eyes. "Hey, listen. You want your story to have a happy ending? Well, your only shot is to begin talking. Or else you're gonna rot in a cell labeled Jane Doe. You're in my world now, you understand? I'm the only one who can change the ending to your story, you hear? I'm the—"

"All right," she said quietly, an almost unnerving look in her eye, like she knew something Benson didn't. "But it's a long story. How much time you got?"

∞

From Annabelle Winters

Thanks for reading.

Join my private list at **annabellewinters.com/join** to get steamy epilogues, exclusive scenes with side characters, and a chance to join my advance review team.

And do write to me at **mail@annabellewinters.com** anytime. I really like hearing from you.

Love,
Anna.

Made in the USA
Coppell, TX
02 December 2019